Twisted Truth

A novel by

Steven Hamilton

ISBN: 978-1-7338778-6-2

Cover Art: Bespoke Book Covers
(bespokebookcovers.com)

With Gratitude

Approaching the publication of a novel, my mind is drawn to those who made it possible. At such times, I am reminded of how much I depend on others to make these stories come to life. And this particular novel is no different. I first give thanks to my Thursday night writer group—NNStoelting, J. Jay Waller, and Richie Goldstein. Despite my bouts of argument, I am deeply indebted for their insight, attention to detail, and their willingness to help me see different ways of telling the story. And as always, I am grateful to Peter and Caroline O'Connor of Bespoke Book Covers for their inspired work on the cover. They never fail to amaze me with their creativity, quality, and professionalism. Finally, I give thanks to my beautiful and talented wife, Mary, for all her editing, inspiration, and... yes... prodding. None of this works without her.

Author's Note

This is a work of fiction. All characters and events are fictional. Any similarity to real people or events is coincidence. Certain organizations, such as police departments and churches, are real, although I have taken a great deal of literary license in describing them in support of the story.

This novel was a long time coming to fruition. I started it nearly three years ago. My first draft was completed within a year and my first shot at editing took about six months. And then it sat... and sat... and sat. The problem was that the subject matter was difficult to deal with. It was never my intent to make statements about the legal system or how it treated people accused of sex crimes. And it was not a novel about sexual abuse of children or abuse of anyone else.

What I was aiming at was a statement about the value of fact and truth. I intended this as a solid endorsement of skepticism. It took me many years to fully understand that not believing something was not the same as believing something to be false. The withholding of judgment pending presentation of convincing evidence is something I have strived for in my more recent years. As I look out now on a world torn asunder by lies, hatred, and accusation, I only wish that more people could adopt a mindset of skepticism.

Chapter 1

That's absolute crap." Lainie Simpson railed at her editor in absentia. The suggestions weren't just fine tuning—Meg Constanzo wanted a completely different story. *Change this, move that, make this lighter, turn that darker.* The nagging pain in her left wrist pulled her out of the rant. She tried to flex it while holding the steering wheel, not doing a very good job of either.

The attorney-turned-novelist nursed a case of tendinitis and a growing agitation with an editor who made increasing demands about the second book in a trilogy of fantasy novels. To round out the misery, she now had to cope with Saturday afternoon grocery shopping.

Lainie glanced from side to side at the rows of cars in the Bellevue, Washington, parking lot as she navigated her Camry in search of a spot. But at least her Toyota was easier than trying to maneuver a minivan. She'd wanted a minivan once, in *those* days, along with kids and all that stuff. Thankfully, she'd gotten past that stage of her life. Lainie sighed. Putting off her shopping trip had seemed like a good idea when she chose to stay home and write Friday morning. In retrospect, perhaps it was a mistake.

Then she spotted it—movement two rows over. Yes, a small green car escaped from its cocoon of a parking spot. Lainie applied more pressure to the accelerator and her car rewarded her with a jump in speed. *Finally.*

Approaching the empty spot, Lainie turned on her blinker and swung wide to ease in. She smirked as she noticed a competitor coming from the opposite direction, blinker also flashing. "Tough luck. I got here first." The spoken words sounded harsher than the ones in her head. Still, she had dibs on the spot.

She avoided the gaze of the defeated driver in the other car. The vehicles on either side of the spot made parking a challenge. One was an extended bed pick-up with a camper on the back. The other was an oversized van. Both protruded out farther than other vehicles. And they both sat right on the yellow line.

She parked with the right side of her car a scant few inches from the van giving her barely enough room to open her door without slamming it into the truck. She dismissed a passing thought about how good it would feel to shove her door open, smacking the side of that inconsiderate bastard. *Bastard? Certainly. No woman would drive such a monstrosity or park like that.*

The need for grocery shopping came around far too often. Lainie had considered switching to online ordering and delivery. But she never seemed to be organized enough. She couldn't even be bothered to make a shopping list. She turned off the ignition and sat, rubbing her wrist and trying to execute an attitude adjustment, without much success.

The shopping aisles posed an even worse problem than the parking lot. Inconsiderate jerks parked their carts in the center of the aisle while they casually read labels, assuming they could even read. She closed her eyes and shook her head, reminding herself that it would soon be over, at least for the day and, hopefully, for the week.

Tomato paste was next on her mental list. Maybe she could do without it. Anything rather than going down *that* aisle. She knew that the small cans sat on the shelf huddled between the ready-made pasta sauce and the Italian seasonings. But in order to get there, she would need to walk past the pasta. Or she could go down another aisle and make her approach from the other direction. *That's stupid. Just go down here and get the freaking tomato paste for God's sake.*

Lainie searched the aisle signs—Canned Vegetables, Baking Supplies, Baby Products... *Ah, there it is*—Pasta Sauce *and* Pasta. She pushed her cart forward. She caught sight of various products as she whizzed by on her way— canned green beans, black olives, flour, sugar. She sped up. Staring directly ahead, she still managed to catch a glimpse of the baby food—applesauce and strained pears. And then they were gone.

She had this stupid argument with herself every single trip to the store. She pushed her cart down the aisle trying to fix her gaze on the cans about mid-way down. But her eyes seemed to have a mind of their own. Despite her best efforts, she saw the packages—spaghetti, linguini, rotini. Her thoughts drifted into the past.

> *She stood at the stove staring at the pot of*
> *boiling water, uncooked pasta in her hands.*
> *The tossed salad sat innocuously to the side.*
> *Her head swam. Her vision blurred. Nausea*
> *swept over her. What was she supposed to do*
> *now?*

She jerked her gaze away from the offending products and her mind back to the present. *Just get the damn tomato paste and be gone.*

*** *

3

As Lainie approached her car, nestled in the tight little parking spot, renewed irritation swept over her. The two overgrown boy-toys still crowded her vehicle. She stared at the situation for a moment and then opened her trunk. No way would she be able to open doors wide enough to get her bags in.

Her wrist throbbed from pushing the cart and handling items in the store. She lifted the canvas bags with her right hand. The third bag felt funny, unbalanced. As she sat it in the trunk, it toppled over spilling Fuji apples, which rolled in various directions. The day kept getting worse. The clerk had put the heavy apples on top of lighter items. *Sheesh. You'd think they'd get some competent help in a place like this.*

Reaching in with both hands to retrieve the runaway apples, the pain shot up her left arm. Frustration coursed through her mind. *Stupid drivers, idiot clerks, tomato paste in the pasta aisle.* Not thinking, she reached to open the driver's side door with her left hand and received an instant searing feedback.

Inside the car and belted up, she turned the ignition. Looking in the rearview mirror, she saw nothing behind her. Unfortunately, the truck and van obscured her view to either side. *Dammit!* She clenched her jaw and closed her eyes. The tension refused to leave. Eyes open again, she pulled the gearshift lever into reverse and pressed the gas pedal, maybe a little too hard.

Thud. She slammed on the brakes. "What the...?" She jerked on the door handle with her left hand but hardly felt the pain. Door open, she poured herself out of the car and stood looking down at a man who lay on the asphalt behind the vehicle.

His eyes wide, he propped himself up, first on an elbow and then moved into a sitting position. A pair of wire-rimmed glasses sat on the asphalt pavement next to him. Two canvas bags lay askew. Green peppers, onions, and an intact jar of pickles had come to rest nearby. As the color drained from his face, a crazed smile developed. The thirtyish-looking man opened his mouth as if to speak. But before any sound escaped, his eyes rolled back in his head and he collapsed backward.

Chapter 2

Lainie handed her driver's license, registration, and insurance card to the uniformed officer. "He's going to be okay, right?" Her gaze shifted between the officer's clipboard, the spot on the ground where the man had come to rest, and the bumper of her car, which gave no evidence of the incident. She massaged her left wrist with her right hand as she watched the officer write. She didn't need this kind of complication in her life.

He responded without looking up. "Can't say. You heard the same thing I did from the EMT—low blood pressure, likely internal bleeding, possible fracture of the left leg, and potential brain injury." The words came out monotone and matter-of-factly. As he handed her papers back, he looked up. "When did you first see him?"

The attorney in her screamed at her to remain silent. But another part of her wanted everything to be okay. And that part won out. "I didn't really see him. I heard or felt the thump and I stopped. I mean, I saw him after I got out of the car." The scene replayed over and over in her head.

The officer knelt and took a photo of the pavement around her left rear tire. "That's a pretty long skid mark for just *easing out*. Looks like you were backing up at a pretty good clip." He stood and gazed at her.

Lainie's legal experience kicked in. "I eased out of the spot. I couldn't see to either side because of these two vehicles." She gestured toward the truck and van that flanked her parking spot. "I was just easing out to try and get a better view, to see if anything was coming. That guy came out of nowhere." A stupid statement to be sure. He came out of somewhere. She just didn't see him.

The officer continued with the notetaking as he spoke. "And when you heard the sound, what did you do?"

That's a stupid freaking question. "I got out of the car immediately. When I saw him on the ground, I called nine-one-one." She left out the part where they'd stared at each other for a few seconds.

"And then?"

"And then what?" She'd called for help. What else was she supposed to do? "I started to ask if he was okay, but he passed out." A red flag whisked through her mind. "And I didn't move him." She looked down at the spot where he'd lain. "Could you call in and see how he's doing?"

The officer kept writing. He paused and inspected her rear bumper, running his hand across the surface. He went back to his report. When he finished, he walked away, taking position beside his car. She could see him using the mike attached to his uniform. After a few minutes, he returned. "He's listed in grave condition. Just going into surgery." He started toward his car, then stopped and turned. "If he pulls through, we'll get a statement from him before we finish this up."

***

Once home, Lainie went about the task of putting groceries away, her heart not in it. With the perishables in the fridge, she haphazardly crammed the other items on the pantry shelf and closed the door.

Grave condition. If he pulls through. Internal bleeding. Brain injury. The officer's words ricocheted through her brain. And things never seemed to go well in hospitals. She introduced a few complementary concepts to the internal discussion—*involuntary manslaughter, reckless endangerment, felony.* The room grew darker as the magnitude of her possible future dawned on her.

She tried to think of any environmental factors that might have played a part but came up empty. The day had been clear, the pavement dry. *What kind of idiot just walks down a row of parked cars without watching?* This was his fault. She couldn't see him, but he should have seen her back-up lights. *What would it have taken for him to just wait until I was out a little farther?*

About four that afternoon, Lainie called the switchboard at Overlake Hospital to try and get an update on his condition. She got the predictable response—patient confidentiality. *Screw it.* She went into the kitchen and started chopping chicken and vegetables.

With a stew on the stovetop, she wandered into the hallway where she needed to make a choice. *Back to the study to write or zone out in the living room?* The novel would have to wait. She shuffled over and plopped down on the couch. Slouching down, she closed her eyes and exhaled. The story of her life—things just kept getting worse and worse.

Lainie picked up the remote from the coffee table and clicked. She rotated through some channels—golf, infotainment masquerading as news, an old movie—before she settled on the local news channel.

As if living through the afternoon incident weren't enough, the station treated her to a thirty second recap ending with a status report. "The individual, whose identity is being withheld pending notification of family, is reported to be in guarded condition."

Guarded condition? Is that good? Better than grave. She turned off the TV, leaned back, and mentally walked through the legal ramifications of the situation. If the man lived, she'd never see the end of the lawsuits. Lainie could envision the medical costs, ongoing rehabilitation, pain and suffering, and on and on.

On the other hand, if he died, maybe there was no family. Then all she'd have to worry about was beating any kind of criminal case that the police threw at her. Not that she wished him dead, but it might make this easier. *Anyway, it was his fault for not watching.*

And on this note, Mildred made herself known.

Chapter 3

Mildred was a relatively new addition in Lainie's life. The snarky, sometimes condescending twit of a conscience had first shown up toward the end of Lainie's legal career. At first more of a sense or feeling, the voice became more demanding, pushier over the past few years. These days, full-blown internal arguments were more the norm than the exception. The name *Mildred* stuck because, well, her conscience sounded like a *Mildred.*

You don't wish him dead but maybe things would be easier if he didn't make it? I thought better of you. Mildred had a way of taking things out of context.

"That's not what I meant, and you know it." Lainie engaged in the never-ending internal argument.

But this is really inconvenient, isn't it? Mildred's sarcasm was hard to miss.

Lainie fought back. "It's got nothing to do with convenience. It was his fault. Now I'm having to pay the price."

Pay the price? Really? What price are you paying? He's probably going to die and you're only worried about responsibility.

"In case you haven't noticed, other people's actions and decisions have a way of screwing me over." The pain, seasoned with a bit of anger, seeped in.

You can't blame this guy for what happened back then.

Lainie shook her head and returned to the moment. Mildred retreated. The local news had morphed into the weather report. She clicked off the set. Forcing herself off the couch, she migrated to the kitchen to consider the stew on the stovetop. She took a head of romaine lettuce and a tomato from the fridge and put a couple of eggs on to boil. Some pepperoncini would round out the salad. Together with the stew, that should keep her alive until the next morning.

Fifteen minutes later, she picked at the stew with her spoon. Moving the pieces around in her bowl seemed preferable to eating it. The diminishing light of the dying day snuck up on her. Before she realized it, the greens, reds, and yellows of the salad had become shades of gray. That made sense. Colorless and tasteless seemed good companions. Rather than turning on the light in the dining room, she picked up the full bowl and took it to the kitchen where the garbage disposal consumed the dinner.

Standing in the hallway once again, she gazed at the open door to her study where a novel in progress awaited. The high fantasy and world-building would have to wait another day. She could not force her mind or her heart into the work.

Lainie considered giving her friend Kelley Vickers a call. One of the few remaining social contacts from her days in law practice, Kelley was always up for a glass of wine and conversation. *But not on a Saturday night.* Her friend had a life that included a romantic partner.

Grabbing her Kindle off the end table in the living room, she sauntered down the hall to crawl into bed with a good book. The digital display on her radio alarm reminded her that it was only six-thirty in the evening. *At least it's dark outside.* Somehow, once darkness had fallen, going to bed seemed okay. She still struggled with the notion of retreating from life during daylight hours. She got undressed and donned the oversized tee shirt that had long replaced the sexier attire from an earlier age.

After brushing her teeth, Lainie returned to the bedroom. Pausing at the foot of the bed, she stared at the e-reader that she mindlessly tossed on her pillow. *Going to bed with a book. Hmmm. Beats going to bed with....*

***

> *She stared at the pot. Why am I boiling this water? Something was supposed to happen. She looked at the spaghetti in her hand. The doctor said I should stay in bed for a while. A sense of impending tragedy coursed through her. She heard a sound in the hallway.*

***

Lainie came awake with a start, her heart pounding and a light sweat bathing her face. She could hear the rain pattering on the window. The light from the street filtered in through her curtains. The shadows created by the wind through the low-hanging branches of her oak tree danced on the wall adjacent to the bed.

She sat up in bed. The clock display read two-thirty-five. The image of the guy lying on the pavement the previous afternoon flashed in her mind. No matter how hard she tried, she couldn't manage to catch a break.

You can't blame him for what happened back then.

Chapter 4

The following Monday afternoon brought a glimmer of good news. Lainie looked at the caller ID on her phone as the ringtone filled her otherwise silent study—Northwest Pacific Insurance. She'd notified the company on Saturday right after the accident. She connected and set the phone to speaker. "Hello." She gazed at her manuscript on the monitor and rubbed her left wrist through the splint as she spoke.

"Hello. Is this Elaine Simpson?" The male voice boomed in over the speaker.

"Yes."

"Hi, this is Carl Nesbitt with Northwest Pacific. I have some news on your claim. The police were able to interview the man, Paul Stafford, this morning. I have a copy of the preliminary accident report. They're listing the cause as human error. He evidently walked out of a blind spot, according to his statement. He said that he wasn't really paying attention and that you probably couldn't have seen him. So, I guess all's well."

She turned from the computer and stared out the window, arching her eyebrows as she considered the unexpected information. "Does that mean the guy's going to be okay?"

"Looks like it. I don't have any information from the hospital, but I guess since the police interviewed him, he must be better." The voice paused before continuing. "As I understand it, there's no damage to your car, is that correct?"

Lainie remembered looking at her rear bumper and wondering how it could do such damage to a man and not even show a scratch. "That's right. Nothing."

"Okay then, I guess we can close the book on this. Given his statement to the police, I can't imagine that he would come back looking for any kind of compensation. But, if something else comes up, we'll give you call." After a pause, he added, "Oh, and I'll e-mail a PDF copy of the police report."

After she hung up, she pondered the news. The attorney in her suspected something was amiss. No one, well, no one except an idiot would admit to being at fault, especially if they ended up in the hospital.

Mildred chimed in. *Not everyone is a bottom-feeder.*

"I didn't say he was a bottom feeder. It just sounds a little suspicious to me, that's all." This conscience thing could be annoying.

Maybe he's just an honest, straightforward guy who takes responsibility for his own actions.

"Humph. Yeah, right. Like that's gonna happen." The problem with Mildred was that she really didn't understand the practicalities of the real world—one of the benefits of being an internal voice.

No comeback—the voice of good and light fell silent.

Before Lainie could relish the victory, the ringtone sounded again. She closed her eyes and shuddered. "Hello, Meg." Her editor was not a patient woman.

No greeting, no small talk. "Did you get the changes I sent you?"

"Yes. I got them and I wondered if we could talk about those." Lainie winced as she spoke. She knew that Meg Costanzo did not *talk* about changes she ordered. She decreed and expected compliance.

Predictably, the woman ignored the comment and moved along. "And what about the five additional chapters you were supposed to have by the end of this week. I assume you are on schedule." The words chirped out at a brisk clip—all business, no wiggle room.

Lainie sighed. "I am. But I had a bit of a problem this weekend, a car accident."

"You laid up? In the hospital?"

She furrowed her brow. "Uh. No. I'm fine. It's just that—

The staccato voice interrupted. "Good. I'm waiting on those chapters. And I want to see the revised material as soon as possible."

***

I suppose it's the least I can do. Lainie carried a vase with a small floral arrangement that she'd picked up at the grocery store. A trip to a legitimate florist seemed extravagant under the circumstances.

The hospital loomed ahead of her, just across the parking lot. With every step, the nausea ramped up a little more. Her eyes found what looked like the windows on the third floor—*that floor*—the one in which her world had begun to fall apart all those years ago. She quickly averted her gaze and banished all thoughts of her own stay in the hospital. She checked for traffic to her right and then kept her eyes focused on the asphalt parking lot surface to keep from sliding on loose gravel—one step in front of another. *Just keep moving.*

As the automatic doors opened to allow her entrance, the smell of antiseptic, burnt coffee, and... something else... blasted her. She muttered as she navigated to the elevators,

"You'd think they would do something about that odor." But a part of her questioned how much of that odor was in her imagination.

She made her way to the nursing station on the fourth floor. "I was wondering if I could visit Paul Stafford. I think he's in room four seventeen." She'd gotten that tidbit of information through a back channel at the police department, an old colleague.

The young nurse looked up at her and then down at a sheet of paper. "Your name?"

She wondered whether this was the same nurse as.... She shook off the thought and focused. "Elaine Simpson." She remembered that the hospital would not give her information on the phone, so they were also not likely to allow her to visit without his permission. She quickly added, "I'm probably not on his list." She tried to come up with the words that would subtly describe her relationship. She came up empty. "I was driving the car." She left it at that.

The nurse looked at the flowers. "Let me check." She stood and walked three doors down and into a room, returning less than a minute later and offering a smile. "You can go in." She gestured toward the room she'd just visited. No, this was obviously not the same nurse as back then. The other one had never smiled.

She took a deep breath and steeled herself for a conversation for which she had no enthusiasm.

Mildred offered her counsel. *At least try to be nice to the guy. After all, he did get you off the hook.*

"Of course I'll be nice to him. And he didn't get me off the hook. He just admitted that he was wrong, which is nothing more than telling the truth." She didn't owe this guy anything.

Mildred didn't answer.

Lainie eased the door open and slipped into the room, not prepared for the wave of memories.

> *From her bed, she could see that the room was empty. Not just empty of people; empty of cards or flowers. A plastic cup with a straw rested on the portable dining tray. Machines beeped. Lights blinked on and off. Distant sounds filtered in from the hallway. Footsteps—someone coming? They passed by. No, not for her.*

Lainie came back to the present. Lying in the bed staring at her, was that same man she'd seen on the pavement behind her car. The smile he'd attempted at the time painted his face as he adjusted the back of his bed up. "Hi. You must be the woman who called the EMTs."

That seemed an odd characterization. "I'm Elaine Simpson, Lainie. I was driving the car that…." She allowed the words to trail off not wanting to give voice to the idea that she'd hit him. Especially since it was his fault. He hit her.

His hazel eyes sparkled. The smile morphed into a brief laugh. "Yes, well, it was nice to bump into you. I'm Paul Stafford." His disheveled brown hair framed a boyish face, which contrasted with a five o'clock shadow of a beard.

Chapter 5

Lainie set the flowers on a small table beside his bed. "How are you doing?" *Other than almost dying because you walked out behind me without looking.*

Paul glanced around the room. He held up his arms, complete with instrument leads and an IV tube, and shrugged. "All things considered, not bad, I guess. How about you?" The words came out soft and low. He nodded toward the brace on her left wrist. "You get that from the accident?"

The first thought that struck her was that the guy was being a wise ass. But the clear, wide eyes and smile seemed to suggest sincerity. "I'm fine. Then again, I'm not the one that got hit. And no, I'm having a bout of tendinitis." She forced a smile and reached over with her right hand to rub the offending wrist.

"Oh, could you put the flowers there on the windowsill so I can see them? They're kind of wasted on the table, wouldn't you say?" He shifted in the bed to try and look at the bouquet.

She spoke over her shoulder as she relocated the vase. "How long do they say you'll be here?"

When she turned to face him, he gazed upward and narrowed eyes as if he were pondering some deep philosophical notion. "That's a good question. I guess I'm kind of okay to leave in the next day or so. But I'm not sure about getting around, what with the broken leg. I'll be on crutches for about three weeks, then on a walking cast for another three weeks to a month." He paused and gazed out the window at the steady rain that had set in over Bellevue the previous evening.

Lainie glanced around the room—no other flowers, no cards, no evidence that anyone beyond the medical staff had been there. "Any family in the area?" *A wife? Children?* Getting around on crutches and living alone would be an interesting proposition.

He shook his head, smile fading. "Nah."

In the ensuing silence, the sounds of the functioning medical equipment became more noticeable. She was ready to go. Not much else to say.

Paul shifted his gaze to her. "Have a seat. You're making me nervous standing like that." He motioned toward a padded chair situated near the bed.

"I need to be leaving shortly. I just wanted to stop by and see if you were okay." She zipped up her raincoat, which she typically left unzipped.

His gaze dropped and his nod barely perceptible. "No problem. It's just nice to talk to someone who doesn't have a big needle or probe in their hand." The smile that returned to his face seemed forced.

Lainie made a preemptive strike to keep Mildred from interfering. "Is there anything you need? Anything I can get for you?" Surely there wasn't.

He looked at her for a moment before responding. "Well, if it's not too much trouble…"

She managed to keep the sigh inside. "What is it?"

He pointed toward a drawer in the small chest on the facing wall. "In the top drawer, you'll find my wallet. If you don't mind, could you grab some money out of there and find a coffee shop in this God forsaken place. I'm in desperate need of a real cup of coffee—large, strong, and black." He stared at her for another instant before adding, "In fact, get us both one, if you have the time."

The nearest coffee shop Lainie could find was on the first floor. As she stood in line, she checked the menu. There it was—*Fresh Brewed Coffee (Dark and Medium Roast): Regular, Large, & Bucket-sized.* The lame attempt at humor didn't impress her. Despite Paul's request, she had neither the time nor the inclination to sit around and guzzle caffeinated beverages with him. She needed to be home working on those chapters.

For God's sake, how much time we talking about here? Ten minutes, twenty minutes? You almost kill the guy and you begrudge him a few minutes of conversation. He's even buying the coffee. Mildred had a way of putting things in the worst possible light.

"I didn't nearly kill him. And I'm fetching his coffee. Besides, I don't have anything to say to him and I doubt that he has anything of interest to say to me." She didn't owe this guy. If anything, he owed her for all the trouble he'd put her through. If it hadn't been for him, she might have knocked out two more chapters over the weekend.

She stepped up to the counter where the young twenty-something barista with a variety of piercings and tattoos waited to take her order. "Could I get two large, black dark roast coffees, please." She could feel Mildred smiling inside.

When she returned, Lainie set the coffees down on the windowsill beside the flowers and dragged the rolling meal tray over to the bed. Putting his cup on the tray, she took her own and sat down, wondering if her conscience approved.

Mildred remained quiet.

Paul eased himself up in the bed, reached over slowly and picked up the cup. He inhaled deeply of the steam that found its way through the small drinking hole in the lid. "Hmmm. Oh yeah." He smiled and nodded to her. Taking the drink, he closed his eyes.

Lainie couldn't suppress a gentle smile. *How can someone in his position take so much pleasure in a cup of bitter liquid?*

He took a sip and nodded as he put the cup back on the tray. "Thank you. Really. I appreciate it."

"You're welcome." She looked at him closely for the first time. His light brown hair just edged over the tops of his ears and was swept back off his brow. The hazel eyes sparkled. She figured him to be early to mid-thirties. Of course, the hospital garb and dreary surroundings tend to add years. So maybe he was probably closer to his mid-thirties. She started to recall her life at that age but pulled herself back quickly.

After taking a drink, she set her cup on the windowsill. "What do you do for a living, Mister Stafford?"

He laughed. "Sorry. It's just that I get that *Mister Stafford* thing all day at work. Paul actually works better for me." The laugh eased into a smile. "I'm the principal at East Rainier High. How about you?"

Lainie hated making small talk. Her vocation was complicated. She sighed and waded in. "I'm a writer."

He arched his eyebrows. "Magazine? Journalist?"

"Novelist." She braced herself for the inevitable, which came next.

"Really? What genre?" He shifted up in the bed even more and adjusted the back to provide support.

"The piece I'm working on now is high fantasy." She changed the subject. "You like working with kids, huh?" But why would she even care about kids? It was too late for her.

Mildred chimed in. *You don't know that.*

She willed her conscience to shut up. Mildred fell silent.

He chortled. "Not at all. I'm really not much of a *kid* person."

Not a kid person. Just as well. Children don't add that much to life. She shook off her cynicism and tried to focus on what he was blathering about.

"In fact, I don't work with them, if I can help it. We have teachers, advisors, and counselors to deal with the students. And I have an assistant principal who takes care of the discipline issues. I work with budgets, personnel rules, and school board meetings."

"Why go into education if you don't like working with kids?" Not that she wanted to work with kids. Not that she wanted anything to do with children at all.

He shrugged. "It's a job. It pays the bills. And I'm more what you might call a 'hands off principal.' I support the staff. They do the real work."

Lainie nodded as she took another drink of coffee and stood. "Well, thank you for the coffee, Mister Stafford, excuse me, Paul. I've got a deadline chasing me and I need to get home. It was good meeting you. Hope your recovery goes well." She walked over and shook his hand. As she turned to go, his voice halted her.

"Thanks, Lainie. And drop back by if you have the time. I'll be here a few more days."

She turned and nodded. "I'm pretty busy but if I'm down this way, I'll try to stop in." And with that she was out the door.

Chapter 6

Lainie logged into her bank account and began the monthly assessment. After the publication of her first novel, she'd granted herself a two-year sabbatical from legal practice to make the leap to a full-time writing career. The advance from the publisher had helped. She was six months into the effort and her finances were not quite what she'd hoped for. A little more wiggle room would be nice. She clicked on the various tabs to show the detail of the different accounts she'd set up. Nodding, she logged off and stared at the desktop screen. She held the regrets at bay. "I knew what I was getting into."

Figuring she could put it off no longer, she opened up a blank word processing document, set the style, centered the cursor and began typing a new chapter of her novel. After a couple of paragraphs, she hit a brick wall and sat, mesmerized by the blinking cursor. If only she could write a new life like the one she created—a new world and a story to go with it.

Other than the soft whir of the computer cooling fan, silence reigned supreme. She had always found it impossible to write with any kind of music playing. Although, sometimes she did talk to herself. Fortunately, Mildred usually kept quiet during these sessions. Usually.

What would it hurt to drop by again?

Lainie closed her eyes and leaned back in the ergonomic chair. "Can we have this conversation another time? This chapter will not write itself."

If the roles were reversed, wouldn't you appreciate a visit?

She laughed. "No."

Mildred fell silent.

Lainie pictured a hospital room, devoid of cards, flowers, and visitors. But it was a different room and a different time. *Well, maybe a little.*

***

She found the door to room four seventeen closed. Although the nurse had told her that she could go right in, she knocked before opening the door just a tad and sticking her head in. "Hey, is it okay to come in?"

Paul looked up from an e-reader and smiled. "Of course, please, come in." He closed the cover on his device and set it on the bedside table.

Lainie set his cup of coffee on the tray table and took a seat in the large padded chair. "Black, if I remember correctly."

"Yes, thanks."

The flowers she'd brought the previous day sat on the window along with one other vase and what looked like a single get-well-soon card. "How're you doing today?" She fought the memories and, at least for the moment, banished them to some dark, recessed corner of her mind.

"Great now. I was trying to figure a way to sneak out of bed and down to the coffee shop myself. Thanks much." He raised his cup in toast to her.

She wondered about the appropriate conversation in this kind of situation. She didn't really know the guy. And it wasn't like she was here in search of a new friend. "Any news yet on when they're going to let you go?"

He furrowed his brow. "Well, they said day after tomorrow. But the social worker was supposed to come by and talk to me about discharge orders. So, I don't really know right now."

Lainie shrugged. What was there to say? She checked her small talk subject inventory, the one that saw little to no use these days. "You live here in the area?" She wondered if maybe that was too personal.

Apparently not. "Yeah, although I keep intending to move farther out. Bellevue can be, I don't know, kind of frenetic, if you know what I mean."

She nodded in agreement and took another drink of coffee as she searched for the next subject.

"I picked up your book on Amazon today. Impressive. I know a published author now." He gestured toward the e-reader.

Lainie laughed. "Well, let's not get carried away. That's the first of a trilogy. I'm working on the second one now."

"Let me know when you publish the next one. I'll definitely buy it. Actually, if you publish a hard copy, I'll buy one and you can sign it for me."

Her laugh softened into a smile. "Deal. I'll let you know as soon as it's ready." She fell silent, not knowing what else to say. And she still had half a cup of coffee left.

He gazed at her for a moment. "Say, when I get out, maybe I could buy you a cup of coffee at a real coffee shop sometime."

A wave of panic shot through her as she envisioned this unmanageable problem that she'd created. "Uh, you know, I stay pretty busy. My schedule's packed most of the time."

His gaze dropped and his smile faded as he nodded.

"But thank you for the offer. Very nice of you."

What a stupid thing to say. Was that supposed to make him feel better about the rejection?

She ignored Mildred. This was neither the time nor the place for such an argument. She stood and walked over to the sink, pouring the remainder of her drink in. "I need to head home. Good luck."

He nodded and forced a smile. "Thank you. And thanks for stopping by. Nice to have the company."

Out the door and striding down the hall, she wanted to put as much distance as she could from that problem and that place.

Chapter 7

Silence and muted tones of gray greeted her as she entered the house through the garage entry. Soft light filtered through the kitchen windows holding the darkness from the hallway at bay. The faint ticking of the wall clock became stronger and dominated the room. After seven years, she should be used to it. *It's called living alone.*

Lainie tossed her keys into the small basket sitting on the rolling cart parked beside the back door. Standing in between the stove and the breakfast room table, she stared at the cupboard, seeing nothing in particular. The day had aged, and mid-afternoon was upon her. The entire morning had been wasted and for what? To make some guy feel better about being in the hospital.

In fairness, you had something to do with his being there.

"Yeah, well so did he." She thought to check the messages on her machine, but the absence of the little red blinking light eliminated the need. She sighed. The only person who would call was her editor, and she'd spoken to her the previous night.

She picked up her landline phone handset, for which she retained a certain fondness. The smart phone was a great tool. But this hefty gray device felt like stability in her hand. Some things remained constant. Lainie pushed the button that brought up her contact list—not quite the sophistication of the smart phone app but, it worked. Using the down arrow, she selected the number and hit the *Call* button.

"Hey there Lainie, how've you been?" Kelley Vickers clearly had caller ID.

Lainie smiled. She and Kelley had been friends since law school. "Oh, same same. You know. Say, I was wondering if you wanted to grab a coffee tomorrow morning, say ten?"

"I'd love to have coffee but tomorrow morning is out. The justice system grinds on. In fact, I'm out straight this week but early next week would work." The regret seemed mixed with some frustration.

You mean frustration as in what you felt when Paul asked you out to coffee?

She ignored the snarky barb. "Yeah, I'm okay next week. Tell you what, give me a call either later this week or on Monday and let me know what day."

"Sounds good. Talk to you later, Lainie." The call disconnected.

It's called living alone.

Daylight had faded and the darkness outside hovered. Lainie stared at the shelves in her refrigerator. Six or seven years ago, she might have tried to talk herself into eating. These days, the internal dialogue centered around what to eat rather than whether to eat. *Progress.*

The carton of eggs caught her eye. She opened the freezer door and pulled out a bag of frozen spinach. Tonight would be a Greek omelet with a side salad. She put some of the greens along with some finely diced onion on to sauté. As she set the container of feta cheese on the counter beside the stove, a random thought flashed through her mind. What was Paul eating tonight? She couldn't imagine anything truly enjoyable coming out of an institutional kitchen.

The kitchen table won out over the dining room. After all, it was just food. She tossed a dollop of plain yogurt on top of the omelet and squeezed some lime juice over her salad of field greens and tomatoes. With everything on the table, silence once again assaulted the room with only the ticking of her wall clock to hold the line. Lainie picked up her fork and cut off a piece of omelet, creating some welcome noise as the silverware interacted with the plate. As she chewed, she tapped her fork on the surface of her plate. *The sounds of being alone.*

***

The agony of the blinking cursor—Lainie sat at her desk searching for the inspiration that had eluded her for the past few days. The story was simply not talking to her. The characters refused to speak. She swiveled her chair to the right, leaned back, and stared out the window at rainy blackness. She saw Paul's face. The bandage around his head reminded her of the encounter. The sparkle in his hazel eyes said something else. Something about hope and humanity. Only those things were not real and anyone who believed in them was delusional.

She recalled the dejection on his face as she told him she was too busy to have coffee with him, ever. No, she really didn't say *ever*. She just said that she was busy.

But "ever" was implied.

"I didn't mean *ever*. I just meant that I'm busy right now. You remember busy, right? It's what I'm supposed to be when I have a deadline, like right now."

Internal silence.

"Anyway, he'll be out of the hospital in a few days and get back to his life. In the meantime, I need to get back to mine." She turned toward the computer and noticed that the blinking cursor had not retreated. Meg Costanzo, her editor, demanded progress and thus far, there was none to be had.

Meg complained that the story was too dark. The protagonist needed a friend or companion—dialogue. But Lainie's story was not about companions or friends and most certainly not about needing anyone.

Mildred intruded. *What's wrong with needing someone?*

"It's simple. The minute you need someone, you open yourself up to betrayal and hurt. If you don't need anyone, then you don't get hurt." Sometimes she wondered if Mildred had even been in existence back *then*.

How can you know joy if you never know pain? How would you know a good day if you never had a bad one?

"Can it with the psycho-babble mumbo jumbo. I've had enough pain to last two lifetimes."

Sitting at the computer trying to force inspiration didn't help. By eleven that evening, Lainie had written and deleted several meaningless pages multiple times. Tossing in the mental towel, she stood in front of the bathroom mirror brushing her teeth. Looking back at her was a woman she vaguely recognized. The brown hair that fell almost to her shoulders had streaks of gray, or were they silver? Did it matter?

She stared at the reflection of her eyes. The blue had faded to pale gray-blue. Small lines emanated from the corners but extended less than an inch into her otherwise smooth complexion.

She stepped back, toothbrush in her mouth, and gazed at her body. Not much there. The flatness of her figure reflected her state of mind. Other than what she managed to generate for her fictional character, Lainie could muster little emotion beyond a pervasive sense of weariness.

She rinsed and put the toothbrush away. Turning out the bathroom light, she went into the bedroom and donned her sleep uniform—the oversized tee shirt. Anyway, she'd had about all the meaning she could handle from this life.

Chapter 8

Lainie braved the cold late March drizzle to have coffee with Kelley the following Tuesday at the Common Grounds Café and Bakery. Stepping inside, she was greeted by a waft of coffee and cinnamon aroma and the sound of dishes clinking. Removing her raincoat, she surveyed the room and spotted her friend sitting at a table near the back.

Kelley stood and waved, offering a broad smile. The two met in the middle of the shop and hugged.

"You look great." Lainie hadn't seen her friend in months. "You've taken off a little weight." Talking about weight was always a dicey issue. But the two of them had engaged in so many discussions over the years that few topics were off-limits.

"A little, I guess." Kelley smiled and then shrugged. "Well, okay, fifteen pounds."

"That's fantastic. It shows." Lainie glanced down at the table. A cup of coffee and nothing else—a true feat of strength for her friend, who had an undying love of Common Grounds' signature almond poppy seed scones. "Let me grab a cup." She headed for the counter, where she made a snap decision to have a latte.

Back at the table, Lainie slurped some of the foam off the top and set the cup aside. "So, tell me, how's Yolanda? You guys have any special vacation plans?"

Kelley beamed. "Oh, she's great. We're going to Europe this summer. We got hooked up with one of those river cruises down the Danube. We're really jazzed. You know we got married this past month?" She looked suddenly a bit sheepish. "Not a big wedding. We just did the courthouse thing."

Lainie threw on her best faux offended look. "And you didn't invite me? What's up with that?" A smile cracked the façade. "Really, congratulations. I'm happy for you." But she wasn't. Marriage was always the first step to disaster. Sometimes it was just hard to see it coming.

Kelley shrugged. "It was a spur of the moment thing. I mean, we've been together for nearly ten years. We didn't even see this gay marriage hoopla coming. But, since the ruling, we figured we might was well get the tax benefits."

The conversation meandered through memories of the past, the progress of Lainie's novel, and the lack of love in her life before settling on Kelley's law practice. "So, you still defending the perverts and rapists of the world?" Lainie meant the question to be light-hearted but it landed differently.

A frown found its way quickly onto Kelley's face.

Before the woman could retort, Lainie tried to salvage the conversation. "I mean, it just seems it would be really hard to believe in those guys." *Ugh, bad to worse.*

But Kelley's face lightened, and she sighed. She seemed to read Lainie's regret. "Ah, yeah, I know. I've come to grips with it over the years. It's not that I believe in them. I don't. I believe in the system and the law, you know, everyone entitled to a defense, innocent until proven guilty, that kind of thing. I know it sounds a bit cheesy but it's how I survive." Then she laughed before adding, "And since they're entitled to a defense, I figure I might as well provide a good one and make money off it."

Lainie chuckled. "I hear you. If my writing doesn't improve here in the near future I may have to revert back to the law." She shuddered just thinking about it.

Kelley drained the last of her coffee and stood. "I hate to run but I have a meeting with the DA in fifteen minutes. I'll give you a call. We'd love to have you over to dinner."

Lainie stood and hugged her friend. As Kelley left, she sat down to finish her latte. Her eyes wandered over the crowd and toward the window and the constant light rain outside. Something caught her eye. A man hobbling into the shop on crutches.

She watched Paul Stafford make his way clumsily between the tables toward the counter. Along with a gray sweatshirt mostly covered by a forest green raincoat, he wore a pair of faded jeans with the left leg slit all the way up to accommodate a cast that extended from mid-calf to just above the knee. He fidgeted and adjusted his stance as the barista took his order. She considered slipping out the door before he saw her.

Lainie braced herself for Mildred's snarky observation, which didn't come. Instead, she stood and made her way, not to the door but to the counter. "Hey Paul."

He twisted and the wide eyes and open mouth morphed into a broad smile. "Lainie. Good to see you." He took his right hand from the handle on his crutch and offered it.

She shook the hand and smiled. "You too. How're you doing. Glad to see you're out and about. When do you go back to work?"

He shrugged. "I was going to try this week but I'm still on pain meds. They make me kind of loopy, so I figure I'll hold off until next Monday."

The barista interrupted the conversation. "Here you go. Grande coffee black." She set the cup on the countertop.

Paul shifted his stance and picked up the cup with his right hand. Awkwardly grasping the lid with his outstretched fingers, he rested his palm back on the crutch handle. All things considered, this was an invitation to disaster.

This was the first time Lainie had seen Paul standing. He was taller than expected. She jumped in. "Here, let me help you with that." She took the coffee from his hand and looked around the crowded shop. "Where you headed?"

"Thanks. Dunno. You see any empty spots?" He craned his neck as he put his weight on the crutches.

"I've got a table near the back. Why don't you join me?" *God, did I just invite him to join me? Crap.*

He looked at her for a moment before glancing to the side and responding. "Oh, there's a spot there at the counter— that stool." He pointed at an open space among the people sitting up at the small eating counter.

She nodded, walked over and placed the coffee on the counter. "Well okay then. Good to see you and I hope things go well returning to work." She smiled and left the shop, feeling a little disappointed.

Chapter 9

Lainie scrolled through the PDF document that Meg had sent her—changes and corrections to past chapters. Later. She opened up a blank document, centered the cursor, and began typing.

An hour later, she read over what she'd written—flat and boring. She debated whether to delete the entire thing or not. In the end, she saved the document, closed out of the word processor and powered down her computer for the night.

Standing, she stretched her arms out to the side and balled her fists. Sitting all evening without getting up left her stiff and prone to cramps. She wandered aimlessly into the living room, plopped down on the couch, and clicked the TV remote.

Talking heads dominated the screen, each shouting at the other about whatever these jerks talked about. Up arrow.

A picture of some kind of garden hose with a special nozzle covered the screen, overlaid with a flashing message—"$49.99 plus shipping and handling." An enthusiastic male voice completed the presentation. "But wait, there's more. If you call within the next ten minutes…" Up arrow.

A local TV news anchor straightened a sheaf of papers and laid them in front of her as she spoke. "Meanwhile, down at Griffin Park, a group of students and parents rallied under the leadership of Pastor Robert Tell, protesting the state's refusal to fund his youth ministry program."

The show cut to a video of a man standing at a makeshift podium outside yelling into a microphone. He appeared to be in his mid-thirties. His dark brown hair just touched his ears. He raised his arm in animation with his speech. "These Godless politicians and bureaucrats conspire to keep the Lord away from our families, our children, and our lives. They hide behind the Constitution, but I tell you this, our founding fathers, men of God all, would never have imagined that their marvelous creation would be used against God-fearing people."

Lainie shook her head as she gazed at the images on her screen. *This guy sure does use the term "God" a lot. Firing for effect, probably.*

The video feed cut again to a man in a coat and tie speaking to a reporter outside a large non-descript building. "We have no problem funding programs associated with churches. But we need the assurances that the programs are not specifically for religion. Churches of all denominations have non-profit arms that work in social and community services. But they need to make sure that there's a secular purpose being served, that's all. If Pastor Tell would like to contact us directly, I'm sure that we can find a way to make this work."

Back to the news anchor. "But while the two sides traded sound bites, there was no visible movement on either side."

Lainie clicked off the TV. Nothing new here. It seemed every few months this Pastor Tell was railing against something in the community. She knew little about him, other than what was on the news. Mostly it involved programs for children, as far as she could tell. "I guess it's good that someone likes kids."

With the house silent and most of the lights off, she slouched back on the sofa and gazed around the room. The steel blue gray walls housed mostly pen and ink sketches, some from Pacific Northwest artists and some from China. Other than the fact that they were all pen and ink, the collection was eclectic. *They* had chosen their art together. *He'd* taken the watercolors with him. And then there were the blank spaces. Gone were pieces that depicted children or childish art. This was probably for the best. Most days the monotone gray reflected her moods.

She stood and stretched once more. Turning off the lights, she meandered down the hall, past *that* room, to her bedroom. She'd start on the next chapter first thing in the morning.

Chapter 10

Y eah, that works." Lainie rubbed her left wrist and vowed to wear the splint more consistently as she stared at the words on her screen. "Sort of." She smiled and nodded. Good progress and it was not yet noon.

The small laser printer situated to the side of her CPU gave the "Toner Low" alert in the control panel readout. Lainie knew she didn't have a spare in the house. Closing her eyes, she shuddered at the prospect of having to get out. After all, she was on a roll. And yet, ordering online would leave her a couple of days with no printer. Besides, she'd been meaning to replenish her supply of printer paper.

"I shouldn't be printing so much. I can read and edit on screen." But she loved the feel and look of the printed page. The emerging story felt more real when she could hold it in her hand. She saved the document and exited the program.

She grabbed her keys from the basket in the kitchen and donned her raincoat as she took a mental inventory of her pantry and refrigerator. Making lunch at home would require a stop at the store. "What the hell, I'll just grab a sandwich while I'm out and save myself some time."

*****

The complex mélange of aromas inside The Crusty Loaf Bakery and Deli never ceased to delight Lainie. The overpowering warm scent of baking bread competed with brewed coffee and cinnamon from the generous-sized rolls in the display case. Glancing up at the menu, she confirmed her choice—the same choice she made every time she ordered lunch here. She joined the queue.

She stepped up to the counter as her turn came. "I'd like a half turkey and avocado on whole wheat with spinach, red onions, and tomatoes. No mayo. Just chipotle." She opened her wallet and removed her debit card.

The young man sporting a stained apron and a nose ring copied the order down on a pad as he spoke. "Will that be for here or to go?" He looked up and smiled.

"To go please." She handed him her card.

Lainie stepped off to the side to wait on her order and began to mentally re-work the last chapter she'd finished. A race of plant-like humanoids seemed a leap. She'd seen it in an online game once and they managed to make it work. Would that be plagiarizing? No, she decided. This was different. Different name, different physical characteristics—just different.

Mildred chimed in. *Ask Meg about it.*

As she glanced around the small bistro, a familiar face jumped out. Paul sat over by the window, a half-eaten sandwich and a cup of steaming liquid in front of him. He seemed engrossed in a paperback. She moved quickly behind a post, hoping he wouldn't notice her.

Success. She loitered out of view for the next few minutes until a voice from the counter caught her attention. "Lainie. Order up." The young man at the counter put a bag of kettle chips in the white sack and handed it to her. "There you go. Have a good one."

She turned toward the door and glanced over to make sure she was still unnoticed. Perfect. The book seemed to occupy his attention. As she glided toward the door, something came over her. She stopped. "I'm behaving like a child.*"* She glanced around as she muttered, hoping no one noticed her talking to herself. With an abrupt change in direction, she walked over to where the man sat. "Hey there. I see you're out and about regularly. She glanced over to see his crutches leaning against the corner of the wall. "Having any trouble getting around?" She offered a reluctant smile. *Let's not go overboard here.*

His gaze shot up to connect with hers. A smile made its appearance. "Lainie. What a coincidence. Hey, we have to stop meeting like this." A chuckle escaped. "Have a seat. Join me, please." He closed the book and set it aside.

She shook her head and remained standing. "I just stopped in to grab something for lunch at home." *What an awkward statement.* "I don't want to interrupt your reading."

He gestured toward the book. "That? Oh, it's just light recreational stuff. Terry Brooks. Have a seat." He nodded toward the empty seat.

Without thinking, she pulled the chair out and set her sack on the table. "Let me grab a bottle of water. Be right back." As she made her way over to the counter, she chided herself for not only wasting valuable time here but also for spending extra money—on water of all things.

Once back at the table, Lainie glanced over at the closed book. She'd read a bit of Brooks in her time. "You read of lot of him?"

"I read the original Shannara series when I was a kid. Over the years I've picked up some of his stuff now and again. Always a good read." He took a bite of his sandwich.

Lainie unwrapped hers and took the cap off her bottle of water. Now that she was settled in, though, there seemed nothing to say. "You come here often?" *How trite and meaningless can I be?* She gestured around the small eating space.

He shrugged as he swallowed. "Not really. Most days I'm working. So, getting out for a leisurely lunch doesn't work. Besides, eating alone in a place like this just feels funny, if you know what I mean. On the rare occasion when I do grab a sandwich or something, I usually just take it home." He took a sip of coffee.

She nodded. Eating alone in a restaurant was a bit unnerving.

Paul set the cup of hot coffee aside and leaned into the table. "Hey, if you have the time, I know a great lunch place at Gilman Village, you know, over in Issaquah. I'll still be off work on Friday if you'd like to go."

Her stomach churned. *This is exactly what I was afraid of. Let's end this right now.* The words that came out surprised even her. "You seem like a nice guy, Paul, but don't you think you're a little young to be hitting on me?"

A dark change swept over the man. His jaw dropped, and his eyes widened. His gaze jerked from her face to the tabletop and then back. He squirmed in his chair. "Uh, I apologize, really, I wasn't hitting on you. I'm sorry if it came across that way." He furrowed his brow and locked gazes with her again. "Besides, I'm not that young. I'm thirty-five." He paused and glanced away briefly. "Almost." Looking back at her, a shadow of a smile returned. "And you're what, maybe thirty-four? Thirty-five?"

Lainie laughed. "Really? Has that line ever really worked for you?" The laugh faded to a smile, which disappeared.

He shook his head and looked down, chewing on the corner of his mouth. "I'm sorry. Have I done something to offend you? That wasn't a line, I don't think." He peered at her as if trying to read her eyes. "And I've never used it before." He lowered his gaze.

She shook her head. "Sorry." She wrapped up what was left of her sandwich and put the cap on her water bottle. "I really need to go." A forced smile was all she could muster.

Paul gazed at her, his mouth drawn into a tight line. No smile, no bright eyes. Just something that looked like pain. "Uh. Sure. Well, anyway, good to see you." He looked away.

Her stomach continued to rebel as she hustled out the door.

The heretofore silent Mildred made her appearance. *You are one cold-hearted bitch.*

Chapter 11

With her left wrist once again throbbing, Lainie navigated her way through the Bellevue streets. "What do you expect?"

That's not his fault.

"Well it's not my fault either." She had to admit, she'd lost control of what little social grace she had. "And I didn't invite his attentions, anyway."

Oh, I don't know. You're the one that approached him the last two times.

She gave up the fruitless discussion—like arguing with a brick wall.

Arriving home, she put her keys away and hung up her coat. Standing there in the middle of the hallway, she tried to coax a decision from her rattled brain. Should she jump back into her writing and knock out the chapters she owed Meg? Or....

"No. I don't owe him an apology or anything else. And the last thing I need is some kid in my life." She shuffled down the hall to her study and plopped down in the chair. "Damn, I left the paper and toner in the car." She leaned back in the chair and closed her eyes. "Just not my day."

She waited for the inevitable argument from Mildred. None came.

"Yeah, with those *innocent* eyes and sad puppy dog look, I'll bet I'm not the only one he's putting the moves on." She heaved herself out of the chair. "I guess that stuff's not going to bring itself in."

Lainie muttered to herself as she stacked the newly purchased reams of paper in the closet. "I didn't ask for this.

Why couldn't he just leave it alone?" With the last of it put away, she shut the closet door and leaned back against it, eyes closed.

Why can't you leave it alone?

She straightened up and exhaled. "What's that supposed to mean?"

Mildred lit into her. *You're the one obsessing. He just asked you out to lunch. You're acting like he assaulted you. You've worked yourself into a frenzy over it and you're behaving like a spoiled child.*

"So, what? I'm supposed to drop everything I'm doing and go to lunch with him just because he's horny?" The instant she muttered the words Lainie knew that she was indeed slipping over the edge. "Okay, okay." She sighed and opened the file drawer.

Extracting the newly created file relating to the accident, she located the police report and found what she was looking for—Paul's telephone number.

Grabbing her landline handset, she took the piece of paper over and plopped down in her large overstuffed chair. After punching in the number, she gazed out the window waiting for an answer, or maybe hoping for an answering machine.

"Hello."

Her gaze migrated from the window to the floor as she spoke. "Hi Paul. This is Lainie Simpson. Hey, I wanted to apologize for today. My social skills could use some improvement. I hope you weren't offended." She nodded as the words came out.

His voice broke a brief silence. "Oh, that's okay. I mean, no, I wasn't really offended. I wasn't trying to…." The voice trailed off. "I guess that I could use some practice at this too.

I don't interact casually much these days." The chuckle sounded forced.

Lainie smiled. "I know what you mean. Look, lunch on Friday would be nice if the offer's still open." Maybe a day trip and some adult conversation might help her.

"Yes, of course. Fantastic. Only, you'll have to drive. I'm still in the cast. I guess you saw that, though."

She felt better after the phone call. Maybe being a shrew wasn't all it was cracked up to be. Lainie immersed herself in the story. She began to see her characters traversing the land. She heard snatches of conversation between them. She furiously typed, trying to capture everything.

She began to feel better about her editor. Meg had been right about the companion. Now, rather than dumping a bunch of information on the reader, the two friends could engage in conversation that spoke to what they saw, what they felt, and what they hoped to accomplish. And the interaction between the two could show more about their characters than might be possible with boring exposition. But she wasn't ready to give in on the romantic interest just yet.

After knocking out a chapter, she powered down the computer and wandered into the kitchen for a cup of tea. While the kettle heated up, she placed a tea bag in the cup and then pulled an ice pack from the freezer and applied it to her wrist.

As she waited for the water to heat, she gazed around her kitchen. Her stove still sat in the same place. She still had the pasta pan, although she had never used it again. Lainie stared at the spot where she had stood that night. Her eyes filled with tears that overflowed onto her cheeks.

How could she have been such a fool? How could she possibly have believed that anything would last forever? "How could I have not seen that coming?"

Mildred took a decidedly different tone this evening. *You know it wasn't your fault, none of it. There's nothing you could have done about him. And the rest, well, it wasn't your fault.*

A bittersweet smile found its way onto her face. She spent the first year hoping he'd change his mind. She imagined him coming to his senses. Maybe the whole thing would have been easier with him at her side. And here she was seven years later, alone. And she hadn't made spaghetti since that night.

Chapter 12

An unexpected turn in the weather produced a sunny but cool early March day. After a quick stop at Paul's house, Lainie turned onto 495 South to catch Interstate 90 East for the short jaunt to Issaquah. "What's this place like?"

He sat with his back to the corner of the seat and the window in order to accommodate his left leg, still in a cast, without it protruding over into the driver's side. "You got your choice. I know of two really good spots down there. One is Italian—makes fantastic pasta—"

"No." The harsh word cut him off in mid-sentence. The half-assed explanation came out softer. "Pasta doesn't agree with me." She touched her stomach with her right hand and hoped it would be enough.

Paul chuckled and shook his head. "That's good, actually. The other place is better. I've only been there once. But I tell you, I had the best blackened salmon salad. And I swear to God, the bread is hot out of the oven. They have sandwiches and other things too, if you don't like fish."

Out of the corner of her eye, Lainie saw him rest his head against the window and smile at her. "That sounds perfect," she said, sighing half in relief and half in gratitude that he'd accepted the lame explanation.

After parking, Lainie went around and helped Paul out of the car. He looked different there in the midday sun. The crisp air evoked white puffs of breath as he adjusted his crutches. The faded jeans and burgundy fleece jacket, complemented by his shock of brown hair and ready smile, made him look more natural and less threatening than when she'd first met him. They embarked on the block and a half

49

walk. Paul, hobbling along on his crutches, offered no complaints. "See that place there?" He nodded to a small bakery to their right. "We'll have to stop there on the way back. Their carrot cake is phenomenal." He seemed given to superlatives. Either that or he had an incredibly positive outlook on life. "I don't think I'll be able to force any dessert after lunch, but I wouldn't mind taking a piece home."

They located the Salty Sockeye with little problem. The aroma of grilling salmon hit Lainie as soon as they walked in. Once seated, though, the scents began to separate— garlic, tarragon, robust beer, baking bread. Lainie closed her eyes and took a deep breath. "I could gain weight just from the smells in this place." And she was hungry.

She looked over the menu for a moment and then closed it. "You know, I think I'm going to go with your recommendation."

He tossed his menu on top of hers. "Me too. Once you find something you like, stick to it. Always works for me."

Their orders placed, they each decided on a mug of draft ale. It had been years since she'd had any alcohol other than an occasional glass of red wine. The combination of the environs, a few sips of the rich brew, and the bustle of people having a good time awakened a sense of contentment, almost happiness.

She set her mug aside and folded her hands on the table in front of her. "So, you decided to go into education despite the fact that you don't like working with kids." She arched a single eyebrow in question.

He laughed. "Yeah, well, there was more to it than that. My wife, or rather my ex-wife, and I married right after undergraduate school. She always wanted to work in marketing and got hired straight away by one of those wireless services. Me, I just couldn't get my arms around any particular career or job. Truthfully, I liked school. And if she would have let me, I might have morphed into a professional student. But the compromise was that I got my master's in education administration. My grad school advisor promised me that I wouldn't actually have to work with students." He shook his head as he looked out the window. "She lied."

"So, you do work with students?" She took a sip and wiped the foam from her upper lip with her napkin.

He shrugged. "I did for a while, in my first couple of jobs. I had to get a teaching certificate before I could be a principal. That meant classroom work. I was an assistant principal and I had to handle all of the discipline issues. The principal didn't like getting her hands dirty. That would have cured me, but I ended up getting this job offer and it turns out that I have an assistant who handles those problems. So, like I said, these days, I work with employees, budgets, and the school board. My assistant principal is incredible. She can handle the toughest kids without breaking a sweat and yet manages a smile for all of them."

The waiter interrupted their discussion. "We have the blackened sockeye salad for both of you as well as a bread basket." He smiled. "Makes it easy. Anything else I can get you folks?" They each declined and the young man made a hasty retreat.

Paul stabbed a piece of romaine lettuce. "Oh. This creamy citrus dressing, incredible." He closed his eyes and chewed slowly.

Lainie smiled inside. It had been forever since she'd seen anyone enthusiastic about mundane things like salad dressing. "Do you mind if I ask you something?" She continued without waiting for his answer, "The first time I visited you in the hospital, I noticed that there weren't any other cards or flowers." It wasn't technically a question, but perhaps he would get the idea.

He paused and stared at his plate for a moment, as though concentrating. Then his face brightened. "Oh, yeah, I remember. I think that first day was either on a Monday or Tuesday. I phoned the vice principal on Sunday. But because it was the weekend, the others at the school didn't even know I was there until Monday morning. The staff sent over some flowers and a card at some point." He shrugged and held his empty fork up in front of him. "How about you? Have you always been a novelist?"

She cleared her throat and took a drink of water. "Uh, no. I was an attorney. Well, I still am. My license is effective. I just stopped practicing. I went to work for a large Seattle firm right out of law school. Lots of grind, lots of overtime. And the pay was good. But after my divorce, I decided to embrace the romantic notion of a private practice, so I hung out my own shingle. Ah yes, the joys of working for oneself—setting my own schedule, being my own boss, coming and going whenever I felt like it." She laughed.

"It took me about a month to figure out that that wasn't how it worked. Instead of having one boss, every single client was a boss. I took more cases to make more money and my schedule turned into a nightmare. Weekends went out the window. I finally said 'enough.' For reasons passing understanding, I had this great idea to write a novel. So I squeezed that into my already impossible schedule. Luckily, I got an agent and landed a contract for my first book. With that and what I had saved, I had enough money for two years and gave myself that long to finish what turned out to be a fantasy trilogy. That was six months ago and I'm on my second book now."

A lull fell over the table as Lainie concentrated on her salad. Despite her misgivings, she was having a good time.

Paul's voice, more serious, broke her reverie. "Lainie, I want you to know that I really didn't mean anything by the age comment the other day. Honestly, it wasn't a pick-up line. I haven't dated much since my divorce and I'm just pretty clumsy at this sort of thing." He peered at her for a moment before dropping his gaze and taking a bit of salmon on his fork.

She chuckled. "It's okay. Kind of same thing here. Anyway, just to set the record straight, I am older than you." She considered leaving it but decided to remove the doubt. "I'm thirty-nine." She watched his muted reaction.

"I take it you don't like younger men." The serious tone continued.

Lainie shrugged. "Not sure I've ever really thought about it, to tell you the truth. I mean, no, I wouldn't be interested in a twenty-something. On the other hand, I'm not looking for a seventy-something either. I guess that within a certain range, it doesn't make a whole lot of difference. Why? Does it matter to you?"

A smile stole its way onto his face. "Probably about the same thing with me. And I'm not saying that just to agree with you." He laughed. "I haven't really thought much about dating at all. I mean, after my divorce, I was really wary about getting into anything. These days, the only people I see are at work and that's a no-no. And since I'm not about to do the online dating thing, it just never seems to be an issue."

She allowed her gaze to rest on his eyes for a moment. "If you don't mind my asking, what was it about your divorce that affected you that way?" She added quickly, "I mean, if it's not too personal."

"Not at all. Well, let's see, I guess I'd say that it was a pretty good marriage, at least to begin with. We had fun and managed our finances pretty well. We decided not to have kids so there was none of that to deal with. But after we'd been married maybe seven or eight years, it just became apparent that we wanted different lives. She liked to be around a lot of friends, you know, going out clubbing, dinner and movies, that sort of thing. I turned into a homebody. I liked stay home on Friday night, throw a disc in the blue ray, a bowl of popcorn. For vacations—Terri liked Vegas. I was happy to drive the Pacific Coast Highway and just visit wine country. As time went on, we drifted further and further apart. Then one night we just talked it out and decided jointly that splitting up was probably the best thing all around. She remarried a couple of years ago. I talk to her now and again. She's happy." He paused and took a deep draught of ale. "How about you?"

She couldn't go there. "I don't know. Things just fell apart. You know how it is. About seven years ago." Lainie stopped there.

"Any children?"

"No!" Lainie fought off the demon and responded more softly. "No. We didn't have any children."

He nodded and left it. They finished their meals accompanied by lighter conversation—the weather, summer plans, and high fantasy. On their way back to the car, they detoured into the Creamy Frosting shop and purchased a couple pieces of carrot cake to go.

She pulled the Camry into in his driveway just after dark. "You need help in with the cake?" The crutches, cake, and house keys were probably more than he could handle.

"Thanks. That'd be great." Easing himself out of the car, he opened the back car door, and grabbed his crutches. "God, I'll be so glad to get off these things."

When they got up on the front porch, he shifted around, reaching into his coat pocket. "Crap, my key's are in in my pants pocket. Would you mind lifting up the mat there? Should be a key underneath it."

She stared at him in disbelief. "Paul. Really? You have a key to your house underneath your front porch mat?"

He chortled. "I keep hoping someone will come in and rob me so I can get new stuff."

Lainie opened the door, stepped inside, and felt the wall, locating a light switch. She looked around at an immaculate living room. The neutral beige carpet complemented the sage green sofa and chair. An eclectic selection of posters and art prints ranging from Pacific Northwest wildlife to pen and ink sketches of Northwest Indians hung on the walls. "Beautiful home." She handed him the key as she gazed around.

He smiled and shrugged. "It keeps the rain off my head. Thanks so much. Fantastic day. I had a great time."

"Where would you like this?" Lainie held up the container of carrot cake.

He pointed toward the kitchen. "Just set it on the counter there." He paused for a few seconds. "I go back to work next week but, if you don't mind, could I give you a call once things settle back down?"

Lainie nodded. "Sure. Thanks." She paused, wondering whether a handshake, a kiss, or just a nod was best. She opened the door and turned. "Have a good weekend, Paul."

He grinned back. "You too. And drive safely."

As she made her way out to the car, Mildred came out of her cocoon. *See, that wasn't so bad.*

Chapter 13

Lainie enjoyed the most relaxing and yet productive weekend that she'd had in years. Going back through Meg's changes and corrections, they all made sense. The companion thing seemed to work well. The dialogue and interaction provided made it easier to desribe feelings. And even the notion of a romantic interest started to make more sense.

Lainie thought a little about Paul. She chided herself for being so hard on him at first. He seemed like a nice guy who struggled a bit with his social skills. *I know about that one.* As Monday drew to a close, she found herself wondering how his first day back at work went. She could picture him hobbling around on the crutches trying to get a cup of coffee back to his desk. He didn't seem like the type to have his admin assistant fetch his beverages for him. She smiled to herself.

She wound down just before eleven on Monday evening. Having fixed nearly half of Meg's "suggested" changes, she felt satisfied with her effort. After putting the kettle on for tea, she wandered into the living room and turned on the TV to catch the late news.

After preparing a cup of chamomile, she set her tea on the small table and parked in her overstuffed chair. With the presentation of the next news story, her sense of well-being evaporated.

> *We have reports tonight from East Rainier High School of possible sexual misconduct by a staff member. The school district is not*

> *commenting other than to say that they are looking into it. Likewise, the Bellevue Police Department will only say that they are investigating a report. But a source within the school district, speaking on condition of anonymity, indicated that Principal Paul Stafford has been placed on administrative leave pending an investigation.*

The photograph of the high school on the screen disappeared only to be replaced by Paul's image. Lainie felt a knot of sickness in her stomach along with a building rage. *That.... I should have known better.* Waves of nausea coursed through her body and her vision blurred. She had sworn way back when that she would never allow anyone in her heart again. And yet, here she was, betrayed for a second time.

Video footage of a man speaking to a crowd took over the screen as the anchor continued to speak.

> *But not everyone is remaining silent. Late this afternoon, Pastor Robert Tell spoke with a crowd outside his Ministry of Light Church.*

The audio cut over to the man who made his points with forceful gestures of his arms.

> *This is what happens when we keep God out of our schools, out of our courts, out of our police operations, and out of our lives. This is the clearest possible signal that our Lord*

has a place at the table. Our children, our most precious resource, are being molested and raped while the school and the police hide behind their rules and procedures. I tell you this, I promise with all of my heart, I will not cave in to this evil. I join the battle with the parents to protect our children.

While Lainie rarely found herself on the same page as this overstuffed demagogue, she hoped he would draw blood from the despicable pervert. The anchorwoman resumed speaking.

Pastor Tell has indicated that he is organizing a group of parents to appear before the school district to demand answers. We'll keep you informed as details emerge.

The station cut to commercial and then the weather. The voices droned on but Lainie heard nothing else. She felt as though her blood pressure, normally good, had skyrocketed. Her chest pounded and she felt her face turning beet red. She sat and waited for Mildred to make an appearance. This was one confrontation to which she looked forward.

Chapter 14

Lainie stumbled through Tuesday. She focused every ounce of her effort on not thinking about Paul. When her mind strayed to the man, a rage crept in, along with an oversized dose of humiliation. Mildred made herself scarce.

Her work in progress didn't fare well at all. Her main character lost all chance at love as Lainie decided against it. "Terrible idea. She's been betrayed by humans, her own race, and nature herself. She doesn't need anyone else to disappoint her. Maybe she doesn't even need a friend."

Lainie considered going back to the changes she'd made at Meg's behest but decided against it. After all, they were already done. No point wasting time on something else she didn't need to do. She forged ahead into new territory, only to hit a brick wall. The story no longer made sense.

She called Meg early in the afternoon but connected with an answering machine. "Give me a call if you get a chance. I have a few questions."

The hours crept by with no progress and no return call. Thoughts of Paul assailed her, but she kept her guard up. She'd wasted far too much time on him already.

After a light dinner of salad and sourdough bread, she decided to give the story another go. It wouldn't write itself and she didn't want her heroine trapped in mid-story forever. She needed closure.

Shortly after eight that evening, the ringing phone interrupted her train of thought. Lainie sat her cup of coffee down and grabbed the phone without looking at the caller ID. It had to be Meg. No one else would call. Her gaze barely left the monitor as she connected and then scrolled to the next page of the manuscript. "Hello."

An unexpected voice emerged. "Hi, Lainie, this is Paul Stafford." The words came out bathed in pain.

"Hello." She had nothing to say to him. She wanted nothing to do with him.

"I guess you heard about my dilemma?" The words seemed forced, reluctant to make themselves known.

Dilemma? So that's what he calls this? She smirked. "Uh, yeah, I heard. What do you want, Paul?"

"Lainie, I didn't do those things. The story's not true." His voice embodied desperation.

She rolled her eyes, wishing that he could see her reaction over the phone. "Hmmm." What else would he say?

"I need help."

The smirk turned to a full-blown laugh dripping with sarcasm. "I guess the hell you do. But, like I told you, I don't practice law anymore. And when I did, I didn't take these kinds of cases." She swiveled her chair to face the window as she spoke.

"I thought that maybe you could just give me some advice or maybe recommend..." His uneven words trailed off giving way to silence.

She closed her eyes and shook her head. "I'm sorry. Can't help you. Contact the bar association. They can put you in touch with someone."

"Okay. Well, thanks. Sorry to bother you."

"Yeah." She disconnected.

Mildred came out of hiding. *The rudeness was uncalled for, over-the-top.*

She responded with the certainty that Mildred was completely out of touch. "What the hell. This guy's a high school principal banging his students. He deserves a lot worse than rudeness."

But the pesky inner voice seemed to have a different take on it. *Maybe, maybe not. But don't people deserve a chance? He said the story wasn't true. What happened to innocent until proven guilty?*

"Even if the details are off, there has to be something there. These stories don't invent themselves."

How would you know? You didn't even listen.

She put Mildred on "ignore" and stared at the handset she'd placed back in its charger. She didn't owe this guy anything last week and she certainly didn't owe him anything now. Besides, even if she did want to help, which she didn't, what could she do? She didn't practice and she had no experience with criminal law. And she damned sure didn't want to be a shoulder for him to cry on.

"Why does this crap always land on me? I'm like a magnet for all the low-life pieces of shit in the world." She shook her head and tried to hold on to the rage. She didn't want to feel any sympathy for this guy.

Then the idea hit. "I know where I can dump this problem. Perfect."

Lainie pulled up the contact list on her phone, made a selection, and pressed the call button.

After a few rings, a somewhat familiar voice answered. "Hello."

"Hi, Yolanda. This is Lainie Simpson. How're you doing? I hear that congratulations are in order." *Or maybe condolences as the case may be.*

62

"Hey there, Lainie. Thanks and we're doing great. How about you?"

Lainie shrugged as if the woman on the other end of the line could see it. "Okay, I guess. Say, is Kelley close by?"

"Sure, hang on. I'll get her."

After a few moments, another voice emerged. "Hi Lainie. What's up?"

Lainie closed her eyes and gave it one last thought. Yes, this is the best way. "Hey Kelley, I was just wondering if you have room in your case load for another loser."

Chapter 15

Lainie gave a thumbnail sketch—some guy she hardly knew got himself in deep trouble and could use legal representation.

Kelley's voice came out sounding all business. "Yes. I do have room in the schedule. So, you say this guy's a high school principal, huh. I guess that means he can pay. I can't afford any more pro bono cases right now. Sure, have him contact me at the office in the morning and I'll take it from there."

Lainie breathed a sigh of relief. She'd done what she could and had passed him off to someone who routinely dealt with that kind of person. She was off the hook. "Great. Will do. Oh, once you two get straight, could you let me know how it went?"

A laugh floated over the line. "Yeah, right. Come on, Lainie, you know I can't do that. Remember the old client confidentiality thing? Sorry." She paused and changed her tone. "By the way, how do you know this guy?"

Lainie had dreaded the question. She described the accident in succinct terms. "We had coffee once and went to lunch." She shuddered as she said the words. They made it sound like something more than it was.

"Wait. Are you telling me you two were—"

Lainie cut her off. "No. There isn't any 'we two.' We were involved in an accident and had coffee and a lunch. Nothing more." She shook her head as she spoke.

"Then why do you want information?" Kelley's question came across like an interrogation.

"I don't, really. I mean, since I referred him, I just kind of wanted to make sure the connection was made. That's all. Once you get into the case, he's your problem." She felt her temper rising again.

"Hmmm. I see."

But it was clear she didn't see. Lainie decided it was not worth the effort to fight it. "Whatever. Look, just forget it."

Another laugh. "Consider it forgotten."

The response frustrated Lainie even more, although she had no idea why. "Okay. I won't keep you. Give me a call if you need anything from me."

After she disconnected, she wrote Kelley's phone number and office address on a sheet of paper before dialing her next number. Tapping her pen nervously on the pad, she waited for an answer.

"Hello." The voice came out tentative and meek.

"Paul, this is Lainie. I have a phone number and address here. Kelley's a good attorney. She should be able to help you." She tried to keep the words and tone as neutral as possible. Hopefully, her anger and disgust didn't come across. But the big thing was that she didn't want to give the impression that she cared in the least.

Chapter 16

Lainie slept better that night than the previous. She'd processed the initial information from the news story, referred the perv to a competent attorney, and disconnected from the process. She could go back to her life, such as it was.

Wednesday morning found her at the computer trying to sort the story out. Friendship and trust seemed absurd given her state of mind. But Meg had a way of insisting.

By late afternoon, she'd run out of steam. She sat staring at a partially completed sentence with the cursor blinking accusatorily. Thankfully, Kelley hadn't called so things must have gone okay with the sleaze ball.

Lainie considered turning on the TV and catching the early version of the local news but decided against it. The media was likely still frothing over the high school sex scandal and she didn't need to know any more about it. She stood, stretched, and began pacing around the house. Her novel needed to move forward and sitting at the computer wasn't helping.

She considered going for a drive to clear out the cobwebs. But then she looked at the clock and remembered the joys of rush hour traffic. Her cellphone invaded the indecision. Glancing at the caller ID, a sense of dread filled her. "I really don't want to take this call." But a sense of obligation overruled her reticence and she connected. "Hey Kelley. What's up?" She leaned back in her chair and stared out the window, dreading what she knew was coming.

"Hi, Lainie. Yolanda's got something going on tonight so I wondered if maybe you'd be up for dinner out." The words she released came sounded a little too rehearsed.

Lainie mentally assembled a list of things on her plate that would forestall the event. Still, Kelley was her friend. She sighed. "Sure, sounds good. Any particular place?"

The response came without hesitation. "How about the Red Pepper Grill? They have cheap hors d'oeurves and decent drinks." This was not a *spur-of-the-moment* thing. "Seven okay with you?"

"Perfect." She tried to sound enthusiastic but the whole situation was anything but perfect.

***

Lainie showed up early and commandeered a booth near the back of the upscale eatery. A mélange of aromas that included grilling meat, garlic, and fresh bread caressed her sense of smell as she crossed the threshold of the establishment. The din of continuous conversation and the clinking of silverware on plates filled the air. Alerting the server that a friend would be joining her, she ordered a glass of red house wine to get started. The drink slid down smoothly, and one more made her even more relaxed.

But as fortune would have it, Mildred had accompanied her. *What have you got to be tense about, anyway?*

Lainie pondered the question. Nothing, really. The book was coming along, actually faster than she'd expected. Her editor wanted changes and had suggestions but that was to be expected. Her finances were doing okay. And best of all, she'd dumped the Paul problem on someone whose job it was to handle those kinds of things. She took a deep draught, closing her eyes as she savored the liquid in her mouth before swallowing.

A familiar voice rang out from across the room. "And there she is, budding young novelist." Kelley made her way to the booth.

Kelley ordered a scotch—neat— and shed her raincoat as the waiter retreated. "So, besides writing the next great million-seller, what have you been up to?" The look on her friend's face seemed too casual, as though it was forced. Her gaze wandered too quickly. And the question seemed especially strange since the two of them had met for coffee the previous week.

Lainie cringed as she waited for some bad news about the case. Not that it should matter. Paul was Kelley's problem. If a good attorney couldn't help him then, well, tough shit. Still, she decided to play for time. "Not much. Life's pretty simple these days. Get up, eat breakfast, write, eat lunch, write…well, you get the picture." As she raised her glass to take another sip of wine, she noticed Kelley clenching her jaw, gaze locked onto hers.

Lainie set her drink down and leaned back in the booth, arms folded on her chest. No point in dragging this out. "Okay, so what's up?" She made a quick attitude adjustment before adding, "I mean, having dinner is great but I get the feeling that there's more to it than that." She forced a smile.

The waiter swooped in with Kelley's scotch. "Anything else now?"

Kelley glanced up and shook her head. "Not right now, thanks." As the young man made his retreat, she rotated the glass in front of her with both hands, staring into the amber liquor. After a few seconds, she took a drink and then set it off to the side.

Leaning in, hands folded on the tabletop, she took a deep breath. "Yeah, you got me." She locked gazes with Lainie and offered a weak smile. "I may need a little help. I got hit with some court scheduling changes today and I'm in a bind. I was wondering if you might be available to do some preparatory legwork on Paul's case." She raised her hands in a gesture that seemed intended to stave off a quick response. "I mean, if you still have your business license, I'd be glad to pay a premium. I'm going to need some interviews done and some background research." She averted her gaze as she finished.

A laugh escaped Lainie despite her effort to remain serious. "Come on, Kelley. You know the deal. Remember? Conflict of interest? He and I had that accident and it hasn't been resolved yet. I couldn't help even if I wanted to." She started to add that she didn't want to but decided to leave it there.

Kelley leaned back and stared for a few seconds. "You didn't say anything about a pending case involving the two of you. He didn't mention it either."

Lainie grimaced. "Well, there's not a *formal* case in progress but it could still happen. The rules are pretty clear about that kind of thing."

"Not really. I mean, yes, they do speak to conflict of interest, but representation is allowed if you feel you can represent him fairly and he agrees. Besides, you wouldn't really be representing him. I'm just looking for some research. I assume you're capable of doing that without bias." She took a sip of her Scotch and set the glass back down directly in front of her.

Mildred offered her thoughts. *Some extra money would allow you to extend your self-imposed deadline.*

Lainie closed her eyes and turned her head to the side as she assembled her thoughts. With the diplomatic refusal all set in her mind, she started to speak but the words that came out surprised and dismayed her. "How much time do you figure this will take? I mean, I'm working on a deadline for my editor."

Kelley's face erupted in a smile. "Not much, really. Maybe a couple of weeks. I have two assistants who are doing the bulk of the grunt work. I just need you to talk to his old boss, his ex-wife, and maybe one or two more people. For the background research, I'm mainly talking about a search of the criminal justice system, financial records, and the like." Her gaze remained locked on Lainie, a look of hope in her eyes. "Come on. After all, he is a friend of yours."

Rage boiled over inside Lainie. "No. He's *not* my friend. In fact, I don't give a shit about him. He's just another perv with a smooth line." Her jaw clenched as she stared daggers at her friend.

She started to go on, but Kelley interrupted her. "Okay, okay. Sorry." She lowered her eyes, her words coming out as a whisper. "I'm just trying to do the right thing here. The guy's under the gun and needs representation. It's what I do. I need some help right now." She took a deep breath and returned her gaze to Lainie. "Look, if you don't want to do it, fine. I understand." She paused and then added, "But I would personally appreciate it if you would."

Lainie cursed herself internally and sighed. "Talk to him. If he's amenable, I'll do what I can." She leaned forward and glared at Kelley. "But my rate is three fifty with a minimum of twenty hours. I'm not going to jump into this nightmare for nothing. Call me after you talk to him."

Chapter 17

Lainie muttered as she stared at the monitor for her still-powered-down computer. "This has to rank right up there with some of the stupidest decisions I've ever made." After dinner with Kelley, she resolved to go home and pour herself into the novel, forgetting the mess she'd allowed herself to be roped into. Alas, no such luck. She couldn't even muster the enthusiasm to hit the power button.

She went to the kitchen for a glass of water. Mildred accompanied her on the journey. *What, you never represented a corporation that misbehaved?*

"That was different—just legal maneuvering. It was never about right and wrong."

How is this different? Kelley asked you to do a simple job. You just have to interview some people and get some background information. You're not the judge or jury, you know.

"The difference is, this guy was porking some kids—a far cry from contract disputes or liability issues."

You don't know that he did anything wrong.

Lainie closed her eyes and shook her head as she walked. Mildred didn't understand. "Like arguing with a brick wall."

Yes, it is.

With her drink in hand, she turned out the lights and started down the hall. She hadn't yet decided whether to go to her work area for one more attempt or head to the bedroom and throw in the towel for the night. The landline ringtone stopped her in her tracks. She glanced at her watch—9:45.

Kelley always called on the cellphone. "This had better not be Paul." She began to mentally formulate the string of expletives she would hurl at him. Instead, she decided to let it go to the message machine. As she entered her bedroom, she listened to her recorded greeting play. As it ended, a voice emerged from the speaker that turned her blood cold.

"Hello, Lainie."

Chapter 18

As the voice sliced through her heart, she mentally retreated into the past.

Lainie stood in the kitchen staring into the living room at the front door through which her life had just passed. Eight years of marriage became nothing. Even what might have been was gone. She struggled to put the pieces together. On top of everything else, now this. Five minutes previous, she'd been concerned with which dressing to pull out of the refrigerator for their dinner salad. Now what? Had she missed something? What was it that he said, something about someone else?

By the time she returned to the present, the message had ended and a blinking red light on the machine urged her to listen. She stared, not sure about that. Did she really want to hear? The flashing LED dared her. She walked over and hit the play button.

"Hello, Lainie. Was just thinking about you and decided to give you a call. I read your book. I'm so proud of you. Maybe we could get together, you know, have coffee and talk. Give me a call. I'm at the same number. Love you."

The machine beeped and the familiar, vague, non-descript voice spoke up. "End of final message."

She hurled her response at the offending machine. "Get together? In what universe would I do that? And the 'love you' crap, really?" Tears gathered in her eyes and threatened to overflow. Her breath came short and her heart ached. "Why? Why can't people leave me alone? Why couldn't he just stay gone? Why now?" She stared at the erase button that taunted her. She reached reach over and depressed it twice, evoking the standard automated response, "Message erased."

She turned and walked into the bathroom to brush her teeth.

Mildred spoke up, albeit much more meekly than usual. *Ignore him. He's a distraction. Don't make him any more important than he really is.*

For once, Lainie found herself in agreement. But her heart tried to argue. She found herself hopelessly mired in a morass of emotional confusion. She wanted to hate her ex-husband but wondered if she should be past this. After all, he hadn't been responsible for all of her problems. As she struggled to force Jason from her mind, his image was replaced by one of Paul, someone else who'd betrayed her.

Before Mildred could object, Lainie swept Paul from her mind. He was a job—one that would bring in a few thousand dollars at least. And once he went to prison, he would get what he deserved. "Screw Jason. Screw Paul." There was only one person in the world upon whom she could rely. She turned out the light as she left the bathroom. Turning back the covers of her bed, she crawled in for a sleepless night.

Chapter 19

Lainie struggled to make sense of the world around her. Regaining consciousness, it took her a few seconds to recognize the surroundings—a hospital room. Amid beeps and buzzes, someone was talking. The man standing there in funky-looking sage green clothes. What had he said? Gone? What's gone? She allowed her gaze to wander the room. Nothing else there. No, wait, a nurse came in. She checked something on a machine and then left. "Jason? Where are you?" What was that she was looking at, over on the windowsill? A card? Some flowers?

The night had turned out to be not entirely sleepless. As Lainie sat up in bed, she found herself wishing it had been. Her breath came hard and fast. Her heart pounded, and she felt her body bathed in sweat beneath the cotton tee shirt.

"Christ, this sucks." She threw the covers back, swung her legs off the bed onto the floor and trudged to the bathroom, glancing at the bedside clock—3:45. On the bright side, though, only a couple more hours before she would normally be getting up.

After washing her hands, she wandered back into the bedroom. Stopping beside the bed, she turned and stared at the door. "Why do I close it? It's not like there's anyone here that will see me." And yet, for the past seven years, ever since… she had closed her bedroom door. The most likely explanation, she figured, was to keep the ghosts out.

As she lay in bed, staring at the shifting shadows on the ceiling, she once again tried to analyze her way out of this case. She had no experience in criminal law. She had a conflict of interest, regardless of what Kelley had said. She was certain Paul was guilty and she hated him for it.

Hate him? Really? Mildred never seemed to sleep. *You don't even know him.*

"I know him. They're all alike. The names change… the dates and places… but it's always the same."

Who are the 'they' you are talking about?

She ignored the voice and went back to the check-off list of reasons to quit the case. She needed to be working on the book. Meg was unrelenting and falling behind would be disaster.

That may be a valid point. Mildred seemed suddenly accommodating… for a moment. *On the other hand, you may want to revisit your financial accounts before making any rash decisions. Things are not as rosy as you expected.*

Lainie threw in the towel. Nights had a way of sucking the life out of her, including her ability to fight with her conscience.

Mildred softly re-focused the conversation. *You're going to have to deal with this, sooner or later.*

"I know. But not tonight. I have a meeting in a few hours. Let me get some sleep, please."

Chapter 20

Lainie took the rickety elevator to the second floor of a building that had seen better days. The hallway reeked of stale tobacco smoke along with a non-specific odor of something less savory. The bare walls, once probably white, had seasoned to a dull shade of yellow. Out of the lift, she turned left and made her way down the hall, watching the office numbers as she went. She muttered to herself as she skulked toward the dreaded meeting. "Terrible idea. Horrible." And the worse part was that she had no idea why she'd gone along with it.

"And here we are, suite two twelve." She closed her eyes briefly, took a deep breath, and opened the door.

A young twentyish woman in jeans and a lavender blouse sat guarding the kingdom. "Good morning. Can I help you?" She offered a smile as she sat, hands folded on the desk.

Lainie nodded and identified herself. "I have a meeting with Kelley."

The woman gestured toward an internal hallway. "You can go on back. Everyone's already there."

Her cellphone chirped just as she was about to enter. Pulling back into the corridor, she checked the display—not a number she recognized. Who would be calling her cellphone? Most everyone she knew was inside the meeting room already. Without giving it much thought, she sent the call to voice mail and set the phone for vibrate. Stuffing it in her purse, she shifted her thoughts to the coming discussion.

When Lainie made her entrance into the small conference room, the discomfort intensified. Paul slouched in a chair on one side of the table. He looked up at her, nodded, and looked back down at the tabletop. Kelley sat at the head of the long, oval table and two other individuals sat opposite Paul.

"Hi. Grab a chair." She gestured with an open hand. "Everyone, this is Lainie Simpson. She's going to be helping out with the legwork on this case." Kelley pointed to the other end of the table. "You know Paul." She nodded toward the two strangers. "This is Andi Perotsky, my research assistant." Shoulder-length blonde hair and brilliant blue eyes dominated the classic features of the young woman who appeared to be in her mid-twenties. Her trim build complemented her medium height.

Andi smiled. "Pleasure to meet you."

"Andi's a grad student—psychology." Kelley gestured toward the other individual, a young man who appeared barely old enough to be out of high school. "And this specimen is Elliott Vanderslyce—my technical magician."

Lainie nodded in his direction.

His disheveled blond hair framed a face otherwise dominated by a set of black-rimmed glasses with thick lenses. The nerdy head sat atop a tall, lanky body. The awkward grin seemed forced. "Sup." He slunk down in his seat, hands resting on the arms of the chair.

Lainie turned her attention to Kelley not allowing her gaze to pause even for an instant on Paul. "Thanks. Pleasure to meet you all." She had known Kelley since law school, but she'd never seen her work. From a legal aspect, this would be interesting, in a morbid sort of way.

"Okay, let's get started. I met with Paul yesterday and went over the basics of the attorney-client relationship and the finances. The purpose of this meeting, other than introductions, is to make sure we're all on the same page. Okay?"

Without waiting for an answer, she plowed ahead. "The status. As of right now, there are no charges so we're playing a contingency game. The school district has put him on admin leave." She turned to speak directly to Paul. "It's not part of our case but I'll give you this advice. Right now, they're paying you for nothing. That means that they'll want to cut you loose as soon as possible. Check your contract carefully. Maybe that's okay with you, maybe not. If you want to fight it, you'll need to deal with that separately from our case." Kelley paused and looked around the table.

Paul nodded as he gazed at Kelley and then back down to the table.

"Moving on. I'm going to lay out some basic rules. Paul, keep in mind that I work for you and you get to make the decisions. But these are things I strongly advise. If you're not inclined to take my advice, then in all honesty, you're wasting my time and your money." She stared at him for a moment before continuing.

"First, don't speak with anyone about this matter without me present. There will be a number of parties that try to isolate you. The police, the press, the school, you name it. Refuse to talk to them. If the police arrest you, go peacefully and immediately request that I be notified. *Do not* answer any questions until I get there. Is that clear?"

Paul mumbled as he nodded. "Yes." He gazed at each person around the room as if looking for some meaning—a lost kid in a large, hostile crowd.

Lainie wondered how he did it—managed to keep up that innocent, injured front after doing what he did. She kept her thoughts to herself.

Kelley continued. "Good. Once I'm there, don't answer any question until I clear it. When they ask, glance at me. If it's okay, I'll nod. If I have a problem with the question, I'll challenge it. But it's kind of hard to deal with it if you've already blurted out the answer." She paused, her gaze resting intently on him with a remarkably neutral appearance, as if she had no feeling one way or the other about the man.

He nodded without looking up.

Lainie allowed herself to watch him for a moment. This was a far different man than she'd shared an ale with just the previous week. His face was dominated by what looked like a combination of fear and confusion. He responded to the comments by Kelley with a mumbled assent and a nod.

Kelley shifted in her seat and tapped her pen on a yellow-lined legal pad in front of her. "A key point that I'm going to come back to again and again—I need the truth from you. We need to know what the other side knows, preferably before they know it. In any case, if and when you have information that's relevant, you need to get it to me." She paused, narrowing her eyes. "And no beating around the bush. For example, if they arrest you, they're going to get a warrant to search your home and seize your computer. Will they find anything that helps them?"

He looked around the table from person to person, his eyes wide. "Like what? I mean, I can't think of anything."

Kelley's laugh came out as caustic and cynical. "I'll be blunt. You visit any adult sites? Do you have any kiddie porn or any porn at all on your computer? Have you signed up for a dating service looking for much younger women? Anything that would help them support these allegations? That's what I'm talking about." She glared at him.

"No. Nothing. At all. No." He shook his head as he accentuated each word. As his gaze came to rest on Lainie, it softened. "No." He slouched farther down in his chair.

Lainie shuddered. This guy had the act down perfect. She ground her teeth and forced herself to remain quiet.

Kelley looked at him for a moment. Any emotion she may have been feeling remained hidden from view. "So far, what we've heard is that three girls filed complaints. We don't yet know exactly what they said. Do you know who they are?" With her head turned slightly to the side, her gaze bore down on Paul.

As he responded, his tone and volume increased as the anger poured out. "I have no idea. They wouldn't tell me. The school won't even talk to me about it. Isn't there some way we can find out?" His gaze flitted from one face to another around the table. He sat up straighter in his chair, his fists clinched tight on the tabletop in front of him. His face turned a bright shade of red.

Kelley shook her head. "Probably not until the police decide to interview you. At that point, they'll have to tell us. She chewed on her bottom lip for a moment before moving on.

"Paul, the way the legal system works in these cases is that the burden of proof lies with the prosecution. They have nearly unlimited resources but that one burden goes a long way toward leveling the playing field. So, as unfair as this may sound to you, we are not out to prove your innocence. Our goal is to poke enough holes in the prosecution's case to either get the case dismissed or have you acquitted. If we start trying to prove innocence in a courtroom, it can have the effect of shifting the burden of proof in the eyes of *some jurors*. They may look to you to convince them that you're innocent. If you can't, they tend to accept the prosecution's arguments at face value. We do not, under any circumstances, want that to happen. So, I say this as a preemptory caution—don't go there. Play by our rules and we stand a good chance, okay?"

Paul reacted immediately. His eyes wide and his hands flat on the tabletop, he insisted, "But I am innocent. I didn't do anything." He looked imploringly from person to person around the table.

"I hear what you're saying and everyone else hears it too. But that assertion doesn't help us. We focus on the evidence. If the evidence takes us to your innocence, so be it. Otherwise, we work with what we have. Got that?"

He obviously didn't *get it*. "No. I am innocent. Whether the evidence says that or not, I am. You're supposed to be my attorney. I don't think it's too much to ask that you at least make the appearance of believing in me." He slapped both hands flat on the tabletop.

Kelley paused briefly and let the silence hold for a moment. When she spoke, it was in a soft but neutral voice—neither supportive nor accusing. "Yes, Paul. I am your attorney. My job, as I have told you now several times, is to give you the best defense I can. My stock and trade is evidence because that's what I have to give to the jury. It's also what I try to pick holes in when it belongs to the prosecution. Whether you are innocent or not, you will get the best defense I can give you. I promise you this, though.

Throwing nothing more than a claim of innocence at the jury is a losing strategy. For the time being, I ask that you trust me. There's nothing we can do about those statements until we see them."

A defeated-looking Paul lowered his head and nodded.

Lainie marveled at his acting skills. He was sitting here trying to pull the wool over all of their collective eyes. Hopefully, the others weren't falling for it.

"Final point today. Assuming that charges are filed, we'll get a copy of all evidence before we go to trial. We'll be able to go through it and find weaknesses. I can pretty much guarantee that, at some point, the DA will come forward and offer you a deal. If we get Eve Lasorda, and I think we will, she's going to want to wrap it up quickly. She's not likely going to be anxious to put those three girls on the stand if she can help it. When the offer comes, I'll bring it to you along with a recommendation. The decision is obviously yours. But I'll tell you right now that my advice will be based strictly on the deal and the evidence. Your assertions of innocence will *not* be a factor for me. You can consider that when the time comes. I tell you this because, when that happens, I don't want you pushing back against me like I'm the enemy. I'll give you the best defense possible. Understand?"

Paul stared at her for a few moments, his eyes narrowing as he shook his head slowly. "You mean I'm supposed to admit that I did something I didn't?"

Kelley gazed at him for a moment. "That's down the road. Until we get there, we don't know what we're facing. I just wanted to alert you to the possibility. Let's not get into the weeds just yet." She took a deep breath and looked around the table. "Anyone have any other questions right now?"

Paul sat up and leaned into the table. "Yeah. I want to know why those girls are saying this? Why are they lying about me? We just need to ask them. This has to be some kind of mistake." He shook his head vigorously.

Lainie felt physically ill watching his act. How could any one individual be so vile and devious? One would think that the least he could do is own up to his actions.

Kelley nodded at him. "Those are good questions and we'll get to them. But there is a time and a way to do that. We first need to see what they said."

He stared with angry eyes and said nothing.

After the meeting ended, Lainie gathered her things and stood. "Give me a call when you're ready to talk about my assignments." She addressed Kelley, taking care to avoid Paul's gaze. As she left the room, she remembered the cellphone call that she'd gotten. she checked her phone and saw the red "1" in the voice mail section. She touched the text and listened.

"Hi Lainie. This is Jason. I tried calling your landline but you haven't returned the call. Not sure if you're checking that these days. Anyway, if you get this, please give me a call. Would love to have coffee with you soon. Love you. Bye."

She shuddered. Yes, she had heard the message left on her landline machine... and ignored it. And no, she had no intention of returning this call either. *Love you? Seriously? He could actually spit those words out after doing what he did?* She almost gagged. She deleted the message and the record of the recent call. Lainie had no need of his phone number. There were no circumstances that she could imagine where she would ever call him.

Chapter 21

Toward the end of the evening, Lainie took a break from her writing to look over the list of assignments in Paul's case. Kelley had apportioned out the preliminary work—mostly background and gathering of records. They had agreed on a sub-contractor arrangement. With her attorney and business license both still in effect, she would just need to develop a time and expense tracking sheet and an invoice form.

Most of what she was responsible for would need to be done during the workday when institutions and offices were open. The only thing that concerned her was an interview with Terri Adamson, Paul's now-remarried ex-wife. The name stared back at her from the page like a playground dare in middle school. No doubt the former Ms. Stafford, if she ever went by that name, would give her an earful.

The other items, checking on Paul's stint as an assistant principal, records searches, and financial status, would be old hat for her. She'd done these things a hundred times before, albeit on civil cases. As she mentally ordered and organized the list, Lainie idly wondered if this was billable time.

Didn't take you long to get back into the lawyer mentality. Mildred had taken the day off until then.

"Hey, I'm helping the guy. Isn't that what you wanted?"

Is that what you're doing? Seems like you were just figuring out how to soak him for more money.

The phone ringing interrupted the internal conversation. Lainie glanced at the caller ID and winced. "Hello Paul."

The response came slow and weak. "Hi Lainie. Sorry to be calling so late but...."

She interrupted him before he could go off on some *poor me* tangent. "Paul, please don't call me at home. We have a meeting tomorrow afternoon. Anything you need to tell me, you can do it then."

"I know." Pause. "I was just, uh, I kind of was hoping to talk."

"No. If you need to talk about this, find yourself a friend." Lainie felt a twist in her stomach as she poured out the words. Not regret, just... something else.

Silence held for a few seconds before he answered. "I thought, well, maybe that you..."

"No. I'm on your legal team. I'll do the best I can for you on that. Anything else, you need to look elsewhere. I need to go. Good night." She closed her eyes and moved the handset away from her ear, ready to disconnect.

She heard the voice emerge from the earpiece like a distant voice echoing off a wall. "Okay. Good night."

She hung up. "That guy's got some freaking nerve. He plays up to me like some shy kid in love for the first time. All the while he's screwing his high school students. Then when he gets caught with his hand in the cookie jar, he comes up with the sad puppy act. Screw him."

You have this all figured out?

"Doesn't take a rocket scientist. It's not like this kind of crap doesn't ever happen. I'm betting his ex is going to fill me with lots of gory details. Just think about it."

I don't think. You're responsible for that part. I just talk to you.

"Then you need to do less talking when you don't know what you're talking about."

Which brings us back to my original question. Are you sure you have this all figured out?

"Go to sleep, Mildred."

Lainie's gaze migrated down to her to-do list. Everybody on the legal team would be out beating the bushes, turning over every rock, doing everything they could to save his hide. All because he couldn't keep his hands off young girls.

Out of nowhere, a question popped into her mind. Where would Paul find a friend at that point? Against her will, Lainie recalled what it was like for the world to crumble and to have no one to whom she could turn. "But that was different. It wasn't my fault."

Chapter 22

The criminal records search—national and state—came up clean. She printed off a copy of the receipt for payment and placed it in the newly created "Legal Expenses" file folder. She'd gone for the high end, expensive search. "Nothing's too good for a perv like that." She took a moment to record her own time on the tracking sheet. If she had to deal with the likes of him, she might as well make money on it.

The phone rang and she answered.

"Hey, this is Kelley. Real quick. The police have Paul and are ready to start questioning. I'm on my way now. You want to come along?"

"I'll pass. No point in padding the bill. I'm sure you can handle it." She didn't particularly want to witness his act again.

"Okay. You have any luck on that background material?"

"Uh, some. The criminal search came up clean. I'm waiting for a call back from the school district on his past performance. I'll start on the financial stuff this afternoon." She looked up at the clock—barely eleven. "Probably be tomorrow before I connect with the ex-wife."

"Sounds good. I'll let you know what happens. Bye." Click.

The afternoon crept by—no call back from Kelley. "Things must really be jumping down at the old cop shop."

If she was listening in, Mildred held her peace.

Lainie plowed through his financial reports, which turned out to be slower and more cumbersome than she'd remembered. Just before three, she got the return call on

Paul's previous employment. The caller ID indicated the West Creekside High School. "Hello."

"Hello, I'm trying to reach Elaine Simpson. This is Sarah Rodriguez returning her call."

"I'm Elaine. Thanks for getting back to me so quickly. I'm on the legal team representing Paul Stafford. Do you have a few minutes to answer some questions?"

"Sure. Is this about the relations with the students over there at his school? Because I really don't know anything about that."

"Yes, it's about that case. But I'm also interested in his time at your school." Lainie switched the phone to her other hand and then cradled it on her shoulder as she prepared to type. She reconsidered. "I'm sorry, could you hold on for a second while I put this on speaker?" Without waiting for an answer, she reached over and punched a button. "Can you hear me?"

The voice boomed over. "Yes."

With the technical arrangements in place, Lainie began. "I understand that Mister Stafford served as assistant principal under you."

"That's right. He was here for, let's see, I think about four years. I can check the records for an exact dates but that seems about right."

"That'll be fine for now. How would you describe his performance?" Lainie had some specific interests but decided to keep the question broad hoping to gather more information.

"Generally, very good. After grad school, he did the standard student teaching stint to get his certificate. We hired Paul right after that. He didn't have any admin experience so there was a learning curve. Not much you can do about that kind of thing. But he came up to speed quickly and did fine."

Not a whole lot there. "What about his relationships with students, any problems there?"

"If you're referring to inappropriate or sexual relations, no, never." The word trailed off as if there was more to come but nothing materialized.

"Okay, anything else, I mean, other than sexual type misconduct?"

"Well, I'm not sure it was really a problem, but he didn't really take to getting out and mixing with students. One of the things that we expect our assistant principal to do is to stay in touch with what's going on. Most people in the position do this by visiting classrooms, hanging out in the lunchroom from time to time, and attending special events going on in school. That wasn't Paul's cup of tea, so to speak. Don't get me wrong, if something came up, he'd handle it. He just never went out of his way to interact with the kids. I have to admit, I was surprised to hear of the problems he's having. That just doesn't sound like him."

Lainie smirked silently. Paul had everyone fooled. "Okay. Any complaints? Parents, teachers, students? Or other staff?"

"Hmmm. Not that I recall. Paul was pretty quiet, you know, kind of reserved. He didn't get close to people. He wasn't rude or anything, he just seemed, I don't know, what you might call socially clumsy." She quickly added, "In an endearing kind of way."

After hanging up, Lainie looked at her notes. This guy really covered his tracks well. She found it hard to believe that he could have gone all this time and not stumbled. She shook her head and chuckled. "I'll bet the ex sings a different song."

Just after five, the phone rang again. "Hello."

Kelley's voice came over ominous and foreboding. "Hey. We got the names of the three students."

"That's good." Lainie shrugged as she prepared to relate the results of her interview with Paul's former boss, Sarah Rodriguez.

Kelley's next words hung heavy. "But we now have a much bigger problem."

Chapter 23

Lainie stared out the window in disbelief as she held the phone to her ear. "What do you mean he intimidated her?" She ratcheted up the volume as she spoke.

Kelley responded, her voice low and steady. "I didn't say he intimidated her. I said the police arrested him alleging that he did. Actually, as I understand it, he never talked to the girl. The parents answered the door and spoke to him. They called the police."

Lainie shook her head and gritted her teeth. "That was incredibly stupid of him."

Kelley chuckled. "You need to spend more time in the criminal justice system. This is nothing. Anyway, he's in lock-up now. You want to go down and get him out?"

"Let him sit in jail all night. It'll teach him a lesson." She paused and thought about it for a brief instant. "You think charges will come from this?" Not that she cared.

"Naw, doubtful. First, since he didn't contact the girl, there's no real intimidation. Second, at the time, there were no charges against him so it's a gray area."

Kelley paused and Lainie could hear her talking to someone else in the room on her end. "Hang on. Don't leave yet. I have a little something I need you to do." Pause. "Sorry, I'm back. Most likely the whole thing will go away. If charges are filed on the sexual misconduct, the judge might increase the bail because of the incident. Anyway, one thing at a time. We need to get Paul out of jail. I'm not sure that leaving him there overnight is such a good idea."

Lainie surprised even herself with a laugh coated in venom. "Do what you need to. For my money, screw him.

I'll do my best to give him a good defense but I'm not going to try and protect him from himself."

Silence descended, broken by a sigh from Kelley. "Okay. Well, I'll take care of it. And we're still on for tomorrow afternoon. Are you going to be able to interview the ex-wife before then?"

"Probably. I'll try to connect with her first thing in the morning."

***

Lainie arrived at the Common Grounds bistro ten minutes ahead of her scheduled meeting with Terri Abramson, Paul's former spouse. Looking over the menu board, she decided to splurge on a latte rather than sticking to her usual black coffee. "I've got a good income stream going. Might as well enjoy it."

She had described herself to the ex on the phone so she sat in plain view and waited, sipping on the rich, creamy drink. Abramson showed up right on the hour.

"Hi, are you Elaine Simpson?"

Lainie wasn't sure what she'd expected, but this wasn't it. The woman stood about five feet seven with a trim figure, dark, shoulder-length hair, expressive brown eyes, and smooth dark complexion. Why would a man divorce something like this and then try to fool around with teenagers? Crazy bastard.

"I go by Lainie." She offered her hand. "Have a seat, please. Can I get you something?"

Abramson smiled and sat. "No thanks. I'm coffee'd out this morning. And I can't stay long. I have a meeting at noon. You said this was about Paul?"

Lainie nodded. "Yes. As I mentioned, I'm on his defense team. I take it you've heard about his problems?" *A polite way of describing his situation.*

She shrugged but didn't respond.

"Right now, we're trying to get as much background as we can. He told us that you two were married for about ten years. Is that correct?"

"Just a little more than that, but it's close enough. We divorced about four years ago." She sat still, hands folded on the table in front of her. Her eyes seemed sad.

"Look, there's really no easy way of asking this but, given the things that he's being accused of, can you recall anything about him that might be relevant?" *Like did he chase teenage girls around?*

Terri shook her head emphatically. "No. And I'm really surprised. I don't believe it."

The response took Lainie aback. Normally, divorced couples didn't have a lot good to say about each other. "Why not?"

The woman turned her head and gazed out the window for a moment, speaking slowly, as if in a trance. "Paul was, is, a good guy. He just wouldn't do anything like that. It's not who he is."

"Could you elaborate?"

"Well first, our marriage was pretty good for a while. But when it started unraveling, it wasn't because there was anything wrong with him. We just wanted different things in life. It hurt both of us to end the marriage but, honestly, staying together would have been worse. Teenage girls? No. Not Paul."

"Why do you say that?" Lainie could see the sincerity in the ex-wife's eyes but she needed more than just speculation. "Anything in particular?"

The woman tilted her head and narrowed her eyes. "I guess I'd say that the times I saw him around attractive teenage girls he just seemed really unfazed. My older brother has two daughters that were drop-dead beautiful teenagers when Paul and I were together. But at family gatherings, it ended up with Paul, my brother, and my Dad sitting out in the yard having a few beers talking politics. He never seemed to even notice my nieces. I know it doesn't prove anything, but that just isn't Paul."

"Have you stayed in touch with him since the divorce?" Lainie wasn't sure why she asked the question.

"Yes, well, sort of. Off and on. I'm remarried now. Paul called to congratulate me and wish me well. This has all been really difficult—the divorce, remarriage, and trying to make sense of things. I guess I'd just say that he made it as easy as it could have been." She shrugged.

Nothing made sense. This guy had been fooling everybody, including his ex-wife for years. Crazy, even now the woman believed in him.

Chapter 24

Leaving the former Ms. Stafford and Common Grounds behind, Lainie stopped at the Crusty Loaf for a quick sandwich before heading off for the afternoon defense team meeting. The aroma of fresh baked bread mixed with garlic and cinnamon—an odd combination but not unpleasant. The bakery prepared the cinnamon rolls fresh each morning. They were a big seller.

She munched on a vegetarian sandwich—cucumbers, onions, peppers, spinach, tomatoes, and alfalfa sprouts with chipotle sauce on one piece of bread and mashed avocado on the other. She picked at the corners of her sandwich, as she tried to make sense of everything that was going on. A deep foreboding dominated her thinking—regret at being manipulated into this whole mess. She left the bag of kettle chips unopened.

Reactions from people she'd spoken to thus far left her perplexed. She knew that men who did these kinds of things were skilled at hiding their true nature. He'd even deceived her for a brief period. But to fool so many people for so long seemed extraordinary, even for a practiced pedophile. The memory of that lunch at Gilman Village made an uncalled-for visit. She abruptly banished it.

Mildred chose that moment to weigh in. *Did you give any thought to the possibility that the ex-wife is right? Perhaps he is innocent.*

Lainie pushed back. "Yeah, that's exactly the way he'd like me and everyone else to think. It's how they get away with it."

She could feel that snarky little bit of conscience smirking. *Ah, we wouldn't want to be made a fool of, now would we?*

A wave of rage came and went within the blink of an eye. "Been there once. Not again, thank you."

Mildred fell silent but Lainie could feel the aftereffects of the assault on her perspective. She thought about continuing the argument but instead, took another bite of her sandwich and gazed out the window at the slow spring drizzle. What if there was something to his story? No sooner had this notion made its appearance than she dismissed it. "Sure, there is—a crock of shit. Probably."

Lainie got caught in traffic and ended up at Kelley's office about ten minutes late. She walked into the small conference room to find a subdued group. Kelley was speaking softly. The others sat. Her attention immediately snapped to Paul. The defining features on his face were a deeply colored black eye and a cut, swollen, and bruised right cheek. His gaze seemed hollow, flat, and devoid of all emotion save defeat. She started to ask about the injuries but stopped herself. It wasn't hard to figure out. The police had roughed him up a bit, just to get his attention. And there wasn't anything she could do about it, even if she wanted to, which she didn't.

"Sorry I'm late. Traffic." She set her briefcase on the carpeted floor and took a seat at the far end of the oval table.

Kelley nodded. "No problem. I was just saying that Paul and I have had a discussion about the witness incident. No need for us to flog that horse here. We can move on." She started to say something else but Lainie interrupted.

"Wait. I want to know what the hell he was thinking." It struck her that she referred to Paul in the third person without even bothering to look at him.

Kelley gazed at her for a moment. "We've already covered it. Let's move on." She shuffled some papers in front of her. "We met with the police yesterday and I think we are close to seeing some charges, just based on their demeanor. I want to go over the different possibilities briefly so that there are no surprises." She gazed at Paul for a moment. He stared blankly back at her.

"First, I'll say that I suspect the delay in seeing charges likely stems from problems with the statements of the girls. We don't know what's in those statements and we're not likely to get any details until they provide us copies. But once they put things together, they'll move quickly. First, they'll arrest Paul."

Lainie watched him wince and lower his gaze.

Kelley paused and softened her tone. "I'll go through that in more detail but first, let me finish up with the charges subject. Once they make the arrest, they'll send the package over to the DA. I suspect that we'll get Eve Lasorda. She tends to end up with these kinds of cases. She'll most likely file directly with the court rather than taking it to a grand jury. From there, we'll have an arraignment where the charges are formally read and a plea is entered. While this is going on, she'll likely try to float some kind of deal to keep this from going to trial. We'll deal with that when it comes. But assuming we go forward, the trial comes after that. Time-wise, we're probably looking at a month to a month and a half if they move it along."

Paul slouched further down in his chair, his eyes glued on the table top. The shallow rise and fall of his chest provided the only real evidence that he was even alive.

Lainie began poring over the copies of news stories that had been placed on the table in front of each of them. "What are we doing with these?"

Kelley turned her attention to Andi and Elliott "Ah yes, the press clippings, as it were. What did you find, Andi?"

"I wasn't able to get anything from it." The young lady seemed nonchalant, almost bored.

Kelley stiffened. "What? You've had these for three days now. How much time do you need?" She stared daggers at Andi.

Elliott glared and opened his mouth to speak, but Andi gently put a hand on his arm. She eased closer to the table and spoke in a soft voice. "It isn't about the time. These releases don't have any direct quotes. They are all summary and I have no idea how much of it is the reporter talking and how much of the police information is there."

Lainie, trying to figure out exactly what was going on, waded into the conversation. "What is it you're trying to learn? And what would you hope to get from the press releases?"

Andi placed her hands on the table and began to speak softly. "It's a form of qualitative analysis. I analyze combinations of words, phrases, and grammatic patterns. I compare that to what I know about the source of the text. From that, I can spot hidden meanings, intentional vagaries, and even stress. I can compare dialogue to patterns typically found within any demographic group. From that, we can spot instances where a person makes a statement that they themselves didn't come up with on their own. In other words, we can spot cases of coaching."

Kelley shrugged. "She can do magic when she has the right material."

Andi continued, "The problem with this material is that it was written by reporters with no direction quotation. Simply put, I can't use this to do qualitative analysis."

Lainie said, "What kind of documents do you need?"

"We need the statements of the girls. Additionally, police statements or summaries are helpful, because they can also show patterns. It's not that unusual to find witness statements that appear as though they were authored by the police and given to the person to either hand-write themselves or through an oral statement. Right now, we got nothing."

After a moment of silence, Andi changed the subject, "You want something to drink, Paul? Water? Coffee? Tea?" Her head tilted slightly, and her intense gaze conveyed true concern.

Lainie did a double take. Really? That little twit's got the hots for this guy. The look on her face was plain as day.

He shook his head a single time without looking up or saying anything.

A heavy, overbearing silence fell over the room bringing an intense level of discomfort to Lainie. The research assistant and technical wizard gazed at Paul, both seemingly worried or concerned. Surely those two, especially Andi, would not be taken in by his injured innocence act. She felt the weight of Kelley's momentary gaze before the attorney shifted back to her discussion.

"Okay, let's move on. We need to talk about the arrest." She paused and swallowed, closing her eyes. When she opened them, they exuded a resolve to plow through the topic without emotion. "Paul, when they are ready, they will come for you. It's not a pleasant process. So, here's what we'll do. We'll put you up in a local hotel under my name. I'll ask the police to contact me with any developments. When they can't find you immediately, they'll call me. I can bring you to the station and have you turn yourself in. That will cut out a lot of the drama. Otherwise, they'll come to your house, handcuff you, and cart you out."

Paul nodded without looking up.

Lainie stared at the crumbling man—the battered face, absence of hope, and the crutches upon which he still depended sitting back against the wall. Up until this point, she'd figured he deserved whatever he got. A doubt nibbled around the edge of her mind. She figured Mildred had instigated it. But what if he didn't deserve it? Her gazed shifted to the window where a steady pattering of rain produced both drops that held their place and rivulets that painted translucent lines down the pane. She found it difficult to look at Paul in his current condition and consider his possible innocence at the same time.

Chapter 25

The group took a short break. Lainie wondered if the pervasive sense of despair was the norm for these kinds of cases. Kelley strode out of the room toward her office. The two assistants walked out together, albeit with less apparent purpose in their gait. They seemed more interested in escaping than actually doing anything. Paul sat as if he didn't even notice the intermission. He spoke not a word. His stare, focused on the table, never wavered. But he continued to breathe.

Lainie stood and walked out. She wanted to say something but wasn't sure what it was. Maybe just acknowledge that he was there. But that was stupid. She knew he was there and he knew she was there. Nothing more needed to be said.

Mildred tossed in her nickel's worth. *Not everything is about you.*

Lainie shook her head as she walked down the hall toward the restroom. "That's a stupid thing to say. I never said it was about me."

Silence from the voice of conscience.

The group reconvened about fifteen minutes later. Lainie wondered in passing if the fifteen-minute break was billable time. She wondered how Paul might feel about that.

Mildred tacked on her perspective. *In the big scheme of things, the cost of this break is meaningless.*

Lainie considered the notion of cost and for a moment entertained the idea that cost included a lot more than money. She'd paid a huge price way back when.

Kelley brought the group back to order. "I want to briefly discuss the police since, at the moment, they're at the center of this. We drew two detectives from Sex Crimes—Tom Burke and Laura Steadman. Burke is pretty steady, rock-solid kind of a guy. He's hard-nosed about these things but he does tend to follow the evidence. Steadman's a loose cannon. This isn't just a *job for her*. It's a mission from God."

Kelley gazed at Paul for a second. As silence filled the room, he looked up at her for the first time since the meeting began. She continued, "Paul, be careful of her. Remember what I told you about talking without me there. That goes double for Steadman. Period. No exceptions. She's going to come at you trying to look like your friend, offering to help you sort this out. Predictable lines—'lawyers just get in the way and confuse things.' 'If you can work with me, we'll get this all over with.' Don't fall for it. She's got you in the crosshairs. Never forget that. She is *not* your friend."

He stared for a moment and then nodded.

It stood to reason that the police were not Paul's friends. But who were his friends? Did he even have any at this point? Lainie wondered if Steadman had been the one who beat him up. She'd never met the detective but, apparently, she and Kelley had history.

The lead attorney brought things back to life. "Okay, now that that's out of the way, let's go over what we've learned from the school. Andi, talk to me."

The lithe blonde research analyst opened her pad and leaned forward into the table. "Not a lot so far. I've interviewed the teachers and administrators." The young woman paused and glanced around the table before continuing.

Lainie nodded but kept quiet.

"Most of the people at the school were tight-lipped about it. But from those that would talk to me, I got the sense that these charges are out of character for Paul. Everyone's a little stand-offish right now but I can't find anything that shows a pattern or even instance of behavior consistent with what the girls are purportedly saying. We should talk to some students but we're going to have to go through the parents to do that. I suggest we get a list of kids—some who have had problems and some who are model students. We can contact the parents and get permission. Best to do it in their homes, if possible. Get them out of the school environment." Andi looked down at her notes, turned a few pages, and then shifted her gaze to Kelley. "That's about it."

Next Lainie recounted her interviews with the ex-wife and the assistant principal. Paul winced and seemed to shrink inside himself when she talked about Terri.

Kelley nodded. "Thanks. So, we have no history of anything that seems to support these allegations. I'll work on the student thing." She turned toward Elliott. "What did you see at the house?" She apparently referred to the home where the alleged witness intimidation had occurred.

The gawky, bespectacled kid shrugged. "Like you asked, I went over to the Smallwood house and checked out their video surveillance on the porch, at least to the extent I could see it from the street. Looks like they got a top-of-the-line system." He slid a smart phone toward Kelley. "You can see from the photo that they have what looks like two different cameras covering the porch. And see there, down in the right-hand corner, the sign giving the name of the security company. Given the neighborhood and the look of the cameras, I'm betting they monitor in real-time over the web. Most of these companies keep archives of the footage for about thirty days. If we think we're going to want it, we should get it now."

"I'll get that started. We shouldn't need it for any kind of intimidation charges, but it may come in handy when we talk about bail." Kelley took a deep breath and turned the page in her pad. "Finally, let's talk about the three students."

Paul jerked his gaze up and toward the attorney, eyes intense.

"We have one girl, a Caryn Smallwood, who is claiming that Paul coerced her into having sex."

Paul visibly shuddered and closed his eyes. Lainie wondered if that was from shock or from the humiliation of being discovered.

"The other two girls both allege that Paul tried to talk them into having sex, but they never actually did. Those two are Deborah Bufford and Marianne Thomas. Our next task is to find out as much about these girls as we can, starting with school records. I'm probably going to have to get a court order to get that information from the school. I'll get started on that right now. In the meantime, Paul, what can you tell us about them?"

He shook his head as if clearing the fog from his brain. "Uh, I don't know much at all. I mean, I don't recall having spoken to Caryn Smallwood. I know she's popular—involved in lots of activities. You can look at the yearbooks over the past few years. It seems like she's in a lot of the photos. From what I've seen, she's a good student." He paused and scratched his head, moving his fingers through the disheveled hair.

"The other two, let's see, Marianne Thomas. She's typically been our top academic performer, so I've seen her name a lot." He narrowed his eyes and rubbed the bruised cheek. "I recall speaking with her about five or six months ago, right after the school year started. It was in the lunchroom. She was with a bunch of other girls. I stopped and asked if she'd begun to look at colleges yet. I mean, with her record, I figured that would be a big thing."

Kelley arched an eyebrow. "And what did she say?"

He shrugged. "I don't remember exactly. Something like she was looking at different schools. Nothing definite. I encouraged her and then left."

"And nothing else after that?"

"No. I don't talk to students very much." He paused and chewed on the corner of his mouth. His demeanor changed. His eyes took on more of a focus. He straightened up in his chair. "As for Deborah Bufford, I'm more familiar with her because she has a borderline learning disability. We have a team assigned for each special-needs student. It involves the parents, teachers, and advisors. Beth Tanis, the assistant principal, chairs all of the teams. I sat in when she couldn't make it. I've met Deborah's parents and I'm somewhat familiar with her performance, but I can't say that I've ever spoken to her."

Kelley nodded as she continued taking notes. "Okay. Let's drill down on these students. We'll start with the school records and move out from there. I'll try to contact the parents and see if they'll allow us to interview the kids. I'm guessing they're going to flat out refuse." She shrugged.

"But maybe we can get some leads from the teachers. Andi, I want you to go back and talk to them who have contact with our three students. Go back all the way to freshman year. And do a routine search on social media."

She closed her notepad and looked out across the group, lingering on Lainie for a moment. "Anything else before we end this?" A palpable silence descended.

Paul's voice, unexpectedly forceful, broke through. "I don't get it. It's like you're just giving up on talking to these girls. Why can't we make them explain? They don't have the right to do this. There has to be something we can do rather than just sitting around and talking about it." He punctuated his words with a fist on the table as he spoke. His face turned red with anger and frustration,

Lainie lashed out before Kelley, who had a sympathetic look in her eyes, was able to speak. "You just don't get it, do you, Paul? You're yelling at us like we're the enemy. But we didn't get you into this mess. You did it to yourself." She glared at the man.

The room went deathly silent. Lainie could feel all eyes on her. Paul's gaze was full of pain. Kelley's look was one of alarm. Elliott sat slouched down in his seat with his eyes wide in what looked to be disbelief. Andi shot daggers of rage in Lainie's direction.

Mildred offered her assessment. *Ouch.*

Chapter 26

Lainie braced for the blowback she knew would come. She could see from the faces around the table that she was being judged unfairly. How could they possibly be taken in by Paul's act? Three different girls told stories bearing a recurring theme. How could this team not see it?

Never far away these days, Mildred intervened in the reverie. *Yeah, right. Only you can see the truth.*

Before Lainie could further engage in the argument, Kelley ended the meeting. "Okay, that's it for today. Andi and Elliott, let's hit it." She strode toward the door, speaking over her shoulder, "Lainie, could you swing by my office before you leave, please?" She passed through the threshold into the hallway without waiting for a response.

Paul gazed at her for a moment, then lowered his eyes without speaking. He slouched in the chair, resting chin on chest.

Elliott stood and ambled toward the door with a shake of his head. His only uttering was a subtle *whew*.

Lainie shrugged and gathered her things to go. She felt a tinge of embarrassment although the silence in the room magnified it. Maybe her outburst had been a little *over the top*. She wondered about an apology but couldn't summon it. She eased out of her chair and into the hall.

As she headed for Kelley's office, Andi called to her from behind. "What the hell was that all about?" She stood, hands on her hips, glaring.

Lainie studied her for a moment without speaking.

The researcher persisted. "Why do you hate him so much?"

Lainie dropped her briefcase and clenched her fists at her side. Taking a deep breath, she clarified her position. "I don't hate him. I hate what he did." She felt it an important distinction.

Yeah, right. She could feel Mildred's scorn.

"And just what is it that he did?"

Lainie rolled her eyes. "Humph." She pointed toward the room where Paul still sat. "You heard what the girls are claiming."

Andi raised her open hands and shrugged. "Okay, yes, I heard the description. Correct me if I'm wrong here, but that is what he is being accused of. Whatever you may think of all this, shouldn't we at least make a show of holding off on the judgment, especially since *we are his defense team*?"

Enlightenment came to Lainie in a flash. It all made sense. Andi was hot for Paul. He'd worked his magic on her too. The glorified admin assistant was always ready get him a drink or do something else for him. Yeah, she would definitely like to *do something else for him*. There was little point in arguing with the little twit. "Whatever." She picked up her briefcase, turned, and strode down the hall to Kelley's office before the young woman could respond.

Lainie stood in the threshold and knocked on the doorframe without speaking.

Kelley looked up and nodded. "Come in, have a seat. And could you close the door, please?"

After closing the door, Lainie set her briefcase on the floor and pulled up a chair. "So, I guess maybe I got a little carried away in there. Sorry." But she wasn't sorry, not really. Well, she was sorry that the others couldn't or wouldn't accept reality. Still, a little contrition might be in order.

Kelley eyed her as she nodded slowly. "You know, maybe you were right about the conflict of interest thing. I guess that there are good reasons for those kinds of rules. I think we've got a handle on things here if you want to go back to your writing. Just send me a final invoice and we'll call it good."

Whatever Lainie had expected, it had not included this. Of course, she wanted out of this mess. In fact, she hadn't wanted in to start with. But this really felt like she was being *dismissed.* Actually, it was a dismissal, plain and simple. She bristled but held her preferred retort. Instead, she picked up her briefcase and stood. "I can get that to you tomorrow." She wanted to argue her case. She wanted them to see her side of it.

But the impassive look, the tight line of Kelley's lips, and the hands folded on the desk in front of her made it clear that the discussion was over. "That'll be fine. Thanks." She picked up a pen and began pouring over some papers in front of her—a signal that the meeting had ended.

Lainie made her way to the elevator, relieved at being set free, but still bristling with righteous indignation at being unjustly fired. Added to this was a building fury at the thought of Andi and Paul in bed together.

Chapter 27

Lainie struggled with the story. Nothing made sense. Her characters refused to speak to her. She sat staring at a blinking cursor that taunted her.

The landline phone pulled her out of her thoughts. Checking the clock, she muttered, "Who on earth would call at this time of night?" A call at ten-thirty could not mean good news. The number that showed up on caller ID looked vaguely familiar but she couldn't place it.

With a sigh, she pressed the *connect* button. "Hello."

"Hi, Lainie. This is Jason. I hope I didn't get you at a bad time."

She had received and not responded to his two previous voice messages. *What part of 'ignoring you' didn't you understand?* "Yes, in fact it is a bad time. But let me be clear, there is no good time for you to ever contact me, period."

"I'm sorry, Lainie, sorry for everything. Look, I just wanted to talk, that's all. I hate the thought of everything we had together completely disappearing."

"It didn't disappear. You killed it. It's late. I have to go. Please don't call again." She disconnected before he had a chance to answer. Her heart pounded as she placed the phone in the charging unit. With clenched jaw, she regretted not saying more to him—how much pain she'd endured because of him. That it took a special kind of narcissist to do what he'd done. That she hoped he rotted in the bowels of hell for eternity. There was so much she wanted to say to him. Then again, sometimes less is more.

Lainie shook her head, as though to remove all of the unwanted thoughts and memories. Her mind drifted to her friendship with Kelley and she winced at the notion that perhaps her outburst had destroyed even that. Pausing for a moment, Lainie picked up her phone and pulled up the contact list. She leaned back in the chair, closed her eyes, and took a deep breath as she waited.

The voice on the other end came out soft and tentative. "Hello, Lainie."

"Hi Kelley. Was wondering if you might be up for a cup of coffee in the morning?"

Kelley's quiet, cautious voice followed a moment of silence. "Sure. But it'll have to be early. Got a lot on my plate tomorrow."

***

Lainie rubbed her thumb across the rim of the ceramic cup as she stared into the black, steaming liquid. "So, I guess that I owe you an apology, big time." She glanced up and across the table at her friend.

Kelley furrowed her brow and tilted her head. "Were you two sleeping together?"

Lainie unloaded. "God no! Nothing like that. Geez, why would you even think that?"

Kelley laughed. "I don't know. Maybe because you've been behaving like a first-year law student coming off a failed relationship. It looks to me like this is really personal with you."

"No, well, maybe a little. I keep thinking about those three girls and what they must have gone through because of him. It's kind of hard to keep that at arm's length." Lainie had anticipated the argument.

Kelley leaned into the table, her hands wrapped around her cup. "Sorry, Lainie. That doesn't wash. I do this stuff all the time and I've learned how to recognize a line of shit when I hear it. This isn't even about Paul. This is about you. I have no idea where it's coming from but it's toxic."

Lainie started to lash out but stopped herself. Maybe it was partly about her. But that still didn't let the perv off the hook. He did what he did. "Look, I just wanted to apologize for the outburst, that's all."

Kelley smiled for the first time since sitting down. "Okay. Accepted. But, thing is, I'm not the one that's owed an apology." She glanced down and cleared her throat. "I spoke with Paul yesterday after you left, you know, to try and smooth things over a bit. Thing is, he wasn't angry at all. Shocked the hell out of me. For whatever reason, he thinks highly of you. Go figure." The smile turned to a brief laugh.

Lainie tilted her head up and sighed. "Well, if you get the chance, tell him I'm sorry." But she wasn't sure she really was. For one thing, he probably didn't really care that much, given that he was in hot pursuit of Andi. "I'd like to ask you something but I want to keep it just between us, if that's okay."

Kelley shrugged. "Sure. What's on your mind?"

Lainie took a deep breath and considered the question one last time. Once asked, she couldn't take it back. "Do you get the sense that there's maybe something developing between Andi and Paul?" The words, given voice, sounded stupid and adolescent.

Kelley burst out laughing, leaning back in her chair and shaking her head. "Sorry, that one caught me off-guard." She chuckled again. "Of all the things you could have asked, that's the last one that I would have expected." As her mirth settled into a broad smile, she continued, "I won't go into it right now, but I can tell you emphatically that the answer is 'no.' I'll just say for the moment that Andi doesn't get involved with clients."

Lainie wasn't sure what response she'd expected. After all, if Kelley had suspected she'd have put a stop to it. Still the laughter was unnerving. "How can you be so sure?"

Kelley gazed across the table for a moment before responding. "We can talk about this later. For now, though, Paul asked about the possibility of you coming back on the case. I advised against it, but he seems to think you should be with us. If you're willing, I'll defer, at least for the time being."

The request shocked Lainie. After the way she'd behaved, whether justified or not, she couldn't imagine why the man would want her around. And given the way she felt about him, going back to work on the case was the last thing she wanted. "Sorry, Kelley, but no. At the end of the day, I just can't shake the sense that he did those things. And at this point in my life, I don't want any part of that. I get that he deserves a defense and that you make your living doing that. I can't. Sorry."

Mildred added a footnote. *Kelley's right. This is not about Paul. It's about you.*

Chapter 28

Lainie slouched in the overstuffed chair and stared at the living room wall. The doorbell roused her from the self-induced stupor. She opened the door to find Kelley's research analyst planted on her porch. "Andi?"

The young woman shrugged. "I got your address from Kelley."

Lainie stood in the doorway, arms crossed on her chest. "And?"

Andi gazed down and she rubbed her right foot on the mat. "Just wanted to talk."

"About what?"

"Can I come in?"

Lainie gazed at her for a moment before nodding and stepping aside. "Sure." She gestured toward the couch. "I can put some water on for tea, if you like." Rather than going to the kitchen, though, she wandered over and plopped down on the couch.

"No thanks." She sat, crossing her left leg over her right. A moment of silence descended between the two.

Lainie was in no mood for conversation, especially with this twit. "So?"

Andi's gaze dropped to her lap. "Kelley told me that you refused to come back to the case. I wanted to make sure, for my own peace of mind, that it wasn't related to our last conversation. I'd hate to think that you'd refuse a client because of something I said."

Lainie smirked. "No. It's got nothing to do with you. I just don't want to be a part of it, okay?" She shook her head. She added, as an afterthought, "Why do you care, anyway?"

"I don't. But to Paul, apparently your opinion matters. He seems to care what you think about him. I figured if it was something with me, we could clear it up."

"There's nothing to clear up. I just don't want to be a part of defending someone who does those kinds of things. I went through all of this with Kelley."

Andi narrowed her eyes and cocked her head. "What makes you so sure he did those things? You seem to be basing everything you're saying on the assumption that he's guilty."

Lainie arched her brow. "What makes you so sure he didn't do those things?"

"I'm not. I'm just willing to suspend judgment and help give him the best defense I can. If he ends up guilty, then I figure the system will deal with him."

Lainie stood and walked over to the window. She stared out at the brown lawn and the bare trees as she spoke, feeling almost like she was in a trance. "Then you're a better person than I." She turned and glared at Andi. "I'm tired of people who behave any way they want, destroying everything around them, and then somehow expect things to be okay."

Andi's eyes widened and she shook her head slowly. "Where the hell did that come from? This is a guy who's been accused of something and you've already decided that not only did he do it but that he's engineered this entire series of events to destroy people. Maybe, just maybe, his life is the one being destroyed."

Lainie considered the young woman for a moment. She could be forgiven her naiveté; she had only just begun life. She would learn about these things soon enough. "I'm sorry you disapprove. And if it makes you feel any better, the biggest reason I won't come back is because I don't think I could contribute, feeling the way I do. It's better for him that I'm not there."

Andi stood. "I've said what I came to say. But I think you're wrong about Paul. You may have been a good lawyer at one time, but I can't say as much for your judgment about people." She strode toward the door. "Sorry to bother you." With that, she opened the front door and was gone without another word.

Lainie stood in the center of the living room staring at the front door through which the young woman had just passed. She felt a strange mix of anger and regret. Despite what Kelley had told her, a budding romantic involvement between Andi and Paul seemed the only explanation for the analyst's aggressive interest.

Mildred had a different take on it. *If that was true, why would she try so hard to get you back on the case?*

"How the hell should I know?"

Well, now, that's certainly a refreshing turn. The all-seeing Lainie Simpson at a loss for an answer.

"Screw you."

Not a very nice thing to say to your conscience.

"I'm not a very nice person, remember? And why should I be? No one else is."

Mildred fell silent. Lainie had gotten in the last word but couldn't shake the feeling that her conscience had won the argument.

***

> *Sitting in her chair staring at the window in the darkness, Lainie heard shuffling from the kitchen. Someone had broken into her house. She turned her head to look but whoever it was remained obscured. Only a wash of light made it into the living room. She heard the clank of a pan being moved on the stove top. Standing, she eased over closer to the door and peered around the threshold into the kitchen. Paul Stafford stood by the stove wearing an apron. He stared at a pot on the stove while holding a batch of raw pasta in his hands. He turned to stare at her, his eyes sad and his head tilted to one side. "Why?"*

Lainie's eyes popped open and she struggled to catch her breath as her heart pounded. She felt her cotton nightshirt soaked with sweat and plastered to her chest. "Just a nightmare." She crawled out of bed and glanced at the clock—2:45. Making her way to the bathroom, she tried to shake it off, but the look of grief in the man's eyes haunted her. If it was a nightmare for her, what must it be for him? Lainie was certain that this was all Mildred's doing.

***

Lainie took a sip of her coffee and sat the cup down next to her keyboard. She had managed to cobble out only two words—*Chapter 27*—and the blinking cursor invited her to continue. Or perhaps it was daring her. Her phone sat within arm's reach and a part of her wanted to call. She reached over, picked it up, and scrolled through her contact list to Kelley's number. That was as far as she got.

With eyes closed, she shook her head. "No. I can't."

Chapter 29

Lainie stood squarely in the front doorway, glaring at the face in front of her. "Paul, what are you doing here?" She stifled the urge to hurl an insult along with the question.

He gazed at her for a moment before lowering his gaze to stare at his feet. "I wanted to talk to you."

"So, talk."

"Can I come in." He glanced up at her. "Please."

This seemed an obscene carbon copy of the visit by Andi the previous day. "What do you want?" She stood her ground.

Furrowing his brow as he spoke, the words came out slow and measured. "I just want to talk. If you could listen to what I have to say, I'll leave and not bother you again."

Lainie closed her eyes and took a deep breath. Stepping aside, she gestured him in.

"Thank you." He slipped past her and stood in the center of the room, his hands clasped together in front of him.

She motioned toward the couch. "Have a seat." She briefly considered offering coffee from the fresh-brewed pot but decided against anything that would prolong the encounter. She pulled in a chair from the dining room table rather than sitting in the overstuffed one opposite the couch. She saw no point in making this a comfortable affair.

Paul stared at his hands, folded in his lap, as he nodded his head. "Kelley told me that you refused to come back on the case."

"And?"

"I wish you would reconsider. I'd like to have you back."

Lainie shook her head. "Why?" She paused before adding the barb that dug into her mind. "After all, you've got a good team. And Andi will...." She caught herself and looked away, clenching her jaw.

He furrowed his brow. "I guess. Yes, they *are* a good team. And I'm sure Andi's a good researcher. Kelley's a good lawyer and Elliott's a good computer guy." He raised his still-clasped hands from his lap as if praying. "And I know they'll do everything they can for me. But, like Kelley said, whether I'm innocent or not isn't that important to them. They're just doing their job."

She smirked. "So? What's that got to do with me?"

He paused and softly said, "At least you care whether I'm innocent or not."

The laugh came out snarky. "Not exactly." Although it reflected her attitude, Lainie regretted the tone. "Paul, I don't believe in your innocence. I fail to see how having me there helps you."

He smiled for the first time. "Yes, I know you think I'm guilty. And that's okay. At least it's important to you. Look, I'm not completely stupid. I know that my life is probably ruined. Even if I'm acquitted or if they dismiss the charges, I'll always be a perv that played the system and won. The only way I'll ever get my life back is if I can prove my innocence. And you're the only one who cares. Maybe you *do* think I'm guilty right now. But at least if you're on the case, you might change your mind. It's possible."

Lainie leaned forward in the chair and prepared to unleash a litany of all the really good reasons why having her on the case would hurt rather than help.

Before she could speak, Paul continued, "I'm not going to lie to you, Lainie. I'm not doing that well. I'm failing fast. It's everything I can do just to get up in the morning and get dressed. And it gets worse every day. I can imagine a day, not too far in the future, when I will cease to care. Right now, while I'm trying to hold on to some small glimmer of hope, I'd like to make sure someone is there when I let go—someone who cares."

"That makes no sense. Why someone who doesn't believe in you?" She struggled to understand what it was he wanted from her.

He shrugged and averted her gaze. "I don't know. Like I said, there's not much hope. Maybe I'm just trying to fix it so that when I'm no longer able to care, someone will. I know you don't trust me or believe me right now. But if you're not around when my own hope is gone, there will be no one at all. At least with you around, there's a slight chance."

He shifted in his seat and leaned forward toward her. "I'm not asking you to believe me. This is not about you changing your mind. All I ask is that, if you do change your mind, you don't stop caring." Tears gathered in his eyes and he wiped them with his sleeve.

Lainie stared toward the living room window and the gathering late afternoon shadows outside. His lopsided argument seemed illogical to her. She expected Mildred to chime in but her conscience remained silent. "I'll think about it." She added quickly, "But no promises, Paul. I'll give it some thought and talk to Kelley if I decide to. That's the best I can do."

He nodded and bowed his head.

Later, she sat at the dining room table staring at the remains of her chef salad. The late March afternoon faded fast, although she hadn't summoned the energy to get up and turn on some lights. She mentally summoned Mildred. "You've been notably quiet today."

Nothing to say. Nothing you needed to hear.

Lainie smirked. "Since when did that stop you?"

Silence.

"I don't believe he's innocent."

I know. But do you believe he's guilty?

"I don't know. And that's as good a reason as any to stay away. That whole line of crap about me being the only one who cares is nothing more than smoke and mirrors. He's playing the *helpless* card. That's all."

What if he's just trying to make sense of it all? After all, that's something with which you have experience.

"No." End of discussion.

Silence.

Chapter 30

Lainie stared at the display. The numbers weren't a total shock, but they gave her no comfort. She had submitted an invoice for just under $4,000 and that would help. But her financial situation had very little wiggle room. For a moment, a short instant, she imagined what a $15,000 or $20,000 infusion of funds would do. Almost immediately, though, a wave of guilt washed over her. She didn't believe the guy. And whether he went to jail or not really wasn't her problem. So why shouldn't she want to make some money off him?

Good question, Lainie. Why not? Mildred was never far away.

But she knew why not. It wasn't right. Whatever else she felt, kicking someone when they were down was wrong.

Nicely done.

"Go back to sleep."

I wasn't asleep. It's the middle of the day.

Lainie closed out the account summary and opened her file directory. She needed to get back on track with the writing. She'd pacified her editor with chapters the past week. But Meg was one of those *what have you done for me lately* people. The hungry beast never let up.

She opened the chapter in progress. Staring at the screen, she had an irresistible urge to print it out and go into the living room and work on it with a pen, while sitting in her easy chair and sipping on a cup of tea. She hit <CTRL><P> to bring up the print menu. As Lainie sent the document to queue, she heard the printer spring to life, although from the sound of it—the creaking and the noisy fan—there was relatively little life remainingg. "A new printer would be nice. Maybe one of those color lasers that connect via the web."

Printers cost money.

She sighed. Mildred was right. Five to six hundred bucks for a new printer seemed an extravagance, especially since she didn't, or rather shouldn't, print that much. She stared at the laboring machine as it cranked out the four pages she'd sent to the print queue. It seemed even slower than she'd remembered. "I don't know, would it be so wrong?"

He asked for you back. You can use the money. But the question is, can you do the work—really do the work?

Lainie picked up her cellphone and opened the contact list.

Chapter 31

By the close of the meeting, they had made the decision to move Paul to a hotel in anticipation of an arrest warrant. And then, one by one, the team picked up their tools of the trade and slipped out of the conference room. Paul slid his chair out and, placing both hands on the arms, he steadied himself as he stood on one leg. He reached around, grabbed his crutches, and started for the door. Lainie nodded to him and tried to smile but couldn't manage it.

He lowered his gaze and kept walking.

Kelley called after him. "Paul, park there in the reception area for a few minutes. We'll be right with you." She grabbed her pad and pen and shouted down the hall. "Andi, hang tight. I have something for you."

Lainie touched her arm. "Wait up, Kelley. You have a minute? There's something I'd like to ask you."

"Sure, what's up?" She plopped back down in her seat.

Lainie peeked outside into the hallway to make sure Paul was not near and then moved up to a chair next to the attorney. "I just wanted to ask, do you think he's innocent?"

Kelley shrugged. "Dunno. We don't really have any evidence yet. We haven't seen what the police have collected. And besides, innocence and guilt are not my issues. I focus on the case, the evidence, and how I can provide the best defense."

"But doesn't it matter?"

She laughed. "Of course it matters, just not to me." The laugh softened to a sad smile as she closed her eyes for a moment and shook her head. "Look, that's a lie. It does matter to me. And that's why I don't consider it. If I get to thinking that a guy is guilty, I run the risk of not doing my best. And then what if I'm wrong? So, I leave the guilt issue to the jury. I do my best. If the prosecutor does her job, the judge does his, and the jury does theirs, then hopefully it all works.

The concept made sense, sort of. "But it doesn't work all the time. Sometimes guilty guys walk free."

Kelley finished the thought. "Yes, and sometimes innocent men go to prison. I know. And if you have a better way of doing this, we'd all love to hear it. But unfortunately, our current system is probably the best we can do, *in this price range*." She chuckled as she tossed out the last few words.

"And what if Paul is innocent?" Lainie gave voice to a concern that had only just begun to take form.

"Then we'd better give him the best defense we can, which is exactly what I would give him anyway." Kelley's words came out sounding just a bit impatient. "Besides, I thought that you were pretty keen on him getting what's coming to him, so to speak."

A current of guilt coursed its way through her. "Yeah. I know. It's just that he looks like he's about ready to crumble."

"He is. And we haven't even started yet. Sometimes these guys can't handle it. Some don't make it." Her voice dropped in both volume and tone.

Lainie sat up straight, her eyes wide. "What's that supposed to mean?"

Kelley locked gazes with her for a few seconds before looking away. "Nothing. I have to go. We need to get Paul situated before the police come looking." She got up and sauntered down the hall toward her office, calling out as she went, "Andi, my office."

***

Lainie didn't sleep that night. The demons called in full force. She saw Paul standing on the edge of a huge gaping black cavern peering in. She knew instinctively that the emptiness residing within that cauldron exerted a powerful attractive force for a man whose life was crumbling around him and who stood devoid of friends.

Still, he may have done this all to himself. After all, if he made the decision to play around with young teenage girls, what else did he expect?

Mildred jumped in to help her out. *But what if he didn't make any such decision?*

Lainie sat up in bed, reached back, and flipped the pillow over before dropping her head back down. "But these stories don't just make themselves up. There has to be some element of truth, even if the details are off."

You're predicating your antagonism towards him on an assumption.

She shook her head to clear the cobwebs. "Why would three young girls fabricate a completely false story? What's the point?"

And that's the right question.

Unfortunately, Lainie had no idea how she would even go about answering such a question without getting into the heads of the girls. And, like Kelley said, permission to interview the girls would likely never come.

***

She'd just poured her first cup of coffee and was booting up her computer when the phone rang. "Hello."

"Hey. It's me." Kelley's voice shot out of the handset. "The police are ready to arrest Paul. Can you get down here to the office pronto?"

"On my way." Lainie poured the cup of steaming liquid into a larger to-go cup, topped it off from the coffee pot, and headed out the door.

Fifteen minutes later, she stepped off the elevator and made her way to Kelley's office. When she opened the door, she found Kelley and Elliott in the main area chatting. The attorney turned and grinned. "You made good time. The cops are pissed. They had me followed when I went to book the room. Guess they know my tactics, huh. Anyway, I had a sneaky suspicion they might try something like this so I also had Andi book a room at a different hotel. We moved Paul late last evening after the police called it for the night. Imagine their surprise when they burst into the hotel room to make the collar." She guffawed and slapped the desk with her hand.

"Not worried about making friends with them, I guess." Lainie did see the humor in it.

Kelley shrugged and arched her eyebrows. "Nope. Steadman and I go back a lot of years. She's got no use for me at all. Nothing I love better than seeing her grabbing thin air."

"What now?"

She narrowed her eyes as she stared blankly at the wall. "Unfortunately, now we have to take Paul down there." She sighed. "At least we spared him the trauma of that unexpected burst through the door with guns in his face." Kelley turned and faced Lainie. "You mind tagging along?"

Chapter 32

Lainie made her way down the corridor from the elevator, following Kelley's lead. They passed through an old wooden door with a frosted glass pane and a placard that identified the area as the Sex Crimes Division of the Bellevue Police Department. A shudder coursed through her body. She'd been in police department offices before, but this felt different—ominous, threatening, dark. A pervading odor of something, a cross between musty and rotten, seemed to cling to everything. The carpeting in the hall gave way to a dingy, worn pale tan linoleum floor.

They found a party of three awaiting them. A chunky, medium height brunette with flashing brown eyes hurled out a challenge before the door had even shut behind them. "Where's your *client*?"

Kelley ignored her. "Good morning all." She nodded in the direction of another woman with jet black hair, sable complexion, and trim build. "Counselor." She smiled and cleared her throat. "Mister Stafford will be here shortly. Maybe we could avoid shooting him, at least until he gets into the room, what do you say?" She tilted her head slightly and arched her eyebrows toward the chunky woman who sported a badge and a pistol housed in a shoulder holster. The female detective glared and turned a dark shade of pink.

"Introductions." Kelley turned and gestured. "This is my associate, Lainie Simpson." She nodded toward the three opposing figures. "Assistant DA Eve Lasorda and Detective Laura Steadman." Facing the lone male in the room she continued, "And this fine gentleman is Detective Tom Burke." The three officials mumbled welcomes. Lasorda, the attractive dark-skinned DA stepped forward and extended her hand, which Lainie accepted.

"Pleased to meet you all." She figured that to be the appropriate greeting although she wasn't really pleased.

Steadman stood with arms crossed. "We haven't got all day. If you just tell us where he is, we'll go pick him up." The scowl defined her face. She reached over and retrieved a tan blazer laying across the back of a chair.

Kelley laughed. "I'm sure you'd love that, Detective. But I'd just as soon you rough him up here in front of us rather than assaulting him in a hotel room. Hope you don't mind." The words dripped with sarcasm.

Lainie winced. Her friend clearly had no qualms about baiting her adversary.

Steadman shot back quickly. "Maybe he should have thought about that before he decided to rape those girls."

The word *rape* had not come up before. The mere mention shook Lainie to her soul. She'd not really thought about Paul's dilemma in those terms. *Inappropriate sexual behavior* sounded more sterile and acceptable for polite conversation. *Rape* conjured visions of violence, forced domination, and humiliation. *Did he rape that girl?* But Steadman had said *girls,* plural. The allegation of sex that Lainie had heard was only for one girl. The others were just attempts.

Kelley's retort interrupted the internal dialogue. "Maybe we could wait until we get a guilty verdict to administer punishment. I know it's a novel and dangerous notion but maybe just this one time?"

Lasorda stepped between the two. "As entertaining as this little exchange is, let's tone it down." She turned to face Kelley. "Can we expect your client soon, counselor?"

No sooner had these words passed the DA's lips than the door opened again and Paul entered, followed by Andi and Elliott. Paul's appearance hit Lainie like a punch to the stomach. His eyes were red and swollen. He had a two-day bristled beard. His thin, gaunt frame seemed to tremble as he walked forward. He looked first at the general group and then shifted his gaze down.

Steadman bounded forward, removing a pair of handcuffs from a pouch at the small of her back. "Paul Stafford, you are under arrest for the statutory rape of Caryn Smallwood and the attempted rape of Deborah Bufford and Marianne Thomas. You have the right..."

The detective's voice blended into the din of the background noise as Lainie watched her jerk Paul around, pull his hands behind him and slap the cuffs on him. Despite what she might have thought about the man before, her heart broke to watch the scene.

Paul seemed to diminish before her eyes. Looking at him, Lainie barely recognized him as the man with whom she'd shared a blackened salmon salad at the Salty Sockeye in Gilman Village just over a week ago.

Chapter 33

Lainie watched Detective Steadman shove Paul toward the door. He kept his eyes down and moved in response to the woman's none-too-gentle treatment. They disappeared into the hallway and the door closed behind them. An awkward lull settled in as Detective Burke and the ADA looked at Lainie and Kelley.

Lasorda broke the silence. "Okay Counselor, let's talk." She motioned toward a small desk with a couple of chairs.

Detective Burke turned toward the door, speaking over his shoulder. "I'll be back shortly."

Lainie pulled another chair up and slid in beside Kelley. Lasorda let a file folder drop from her hands onto the desk—*slap*. Leaning back in her chair, she ran her fingers through the jet-black hair at her temple. "We can do this the easy way or the hard way." Her tone was quiet but firm, oozing confidence.

Kelley smiled and arched her eyebrows. "Why *whatever* do you mean, Counselor?"

The ADA exhaled and shook her head as she drove her finger down on the file folder. "Come on, Kelley, we got this guy. I got three solid statements here. You know the drill as well as I do. We can go through the motions if you want. But, frankly I'd rather not put these three young girls on the stand. They've been through enough."

Kelley smirked. "And so, what, we just go ahead and convict him and call it a day?"

Lasorda rolled her eyes. "You can lose the theatrics. There's no jury or cameras in here." She paused and opened the file folder. "I'm prepared to offer sexual misconduct with

136

a minor, second degree—gross misdemeanor. We're talking max one year and a fine. If you force me to put those girls on the stand, I'm going for first degree and I'll get it. That's a class C felony—five years and ten grand. And I can promise you that a jury's not going to take kindly to a principal using his position to seduce young girls."

Kelley gazed at her for a moment before reaching down for her briefcase. "I'll take the offer to my client. His decision. By the way, when can I talk to him?" She stood.

The ADA remained sitting. "Just so you know, I'm shooting for arraignment tomorrow morning so don't take too long. This is a limited-time offer." She stared up at Kelley.

"Assuming the gestapo here will let me in to see him, I'll get with him this afternoon and give you a call." She turned to Lainie. "Let's go."

Stunned by the speed and emotionless exchange that had just occurred, Lainie followed her associate and friend. A man's life was being negotiated away and she felt powerless. She wondered as she exited the room why she even cared.

They got in to see Paul just after two. The orange coveralls combined with his swollen eyes and haggard face painted the picture of a man with no hope. They met with him in a small room that contained a table and four chairs. He slunk in his chair, staring down at the tabletop. Lainie glanced at him but quickly averted her gaze. For his part, he seemed not to even notice her.

Kelley started by repeating what she had told him earlier. "Paul, I need you to listen to my words closely. Remember several days ago that I told you the prosecutor would offer a deal. She has. I am obligated to present this deal to you." She went on to describe the offer.

At first, he continued to stare at the tabletop, a blank, empty look on his face. As she walked through the details, though, he looked up, his eyes widening. When she finished speaking, he looked back down for a moment before sitting up and leaning into the table, responding, "So, what? You're saying that if I don't agree to admit this they're going to put me in prison for five years. But if I say I did it, I would only be in for a year, is that right?"

Kelley nodded but remained silent.

Paul narrowed his eyes and shook his head. He slunk back down in the chair. "There's nothing in there about me being innocent. It's like everybody's already decided I did it without even bothering to look for the truth."

Conflict tormented Lainie. On the one hand, he was right. Other people were trying to make deals that would put him in prison for a greater or lesser time. And even after that, being a convicted sex offender, there would be nothing left for him. But what if he *was* guilty? What if he was just an incredibly good actor?

Kelley's voice interrupted her thoughts. "Like I said, I'm obligated to bring this to you. I didn't say I recommend it. I haven't seen the statements yet and I haven't heard a peep about any other evidence." She paused and furrowed her brow. "The ADA wants to fast-track this. She wants a deal in place before arraignment and she knows she has us at a disadvantage. She's seen the statements and we haven't. One thing we could do is to let it go to arraignment and get a trial date. At that point, they have to provide us with all the evidence."

"What difference would that make?" He stared across at her without blinking.

"It means that we go in tomorrow with no deal in place—nothing on the table. She sat up straight and leaned into the table. "Here's what I think, at least for now. Let's call her bluff. If she truly wants to keep those girls off the stand, she'll do the deal even at the last minute. I need to see those statements."

Paul nodded. "And so?"

Lainie thought she saw a hint of sparkle in his eyes, something like hope.

Kelley took a deep breath. "The arraignment will go tomorrow morning, most likely. They'll read the charges against you and ask for a plea. When they do, you are to say only four words—*not guilty, your honor*—nothing more, nothing less. Do *not* try to elaborate, don't discuss it, or anything. Understand?"

"Yes." His eyes dropped again.

Kelley continued, "The judge will fix bail. The prosecutor is going to request that you be kept in custody. I'll ask for release on your own recognizance, that is, release without bail. We've got some things working for us here. You've got no record. You turned yourself in. You don't have enough resources to flee the country and live elsewhere, I assume. And I'll present all of that."

She shifted in her seat and leaned back, watching Paul for a moment before continuing, as if she were assessing his ability to hear what she was about to say. "The prosecutor is going to remind the judge of the heinous nature of the accusation. She is going to bring up the fact that you tried to contact one of the girls. She's going to call it a threat or

139

intimidation and say that the girl's safety is at risk. Fortunately, I managed to acquire a copy of the video that shows exactly what happened. All in all, I think we stand a pretty good chance of getting off light on the bail. *But*, and this is important, whatever bail is assigned, you will either have to come up with the cash or work through a bail bondsman. A bondsman will put up the bail and charge you a percentage as a fee. If you've got available resources, you are far better off putting it up yourself since you get it back when you show up."

Lainie's stomach continued to churn as the discussion became more and more specific. Reality set in. She watched with an overwhelming sense of sadness as a man that had, at one time, seemed a kind and gentle soul crumbled before her eyes.

Chapter 34

After the experience at the police department, a darkness settled over Lainie's heart. Despite the mental preparations for what she knew would be coming, seeing Paul handcuffed and shoved out the door toward fingerprinting, the mug shot, and a cell for the night threw a bucket of cold reality on her warm self-assurances. What would he do all evening?

Mildred provided a ready answer. *Try to stay alive among the throng of men for whom jail is no big deal.*

She offered perspective. "It's only for one night. We'll get him out in the morning."

Oh, so you care now?

Lainie hit the power button on her computer. While it booted up, she went into the kitchen and put the kettle on for tea. Selecting a peach ginger, she decided on a shot of honey—something to take away the bitterness. When the phone rang, she checked the caller ID. "Hello."

"Why am I sitting here with no chapters in front of me?" Meg's words carried their usual sarcastic condescension.

Lainie took her landline handset into the living room and plopped down in her overstuffed chair. "Hi Meg. I apologize. The world turned upside down the past few days. I'll finish them and get them right off." She took care not to specify when, an oversight that Meg did not miss.

"And when, pray tell, might I be graced with said chapters?"

"I have one ready. My computer is booting up right now. I hope to have another two of them ready by the end of the evening. I'm tied up tomorrow morning but should finish the

other two by tomorrow night. I'll send them to you then."
She shuddered at the idea that she'd just committed to
producing four chapters in two days, something she had
never in the past accomplished.

"Your personal commitments are not my problem, dear. I
need those chapters."

Something snapped inside Lainie. "You know what, Meg,
if what I'm doing isn't working for you, screw it. People's
lives are crumbling here, and you're worried about a fucking
elf and her friend in some God-damned fantasy world. To
hell with it, I'll return your advance and do this myself."

She gritted her teeth against the rage at the same time she
felt her stomach doing somersaults. She'd struggled to get
this chance and now she was throwing it away.

Mildred interjected. *Still not as bad as what Paul is
facing.*

Lainie forced her attention back to the phone in time to
hear a subdued comment. "Get the chapters to me when you
can." Click.

***

Lainie propped up in bed on one elbow and looked at the
clock as the phone rang a third time—one-thirty. The blur in
her eyes made caller ID useless. And at this hour of the
morning, it couldn't be good news. She connected. "Hello."

Kelley's voice floated over. "Hey, it's me. They admitted
Paul to the hospital a little while ago. I'm headed there now.
Not sure what happened but he's in intensive care. I'll give
you a call when I know something."

Lainie tried to shake the cobwebs from her brain. "What… how?"

"Dunno. They were pretty vague. Could have been some of the other prisoners or maybe the guards. Hard to say right now. Call you soon."

"I'll head over too." She knew it had to be the Overlake Hospital—fifteen minutes from her house.

"See you there."

***

Lainie thought she'd prepared herself. She was wrong. The sight of Paul lying in the bed, handcuffed to the bedrail, nearly brought her to her knees. His face was swollen and deep purple with a bandage around his head. He had a number of tubes attached, one of which appeared to be providing blood. Waves of nausea flowed over her.

Kelley, who had been sitting in a chair beside him, stood. "Not a pretty sight, huh? He's under sedation right now but they said he should be conscious within the hour. We might be able to get a plea entered telephonically so that we can get bail. I don't think it would be very productive sending him back to that hole." She shook her head, alternating her watchful gaze between Lainie and Paul.

"What the hell? How did this happen?" Lainie stared in shocked disbelief.

Kelley shrugged. "They're not talking right now. The guard outside is just a rent-a-cop and doesn't know anything. The staff down at the holding pen are all circling the wagons. But I'd guess one of two things. Either the guards decided to make an impression on him or they leaked his offense information to the population of prisoners and let them handle him. Either way, they made their point."

The door opened, and Detective Steadman strode in. She barely acknowledged the two women and then shifted her look to Paul.

Kelley moved up closer to the woman. "Well, now, that didn't take long at all, did it?" She glared at the detective in an obvious challenge.

Steadman met Kelley's *if-looks-could-kill* stance for a moment and then looked away. "I had nothing to do with this."

Kelley howled with sarcastic laughter. "Oh yeah, I know. You'd *never, ever* do such a thing."

A nurse stuck her head in with a finger over lips and a reprimand in her eyes.

The detective glanced at Kelley for a moment and then quickly away again. She said nothing.

Kelley moved up close to Steadman and stared, eyeball to eyeball. "The guy's unconscious and handcuffed. And even when he wakes up, he has severe internal injuries. He's not going anywhere. Why don't you get the hell out of here? Or do you want to add your nickel's worth."

The glaring Steadman turned beet-red. Whirling around, she stormed out of the room.

"Fuck her." Kelley spit the words out.

Lainie sat down as confusion set in. Kelley never worried about guilt or innocence and yet here she was, playing nurse maid to this guy she didn't even know. "Impressive. She's going to be your friend for life, I'm sure. But why take her on like that? I assume she didn't do this."

Kelley turned and gazed at Lainie for a few seconds. "No one deserves *this*. He may end up being guilty. But that's for a jury to decide and sentencing comes from the judge. That bitch doesn't get to play cop, judge, and jury. She may not have done this directly, but she's a part of it. One of these days I'll bring her down." She shook her head and again commenced watching Paul.

Lainie could see the rage building in her friend, but she wasn't sure who the target was. Steadman was definitely a candidate. But it felt like there was something else.

Chapter 35

Lainie and Kelley ended up in an all-night diner two blocks from the hospital. Lainie stirred the black java without thought as if somehow a sense of understanding would percolate up. "For Christ's sake, he just went in yesterday." She shook her head and furrowed her brow.

Rain pelted the window creating a steady rhythm. Kelley seemed entranced by the darkness outside. "It happens." The words came out soft, as if not meant to be heard.

Lainie stared at her and waited.

"Could have been either the guards or the prisoners. Either way, the result's the same. He's battered to hell and *they're looking into it.*" Her coffee sat untouched. "Detectives will tell you that child molesters and the like don't fare well in the slammer, which is true. What they don't tell you is that they make sure the word is passed to the prisoners, who do the dirty work. No one is ever held accountable. Not the guards, not the cops, and not the prisoners."

"I've never seen you like this, Kelley. You're always so self-assured and laissez-faire about things. What's got you so upset this time? Is it Paul?"

Kelley turned her head and stared at Lainie for a moment. "I've had guys get knifed in lock-up and die. Never went to trial. Maybe they were guilty, maybe not. But they paid the price." She took a drink of what was probably room temperature coffee. "This whole jailhouse justice thing throws the system on its head. But the worst part is that the cops don't care. Well, in fairness, I'm talking about Steadman. Her pat line is that it saves taxpayer money."

146

Lainie tilted her head and arched an eyebrow. "The bad blood between you two—what's that all about?"

Kelley shrugged. "She sees herself as a one-person crusade to save women and children, at any cost. And the worst part is that, on some level, I agree with her. The kids and women who are brutalized and violated deserve that kind of protection. But it's not black and white. She believes everyone she arrests is guilty and I can also understand that. Her biggest problem is that she makes a decision early on and then sticks to it no matter what. Paul happens to be her target right now. Nothing we say or do will matter one whit. If she senses that the case is struggling, I wouldn't put it past her to invoke her own particular brand of justice."

"Any idea where this comes from?" Lainie couldn't imagine someone so narrowly focused.

Kelley shook her head. "Dunno. I suspect that she's carrying around some baggage, but I have no idea what it is."

"Maybe we should try to work more through the partner. Burke, right?"

A smirk preceded the response. "Burke's a good cop but Steadman's got seniority. For now, she calls the tune and he dances the dance. Anyway, at this point we're connected to the ADA. Lasorda's okay, but she's just after another notch on her gun. If we can discredit the evidence, then she'll throw in the towel. She doesn't like getting her butt kicked in court. And it'll hurt especially bad if we have to take those girls apart on the stand."

Lainie felt another wave of sickness. She'd heard the stories of defense attorneys attacking rape and molestation victims in court and it didn't feel like something she wanted to be a part of.

The blackness outside gradually gave way to a dusky gray and the pelting rain to an incessant drizzle. An hour later, the two paid their bill and trudged out into the dismal morning.

Once home, Lainie showered, grabbed a bowl of oatmeal and a couple slices of whole wheat toast with strawberry jam. As she washed the dishes, she wondered if Paul had regained consciousness. Maybe she should swing by and check on him. But she reminded herself that Kelley was going to arrange for a phone call from the court if he was able. No need to have two people checking on him.

She sat in the living room staring out the window. Having guzzled coffee since about three, she wasn't anxious for more. Conflict gnawed at her. She felt bad for Paul. But, if he'd done what they said, then maybe he deserved all this, and more.

Who gets to decide?

Lainie pushed back at Mildred. "A jury decides."

And what if the jury gets it wrong?

Juries did get it wrong sometimes. Innocent people went to prison. Innocent people have been executed. What if the jury got it wrong on Paul? And they could get it wrong two different ways. They could convict an innocent man. Or they could acquit a guilty man. Who answers for that?

The ringing phone broke her train of thought. The caller ID indicated Kelley's cell. "Hey, any news?"

Her voice sounded a little more upbeat than it had several hours ago. "Yeah. He regained consciousness and they upgraded his condition to *good*. They're moving him up to a regular bed. So, we should be okay for arraignment by phone, provided the judge will go for it. Also, I swung by the office. We got the digital file for the security video recording of the Smallwood's home. It'll help his cause."

Lainie closed her eyes and breathed deep. "Good. That's great. I'm getting ready to leave. I'll see you at the courthouse."

Chapter 36

Lainie took a seat beside Kelley at the defense table. The two assistants, Andi and Elliott sat with Paul in the hospital. A low buzz of background noise filled the courtroom. She'd never done criminal work but had been exposed to enough in law school that she knew what to expect. Across the aisle, Eve Lasorda leafed through a stack of papers. Detective Steadman sat beside her, staring in the general direction of the bench. Neither of the two women cast a view toward the defense table.

At ten, the clerk picked up the phone handset and dialed a number. After a few words, she hung up and dialed another, longer number reading from a sheet of paper in front of her. She uttered a few words into the receiver and then turned to watch the area behind the judge's bench.

As the door opened, the clerk stood and announced, "All rise, superior court for King County is now in session, the Honorable James Foster presiding."

The fiftyish, stocky man outfitted in a black robe entered. "Please be seated." He turned to the clerk. "Are we ready to proceed?"

The clerk nodded. "Yes, your honor. The defendant will participate by teleconference from his hospital room."

The judge turned to the defense table. "Counselor, I assume that your client is medically unable to attend the hearing in person?"

Kelley stood. "Your honor, Mister Stafford had every intention of being here today. Unfortunately, he just left intensive care a few hours ago. He's hospitalized with severe internal injuries and possible concussion, courtesy of

Bellevue's finest." She gestured toward the prosecution table.

Steadman turned a deep shade of red and stared daggers at Kelley. Judge Foster rolled his eyes. "Thank you for the information but I can do without the color commentary."

Kelley lowered her head. "Yes, your honor. If I may approach. I have a photograph of Mister Stafford as of three this morning. I offer this as validation of the condition that prevents his in-person attendance."

The judge beckoned her up even as the DA rose and spoke. "Your honor, prosecution is willing to stipulate." The words came too late.

The judge studied the photo of the battered man unconscious in the hospital bed. He stared at the prosecution table for a moment. "Yes, well I see the defense's point." He cleared his throat. Okay, we'll proceed telephonically. Are you there, Mister Stafford?"

A weak, slow voice flowed over the speaker. "Yes, your honor."

The judge leaned forward and read the charges, after which he asked, "How do you plead, Mister Stafford?"

A moment of silence was followed by a weak and uncertain voice. "Not guilty, your honor."

The judge leaned back in his chair. "Very well. The defendant has entered a plea of not guilty. We'll set this on for trial. Miz Lasorda, where does the prosecution stand in terms of time?"

The assistant ADA stood. "Your honor, we don't anticipate delays, but I would like to have at least three months to prepare the case."

151

"Noted." He turned his attention to the defense table. "Miz Vickers?"

"Your honor, the Sixth Amendment to the U. S. Constitution guarantees my client's right to a speedy trial. Washington State Court rules specify sixty days if the accused is in custody and ninety days if he is not. We would like to have this resolved as quickly as possible. I haven't gotten copies of the statements from the DA's office yet, so I'm reluctant to say more than that."

The judge nodded, his eyes betraying a bit of weariness. "Yes, yes. Well, we're not at that point just yet. I'm sure ADA Lasorda will provide those statements in a timely manner." He paused and glanced at each of the attorneys. "With speedy trial provisions invoked, we have a maximum of ninety days and the defense desires sooner rather than later. Is that a fair representation?"

Lasorda and Kelley both assented.

He punched a key on the notebook computer sitting off to the side. "Very well, then, let's set this on for, say, one month." He stared at the screen for a moment. "I'm calendaring this for Thursday, April twenty-sixth, nine a.m. Please notify the court as early as possible if either of you need to adjust that." He paused and looked at the prosecution. "Bail?"

Eve Lasorda stood. "Your honor, the people seek remand. Mister Stafford committed a particularly vicious crime against three young girls. Additionally, he visited the house of one of the victims and attempted to intimidate and threaten her. He constitutes a danger both to the community and to the victims. We ask that he be held without bail pending trial."

The judge turned his head to face the defense table. "Counselor?"

Kelley stood. "Your honor, first, we've seen no evidence at all of this crime other than the third hand report that some girls may have said something. We have not yet been provided with copies nor have we been allowed to view the statements. We have also not seen or heard of any other evidence supporting this allegation. So, if I may, I'd like to offer a friendly amendment to the DA's statement—the crime he allegedly committed." She cleared her throat as the DA shook her head.

"A search of all criminal databases has not revealed any indication of prior criminality. Interviews with former employers, co-workers, and family members indicated no such prior behavior. And we also ask that you consider the fact that, when charged, Mister Stafford presented himself to the police to be taken into custody. He has been an upstanding member of the community. He does not have assets that would allow him to flee the country. And as you can see from his photo, he's hardly in any condition to do anything. We ask that Mister Stafford be released on his own recognizance." She looked down at the table as a smile stole over her face.

"As for the *threats* and *intimidation*, we've obtained video footage from the home security system showing the encounter. I have it queued up. With the court's permission, I'd like to play it so that we can all see this incident."

The judge nodded. "Very well."

Kelley walked over to a notebook computer sitting on a small table beside the clerk. She tapped on some keys and stood back. The screen mounted on the side of the room opposite where a jury would have been sitting jumped to life. Over the course of the next three minutes, viewers could see Paul Stafford pleading with a man and a woman, wringing his hands in front of him. "Please, I just need to understand…" "I didn't do any of that. I don't know why she…" "Please, I just want to know…" The display showed Paul walking away from the house, hands in his pockets and then cut to black.

The image burned into Lainie's brain. He could still be lying, but to all appearances, this was a man who had stepped into something of which he knew nothing. His defining characteristic seemed to be confusion. She envisioned his options and choices being eliminated one at a time.

Kelley returned to the defense table. "Your honor, this was clearly not intimidation nor threatening." She gestured toward the now black screen. "On top of that, he never even spoke to the victim. When her parents asked him to leave, he did so, peacefully."

The judge stroked his chin. "I have to agree with defense on that point. It hardly seems threatening to me. On the other hand, I can see how this might be upsetting to the parents. I'm going to split the difference. I'll release O—R. Mister Stafford, are you still with us?"

A weak response. "Yes, your honor."

"Good. Mister Stafford, I order you to have no contact whatsoever with the victims or their families. Furthermore, you are to remain at least one thousand feet from their residences, schools, and churches. Is that clear?"

"Yes, your honor."

"Anything else today?" The judge appeared ready to make a retreat.

The two attorneys remained standing, both responding. "No, your honor."

"Very well, court is adjourned. We will see you all back here on April twenty-sixth." He stood and departed.

As the various people stood to file out, Kelley strode casually by the prosecution table. "What happened, Steadman, you didn't pay the guy with the knife enough?" She chortled and moved on before the detective could respond.

Lainie hurried after her associate. "Christ, Kelley, are you trying to stay on her bad side?" This seemed illogical.

Kelley smiled and shook her head. "I certainly hope so."

"You sure about that?" Lainie wondered what goading Steadman would accomplish.

Her friend filled in the blanks. "Oh yeah. I'm just praying for the day she takes a swing at me. And it's coming, I can feel it." Once outside the courtroom, she turned to Lainie. "I'm headed over to the hospital to see Paul. You want to meet me there?"

Lainie searched her heart—did she want to meet Kelley there? No, she didn't but she wasn't sure whether it was the pain of seeing Paul in that condition or her lack of belief in him. "I've got some things to take care of today. I'll give you a call later."

Chapter 37

Once home, Lainie fell into bed face down. Exhaustion from being up most of the night and sitting through the courtroom drama had taken its toll. Beneath the heaviness of the physical load lurked an emotional beast. She wasn't sure whether she believed Paul or not. But more than that, a deeper uncertainty haunted her. Did she even *want* to trust him?

Mildred spoke up. *Don't want to be made a fool of again?*

Lainie was too tired for this argument. "Let it go. That was different. One's got nothing to do with the other." She rolled over in bed and stared at the ceiling.

Whatever.

She hated it when Mildred threw that at her. Lainie could think of little worse than being dismissed by her own conscience. She closed her eyes.

***

Lainie awoke as the late afternoon light through the window brightened the bedroom. Her stomach reminded her of the fact that she hadn't eaten all day. After taking a few minutes to gather her thoughts, she rolled out of bed and stumbled into the bathroom to regroup.

As she made her way to the kitchen to create some kind of meal, her thoughts turned to Kelley and Paul. The microwave clock informed her that it was after five. She picked up her landline handset and dialed Kelley's cellphone number.

The attorney picked up on the first ring. "Kelley Vickers."

Lainie leaned back against the kitchen counter, looking out the window as she spoke. "Hey, it's me. How'd it go at the hospital?" She felt oddly uncomfortable saying Paul's name.

When she responded, her voice came across as soft and understated. "Okay. His condition is still listed as good. They're going to keep him another couple of days."

Lainie wasn't sure what to say. Was that good news or bad news? Did she even care? "What's next?"

"I don't know. Actually, I need some sleep before I start thinking about that. Give me a call in the morning." The words and tone sounded distracted, almost disconnected.

"Sounds like a plan. Have a good night." Lainie cut the connection and placed the handset on the counter. Surveying the kitchen and mentally taking stock of potential meals, she settled for cold cereal.

Despite a lack of appetite, she spooned in the milk-soaked raisin bran. The fading light of day deserted the kitchen allowing darkness to creep in. Lainie put her bowl, spoon, and glass in the sink and made her way into the living room, swapping one dark space for another.

You need to sort this out. Mildred seemed oddly non-confrontational, almost gentle with her.

"I know." She understood exactly what her conscience was talking about. She plopped down on one end of the couch. After a moment, she swung around and slid her legs up, resting her head on the arm of the sofa while she stared at the gray ceiling. "I don't owe this guy anything."

Nobody said you did.

"Nobody showed up when I needed it."

And how did you feel about that?

157

"Let's not go there. And why should I even care about Paul?"

Because you do.

This wasn't helping. What was it she cared about? "I care about being hurt again, being betrayed."

What about Paul? How do you think he feels right now? Betrayed maybe?

"That's not my problem. I'm just helping him with the case. That's what I offered to do."

Can't you, just for one minute, try to see all of this through his eyes?

"No, because I have no idea whether he did those things or not." She pulled her arms up and locked her hands behind her head as she continued to stare upward.

If he did, he's certainly paying for it. But if he didn't….

She closed her eyes and shook her head slowly. "I know. And we'll do our best to defend him. Isn't that enough?"

Is it?

***

Lainie came awake with a start. Darkness enveloped everything. She thought she'd gotten past this little habit of falling asleep on the sofa. She pushed herself up into a sitting position and squinted to see the display on her DVR—just past three. Standing, she stumbled down the hall and fell into bed, fully clothed. She did her best to avoid entertaining any thoughts at all. Just before she drifted off, though, an image of Paul lying bruised and battered in the hospital bed pried its way into her thoughts. The image faded to black.

Chapter 38

The next morning, Lainie made her way through a cold drizzle to Kelley's office. She was running a little early for the ten o'clock meeting. On this day, though, her walk from the parking lot to the building took her through the middle of a mini-protest of sorts. Four women with placards demanding Paul's imprisonment and banishment to hell walked back and forth right in front of the entrance. She walked past them without comment, making an effort to avoid any reaction at all.

When she arrived in the conference room, Kelley was setting her coffee and writing materials on the table. The space was otherwise empty. "Are Andi and Elliott going to be here?"

"They should be in shortly." She glanced at her watch. "Still early. Get any rest last night?"

Lainie shrugged. "Some. I fell hard asleep yesterday afternoon. I'm getting too old for these middle-of-the-night parties. But, yeah, I guess I slept okay last night."

Mildred chimed in, *Probably better than Paul.*

The two assistants strolled through the door about fifteen seconds apart. Each nodded and said their good mornings. Surrounded by steaming cups of coffee, the party of four got started.

Kelley glanced around the table, tapping her pen on the pad in front of her. "We all know how court went yesterday. I count that as a big win for the home team. We're now headed into a lull. The trial starts in a month. Let's go around the table. Andi, you have anything on the three girls?" She turned toward the research assistant.

"Not much more than we already knew. Caryn is an honor student. She's popular, lots of extra-curricular stuff. Doesn't date any one specific guy but doesn't seem to have trouble filling her dance card. Family is well off. Word is that her parents are angling for her to get into an Ivy League school. Not much info on what she wants." She glanced around the table before continuing.

"Deborah Bufford has a learning disability. I don't really have anything to add beyond what Paul told us. No apparent connection to Caryn. And Marianne Thompson is an A student, quiet, reserved. She's not overly popular but neither is she disliked. The teachers all seem to respect her, and she doesn't get into any trouble. No apparent connection to Caryn or Deborah." She looked up from her notes. "I guess that's what strikes me about this. At least with regard to school, there doesn't seem to be anything that links these three together." She shook her head.

Kelley made a few notes. "Not sure whether I told you all or not, but the parents said *no* to the interviews. So, until we get the statements from the ADA, we're shooting in the dark." She pulled her cup over in front of her but left it on the table. "Elliott, I have something for you. This afternoon go to the hospital and get a release of information from Paul. I want to see his phone records for the past, oh, let's say six months."

The gawky young man swiped the shock of blond hair from his brow and nodded.

Lainie jumped in. "Why do we need those?"

Kelley gazed at her for a few seconds. "No particular reason, other than the obvious. Mostly because the police are going to get them, and I want to know what they know." She paused and looked down at her notes for a moment. "The eight-hundred-pound gorilla here is the statements. I haven't heard about anything else from the DA or the detectives. All else being equal, that usually means they have nothing. I could be wrong. They could spring it on us with the discovery package. Honestly, though, that's not Lasorda's style. Also, if they had something else, she'd have trotted it out when she put the deal on the table."

Lainie wondered if the discovery process worked the same in criminal as it did in civil cases. "How soon do they have to give us the package?"

"It's not hard and fast. They can't spring everything on us the day before trial. But they don't have to give us everything a long time in advance, either. If I feel they've sandbagged us, I can move for continuation to give us time to prepare. But Lasorda's pretty good about this stuff. In fact, given that the police had the statements days ago and there's not really anything else they've talked about, I'm surprised we don't have them already."

Lainie nodded. "Doesn't sound that different from civil." A lull fell over the room. She got up and stretched. Walking to the window, she looked down to see the four women still milling about near the entrance to the building. "Hey Kelley, what do you make of this?" She gestured toward the window with her head.

Kelley stood, walked over, and looked down. "I've had some of these in the past. Usually concerned parents or family members who feel they're not getting justice. First reaction is to always blame the defense."

Lainie focused on the women. "Something kind of wonky about this, though. Look at them. Three have handmade signs with different slogans. The fourth one has a professionally made sign. It has Paul's photograph in color. The lettering is made to look hand-printed but it's not. Look at the reflection when she turns. The whole package is protected by a plastic coating of some type. This woman didn't just wake up this morning and decide to protest. She planned this."

"Yeah, well, maybe it's important to her." Kelley motioned Andi and Elliott to the window. "Find out about them—names, addresses, phone numbers, and such. Most important, though, I want to know if there are any links between them." She gazed down at the women in the street with a growing interest in her eyes. "It might be nothing but you never know."

Lainie shifted her thoughts from the four women to the statements from the girls. "Let me ask you, you said that Lasorda normally gives you discovery stuff in a timely manner. What do you make of her delay?"

"I'm not sure I'd call it a delay. After all, arraignment was just yesterday. But, assuming she's not anxious to provide them, I'd say that she probably has some concerns or reservations about them. Maybe she's having the detectives drill down on them to fill in the holes." She turned and sat on the windowsill facing the table.

Elliott and Andi returned to their seats and jotted down notes. Kelley alternated her view between the conference room table and the small parade down below. "Okay, if there's nothing else, let's hit it."

Lainie moved over closer to Kelley. "Anything for me?"

"Not right now. Mainly I'm just marking time until we get something from Lasorda. I'm going to swing by the hospital later and check on Paul, unless you want to." She arched her eyebrows.

The excuse on the tip of her tongue wouldn't come out. Instead, she muttered the truth. "I'd rather not."

Chapter 39

That night, Lainie made another stab at peace with Mildred. "I want him to get a fair shake. He deserves the best representation we can give him."

Is that really what he needs right now?

Lainie knew exactly what the snarky voice was getting at. "I'm sure he needs a lot of things. But what I can give him is the legal piece."

Do you believe he's innocent?

"I don't know. And like Kelley says, that's not my concern. My job is to do the best I can do." Lainie had to admit, that line sounded better coming from Kelley. Then again, Kelley didn't really know him. Paul was just a client to her.

And you have a connection?

"I knew him before. That's all." She could feel Mildred collecting her thoughts for another assault. She made a preemptory strike. "I'm going to give it everything I have. We will get him off."

Mildred's silence was a disapproving one. Whatever peace Lainie had achieved felt tenuous at best.

She caught the eleven o'clock news later that night. The story about Paul's arraignment and release had aired the night before, so she assumed there wouldn't be much about it in the media. No such luck.

The second story in the show was Pastor Robert Tell making another speech, this time outside the Bellevue Police Department. *Locations change but the message remains the same.* He called Paul out by name, deploring the preferential treatment being given him by the legal system. "He's

164

walking free among us, molesting our children, raping our young students. And what do our trusted legal officials do? They let him out of jail and put him on the streets with no restrictions. He goes where he will. Does what he wants." His words were inaccurate but no one at the TV station seemed to pick up on it.

The firebrand minister raised his right hand into the air as he continued to shout. "What we are seeing here is the systematic destruction of all that we hold dear. We have locked God out of the house. We have invited Satan to the table."

He paused, nodded, and smiled. "But we, the faithful, are not defeated. Nor are we discouraged. We fight on. We fight for our children, our young adults, and our God. I ask that you join me. Together, we can take back our city and put our Lord in the place rightly belonging to him."

Lainie clicked off the TV. But the image of the man remained in her head. And a question—what was his connection? After all, a lot of sexual assault cases passed through the court system and she'd never seen him take a direct interest. Not that she followed these things carefully. But still, he seemed to be making quite the splash over this. Suddenly the image of the four women struck her—a connection perhaps?

She got her answer the next afternoon. Once everyone was seated, Kelley turned to the tech wizard. "So, my good man, you have something for us?"

Elliott had been fidgeting, apparently ready to talk. When called on, he sat up straight, glanced aside at Andi, and started. "I do. The four women are Emily Banks, Susan Thornhill, Ann Miller, and Toni Carter. Individually, there's little of interest. But they all have a connection to Robert Tell's church." He looked again at Andi and then added, "There have been calls to and from the minister's cell phone, a bunch of them within the past few days. I—well, we—also managed to find out that the custom placard carried by Banks was printed at Cascade Printing and Graphics and charged to the church's account." He put his hands flat on the table and smiled at the group of rapt listeners.

Lainie shook her head. "Uh, excuse me for asking, but how did you manage to get that information?" Without a court order or subpoena, that should have been out of reach.

Kelley waved her hand as if half-heartedly swatting at a buzzing insect. "I don't need to know. We're not going to use it." She grinned. "But it is interesting information, wouldn't you say?"

Lainie shrugged. The information was consistent with what she'd seen on TV last night. "I don't know. Tell's made no secret of his interest in this case. Not surprising, then, that he's using people he knows to multiply the pressure."

Kelley's retort echoed what she'd asked herself the previous evening. "Ah yes, but the question is, *why*? Of all the cases, why this one?"

The room fell silent. Short of asking the minister, Lainie couldn't think of a particularly good way to answer that. An idea wormed its way into her mind. "Wait. Is it possible that one or more of the young girls are connected to the church? I mean, if that was the case, it would certainly explain his interest."

Nods all around. Kelley spoke up. "Yeah. Sounds right. But that takes us nowhere, at least for now. If they are connected to the church, then it would only seem reasonable that he took up the mantle on their behalf." She turned to Andi. "Dig deeper on the girls. Elliott, you help. If there's a connection, I don't expect it'll be hard to find, especially given his high-profile exposure. There's bound to be something on social media."

She gathered up her papers and then sat still for a moment. "Looks like Paul is going to be released tomorrow, although he'll have to spend a few days in bed at home. I'll pick him up and take him to his house. I know it's outside our area of responsibility, but maybe we could take turns preparing some meals for him. He's not going to be up and around well enough to cook."

Andi spoke up first. "No problem. I can throw something together tomorrow night."

Elliott shrugged. "I'll do the next night, if he's willing to eat it. I'm not the greatest cook. I make no guarantees."

Kelley finished it the round. "Yolanda and I will take care of the night after. That should do it. After that, I hope he'll be on his feet again. Okay, thanks all. Let's hit it."

Lainie pondered what she'd just experienced. The group never even looked at her. They wrapped around Paul like a warm quilt on a cold night, not needing any help from her.

Mildred weighed in, *And that's a good thing?*

Chapter 40

Kelley, you got a minute?" The others filed out of the conference room on their way to important tasks. "Anything I need to be working on?" Everyone had an assignment but her.

The lead attorney paused at the threshold. "No. we need to see the statements, which will come with the discovery material. Andi and Elliott can dig around a bit, but I'd rather not pad the bill any more than we have to. If my two henchmen come up with anything interesting, I'll give you a call. Otherwise, I guess you can jump back into your writing."

Lainie felt conflicted and that bothered her. She needed to get back to the chapters, and she probably owed Meg an apology. But the notion of sitting around not working on the case left her uneasy.

Leave it to Mildred to exacerbate a trivial internal conflict. *Maybe you care more than you think you do?*

"Of course I care—about the case."

The inner combatant backed off, sort of. *If you say so.* She seemed to always want the last word.

Lainie walked through the door into the kitchen from the garage just before two. Glancing at the clock, she knew she had time. She picked up the phone, searched the directory, and dialed.

A clipped, all-business voice emanated from the handset. "Meg Costanzo."

Lainie closed her eyes and hoped for the right words. "Meg, this is Lainie Simpson. I wanted to apologize for the other day. I had some things going on. That is no excuse and,

I am sorry." What surprised Lainie most was that her feelings weren't really about salvaging the professional relationship with her editor. She felt bad about her outburst. After all, the upheaval in her life wasn't Meg's fault.

A softer voice followed a brief moment of silence. "So, you're back on schedule?"

Lainie smiled. Based on conversations she'd had with the woman, this was probably as close as Meg came to a personal exchange. "I'm shooting for the end of the weekend on the five chapters. Have some of it done already." She started to elaborate but decided this was enough. After all, this conversation was not about the novel.

Things improved in the hours that followed. The words, sentences, and paragraphs came easier. The blinking cursor welcomed rather than intimidated. The fictional characters continued their friendship. As for the romantic interest, no.

By eleven, Lainie had run out of steam. She struggled through the last paragraph of the night and then closed out the word processor. As she started to shut down the computer, a thought came to her. She opened the web browser and typed in the search box—"Robert Tell."

The first four links led her to media stories regarding the good pastor's ongoing fight with state and local officials over funding, or rather, the lack of it. Most of the media content repeated what she'd already gleaned from the video clips she'd seen on TV. The one new piece was the name of his church—Word of the Light Temple. She was familiar with the usual denominations, such as Catholic, Presbyterian, and Methodist. But Tell's organization didn't seem to fit into any pre-defined group of which she was aware.

After the media stories came links to social media—Facebook, Twitter, and the like. When she tried to access the links, all of the sites wanted her to set up a membership and that wasn't going to happen, at least that night.

Scrolling farther down, she ran across another media story, this one from the *Coeur d'Alene Press*. From this, Lainie acquired two interesting pieces of information. The first was that Tell's fight with Bellevue and Washington state officials were largely a repeat of similar conflicts with Idaho officials about eight years previous. The government there finally caved and provided funds to his church for youth outreach programs. Less than two years later, the church closed its doors with no warning. The story cited vague accounts of financial difficulties.

The second bit of information was that there were allegations of misconduct on Tell's part—affairs with several married congregation members. With no names given and no other related links, Lainie printed the story, closed the browser and powered down for the night.

Chapter 41

Not knowing about religious practice and organization hampered Lainie. She had read the media reports but still couldn't get her mind around the crux of Tell's acrimonious relationship with local and state governments, other than him wanting money and them fighting it. Surely this was not an isolated issue. She wondered if other churches had this problem. These questions kept her awake most of the night, but she was at a loss as to why it seemed so important. What did this have to do with the case?

The next morning, she fired up the computer and started the search process again, this time focusing more on churches in general. It took no time at all before she ended up on the website of the Church Council of Greater Seattle. Within a few minutes of reading the organizational background material, she found her way to the directory of members. To her surprise, she found that Tell's organization was indeed a member, but was categorized as a faith-based organization rather than a church.

Perplexed, she dug for additional clarity but the vague description of categories on the website told her little. She did come away with a potential lead—one of the governing board members was a Methodist minister in Bellevue— Reverend Janet Polasky. Lainie copied down the contact information and turned off the computer.

As she absent-mindedly spooned the raisin bran to her mouth, she wondered where to take it next. Part of the problem is that she had wandered into this area of inquiry without direction from Kelley. An hour or two of pro bono research wasn't such a big deal but embarking on a major time-consuming search was a different story.

Mildred made her first appearance of the day, having remained silent all through the sleepless previous night. *Why not just talk to the Methodist minister? It won't take long and, if there's anything of interest there, you can run it by Kelley.*

***

"Thank you for meeting with me, Reverend Polasky." Lainie sat at a small wooden table with the minister across from her.

Polasky studied the business card in her hand. "Certainly, Miz Simpson. How can I help you?"

"As I told you on the phone, I'm with the defense team in the Paul Stafford case. I'm really looking for two things. First, I'd like to better understand the issue around public funding and church programs—how that all works. Second, more specifically, I'm looking for information about Pastor Robert Tell."

A dark look swept over Polasky as she stared at Lainie. "And what led you here. if you don't mind my asking?"

"I was looking at the website for the Church Council of Greater Seattle and noticed that you're on their governing board. Since your church is here in Bellevue, I figured this was a good place to start."

The minister nodded, her gaze softened slightly. "With regard to the money issue, public funding for faith-based programs is contentious. You know, separation of church and state. Different groups see this differently and there is plenty of conflict to go around. If you want to know how this is playing out with Tell, I suggest you contact him. You can also talk to local and state officials to get their side of it. That should at least give you a better idea of what his particular issue is." She leaned into the table, her hands flat on the surface. "But what does this have to do with the case you're working on? Isn't that the one with the high school principal and the girls?"

Lainie sighed. "Yes, it is. But I do have a question about his church and the council. I noticed that his is listed as a faith-based organization rather than a church. What does that actually mean?"

Polasky's smile seemed forced. "Because of the large number of member organizations—we have over four hundred—we put them into categories to help visitors to the website find what they want. Faith-based organizations are those that, while they have a spiritual or religious component, their primary focus is on service to the community. Honestly, there is some ambiguity there. Most churches have a service element, and faith-based organizations have parts that look like churches to some people. So, the assignment to categories can be subjective."

"Tell's organization is more of a charity than a church?"

The minister pulled her mouth into a tight line and her eyes narrowed. "I'm not prepared to discuss that. The council is not an information source about its members. If you want to know more about what he does, ask him." She relaxed as she leaned back in her chair. "But you still didn't tell me what all this has to do with your case."

Lainie stood. "Thank you for your time, Reverend. You have my card if you want to contact me."

Chapter 42

Lainie opened the file drawer and reached into the very back—behind the tax returns, the title to her car, and her professional license. She withdrew a small, powder blue envelope. Her eyes grew misty. Without closing the drawer, she swiveled the chair away from the cabinet and held the memory in her shaking hands.

Opening it, she pulled out a "get well" card with a watercolor image of a floral bouquet on the front. She stared at the flowers, a collection of yellow, blue, and pink. A tear trickled down each cheek. She gently ran a finger over the image and her heart ached.

Inside the card, she found a dried flower, although she had no idea what kind it was. At one time, it might have been red or pink. After all these years, though, the color was a faded ochre. She set it on her desk as she read the hand-written note.

> *Lainie,*
> *My heart breaks to think of what you are going through. Please know that I am here for you. Kelley.*

The memories flooded back. She remembered lying in that bed, staring up at a doctor who seemed uncomfortable with the news he was delivering.

> *I'm so sorry....*
> *We did everything we could....*
> *You will be able to have another child....*

Lainie remembered that, at the time, she wasn't sure how she was supposed to respond. She recalled feeling numb. Nothing mattered. After the doctor left, the room was empty, save for her. She wanted Jason to be there, but he wasn't. She had no idea where he was. She had left a message for him at his medical practice when she'd taken a cab from her office to the hospital. She had called his cellphone—it went straight to message. That had been five hours earlier. Still no word from him. Calling her best friend had almost been an afterthought.

And then Kelley had shown up, flowers and card in hand, offering a genuine smile watered by tears on her face. Lainie hugged her as best she could, what with the tubes and wires. They talked for several hours. Kelley seemed to know what to say.

"She was there for me." Lainie mused out loud, tightly tracing the dried bloom in her hand.

That's what friends do. Mildred's "voice" was soft and understanding, for a change.

"And that's what husbands are supposed to do." The bitterness crept in.

Yes.

"Is it any wonder I feel the way I do?" She wanted absolution from Mildred.

No response.

An image washed over her—Paul lying in that hospital bed the first time she'd met him, alone in the room, no flowers, no cards. She remembered his later explanation—he'd only just called his school. They sent him flowers and a card later. But he'd seemed somehow okay with being alone. Except that, for reasons Lainie only now began to understand, he seemed delighted to see her. He savored the coffee she brought him as if it were a gourmet treat. Maybe, in his mind, it was the culinary equivalent of a heartfelt get-well card.

Simple things—a cup of coffee, a kind word, a smile—that seemed to be what he wanted. They brought a smile to his face. And yet she had tried desperately to deny him those things. And it was all because of....

Chapter 43

Lainie awoke the next morning ready to write. She re-read the last two chapters that she'd shoehorned into the manuscript. But her characters still seemed flat, unalive.

She created a new document and saved it as *Cast*. Using bullets, she began to describe her characters, not just their appearances but feelings, history, beliefs, and dreams. The two companions came from different worlds, and yet they had been thrown together by the story. And somehow, they made it work.

As her fingers flew across the keyboard, thoughts took the form of words on screen. She began to like the two. She teased at the edges of dissipating suspicion and the dialogue began to flow. Emboldened with new enthusiasm, she filled her coffee cup for the third time and started in on the next chapter. By late afternoon, she had the requisite work product for Meg. She nodded as she created PDF copies and then forwarded them with a contrite note apologizing for the delay and a promise to do better.

Powering down her computer for the night, she felt a weight lifted from her shoulders. She wondered, though, whether that was from the completion of the chapters or from her newfound understanding of the beings that inhabited the story. The phone interrupted her satisfied musings.

Lainie checked the caller ID. "Hi Kelley."

"We're going to meet tomorrow at two. Andi and Elliott have a rundown for us."

Lainie turned and leaned back on the kitchen counter as she spoke. "How's Paul doing?"

"He's okay. See you tomorrow." The response seemed...
off.

***

"Hey everyone." Lainie strode to her usual seat at one end of
the table. Kelley sat opposite her at the other end. And true
to form, Andi and Elliott sat next to each other on the side.

"Afternoon." Andi nodded and smiled.

"Sup." Elliott tossed out his typical greeting, although
Lainie had no idea what it actually meant. She figured it sort
of a "how're you doing" when the greeter didn't really want
to know.

Kelley continued to flip through her notes. After a
moment of silence, she looked over at the pair. "Okay, talk
to us."

Andi leaned forward into the table, looking alternately at
Kelley and Lainie as she spoke. "The three girls—still don't
know as much as we'd like but we have a few things. The
most obvious is that the two alleging that Paul *tried* to coax
them into sex are connected to Tell's church. Deborah
started attending about three months ago. It's been roughly
eight months for Marianne. Most of what we got was from
social media. The third girl, Caryn, doesn't seem to have had
much to do with the guy, at least not up until now. There
doesn't seem to be any friendship or social connection
among any of the three."

Lainie jumped in when Andi paused. "Is it possible that
the church is kind of a social nexus? Maybe they're not
school friends but connect there, you know, at activities and
such."

Andi furrowed her brow and nodded. "Yeah. That could be. I was assuming that any connection there would overflow rom the school setting, but you may have a point." She shifted in her chair and set her notes aside. "However, Caryn hasn't been connected with the church and the three girls definitely *do not* run in the same circles at school."

Lainie mentally arranged the puzzle pieces, which still made little sense. "You said that Caryn hasn't been in that church *up until now*? Did something change?"

Andi looked over at Elliott for a moment before responding. "Well, yes, sort of. While there's still nothing to indicate she's attending any kind of services or church activities, there exists the possibility that she's had telephone conversations with Tell." She fell silent and looked down at the tabletop, fidgeting with her pen.

Lainie started to ask how she knew that, but the look on Kelley's face warned her off. An emerging understanding of Elliott's talents began to take form. She shook her head in wonder. Either he was going to make a fortune or end up in jail.

When Andi continued, she moved into different territory. "We still don't have access to their school records. But I have gotten some informal information. Caryn Smallwood gets good grades, very good grades. But I haven't met anyone yet who said that she's a good student or that she's smart. Maybe it means nothing. Still, kind of interesting."

Kelley stared at her for a moment before looking down and scribbling some notes. "Go on."

Andi flipped the page on her pad. "Deborah Bufford, pretty much what we talked about before. She has a learning disability. She struggles academically but manages to pass.

Nothing special. No discipline stuff that I've heard about. I assume we can verify that if we get access to the records." She paused and looked up.

Kelley shrugged and nodded without speaking.

"And finally, we have Marianne Thompson. She's smart and a great student." She paused and looked around, as if to make sure that the distinction and difference from Caryn was noted. "Gets straight As. No discipline at all. By all accounts, a model student. Respected by the staff. She *gets along* with other students, but I get the sense that she's not what you would call popular."

Lainie mentally returned to the church connection. "You say that she's been hooked up with Tell's church for, what, about eight months?"

Andi nodded. "Yeah, at least that was what I was able to infer from the different conversations. There was some sense that she changed, although the descriptions were vague and sometimes conflicting. Generally, though, there seemed to be a consensus that Marianne kind of *pulled in* a bit, if you know what I mean. She became a little quieter, a little more withdrawn, while at the same time...I don't know, more, I guess, *at peace*. At least that's what a couple of people told me."

"When you say *people* told you, who are you talking about? Students? Teachers?" Lainie knew that talking to students would have been difficult to arrange. And teachers would have a different perspective than kids.

Andi tilted her head and arched her eyebrows. "Teachers and staff. No way I can talk to kids without parents okaying it. I did get some of this from social media, but neither Deborah nor Marianne are big into that. Caryn's Facebook account, on the other hand, is literally blow-by-blow of her life." She chuckled.

Kelley took control of the meeting. "Nice work, you two. This does give the church a seat at the table, so to speak. But it doesn't move us any further along in the case. At the end of the day, we still have three girls accusing a man. One could argue that Tell is providing emotional and spiritual support while, at the same time, advocating for them."

Lainie shook her head. "I don't know, that guy gives me the creeps. Somehow I can't see him giving spiritual support to anyone." She knew that part of this came from her research that she'd been told not to do. She decided not to comment any further.

Kelley gazed down the table at her for a moment. "While I might personally agree with you, we don't have anything to hang our hat on and, on top of that, I still don't see the connection to the case." She sat back in her chair and closed her pad. "I think that's it for the case today. Andi, how'd it go last night?"

A pang of guilt struck Lainie as she realized that they were referring to Andi taking dinner to Paul.

"I took over some homemade chicken vegetable soup and biscuits. He had a couple of bites but, not much. He looked...." She stopped mid-sentence and bowed her head.

"Not surprised." Kelley shook her head. "He's in a pretty bad place now. His house has been vandalized. And he's gotten some really nasty phone calls on his answering machine." She looked over at Elliott. "Could you see what kind of information you can get. I checked the machine and the numbers all showed up as private callers. He has an unlisted number so I'm curious how those people found out."

Lainie stroked her chin as she gazed at Kelley and then at Elliott. She started to formulate a question about how he might go about that. She decided she didn't want to know.

Kelley's voice interrupted her thoughts. "Let's try to get together this Friday at, say, ten. I'll check with Paul. Hopefully he'll be well enough to make it in for that. And Elliott, I'm betting that he's not going to want any pizza tonight. Use a little imagination."

Chapter 44

Lainie arrived home that afternoon to find an e-mail from Meg in her inbox.

Got the new chapters. Will get back to you in a few days. Like the direction. M

How uncharacterically charitable of her. She pulled up the last chapter and re-read it, nodding as she felt the pace of the dialogue. As she plowed through the rest of it, she finished with a sense that not only did she like the story, she was also beginning to genuinely know the characters.

Lainie felt excited. And she reminded herself that she needed to repair some things with Paul. "First thing in the morning, I promise."

***

She stood over the stove sautéing slices of chicken breast and a medley of vegetables—broccoli, cauliflower, onions, and asparagus. She crushed some garlic and grated ginger into the mix before adding a sparse helping of bottled stir fry sauce. She looked up and gazed out the kitchen window into the dying light of the early April evening. *What would Paul be eating tonight, if not pizza?* She tried to picture Elliott preparing something that was, at the same time, healthy and palatable. She came up empty.

"I should have volunteered." The others had not even questioned her silence. Kelley had stopped asking if she wanted to go with her to visit Paul. They'd no doubt noticed her antagonism toward him. "It's not antagonism. I just wanted to keep that professional boundary."

Mildred didn't accept the answer. *Is that what you call it?*

This time, she knew her snarky twit of a conscience was right. She had indeed been a cold, hard bitch. She resolved to talk to him on Friday.

***

Thursday flew by. Lainie cranked out three chapters—bam, bam, bam. The story grew richer, more satisfying.

At the same time, Lainie felt her bond with Paul growing stronger, except that he didn't know it yet. For the first time, she realized that she'd stopped thinking about how to win the case and had begun thinking about establishing his innocence. That seemed such a subtle distinction. And yet now she could see the difference as plain as day.

Kelley phoned just after seven. "Just checking in. We're on for ten tomorrow morning." No mention of Paul.

"How is he?"

A moment of silence. "About the same." Pause. "I'm going to give Lasorda a shout tomorrow morning, see if I can pry that discovery package from her."

The speed and lack of emotion with which her friend had passed over the subject of Paul disturbed Lainie. Still, it was nothing she could solve at the moment. She would make it right the next day.

***

Lainie strode through the middle of the four-woman protesting party that had re-formed this morning. With her head down, she bumped into one of the women. When she glanced up, she found herself face-to-face with a glare that seemed hot enough to burn through metal. She resisted the urge to sling an insult and sidestepped the woman, continuing toward the building door. She entered the upstairs conference room to find Kelley and Elliott chatting. "Hi. I see our friends are out there again." She removed her jacket and hung it on the back of her chair. "Andi and Paul not here yet?" She stated the obvious.

Kelley nodded. "Morning. No, Andi's picking him up but I'm thinking we might want to delay that a bit." She pulled out her phone and pressed the screen a few times. Putting it to her ear, she gazed around the room. "Oh, yeah, hey. You at Paul's yet?" She furrowed her brow as she listened.

"Okay, listen, if you can sit tight there, maybe you guys can shoot the breeze. Or if you want, maybe stop somewhere for a coffee and scone. We have what you might call an emerging opportunity here. Give us about an hour and a half. That work?" She listened and nodded. "Good. See you then."

She put the phone away and picked up a single piece of paper. Lainie noticed that she also had a notebook computer open with a thumb drive in the USB port. "Elliott, if you'd excuse us for a bit, I think Lainie and I are about to have company."

The gawky nerdish kid grinned, swiped the shock of blond hair from his forehead and sauntered out the door.

Lainie stared alternately at Kelley and the computer. "What's up?"

The lead attorney stood and walked over to the window. "See that woman down there, the chunky one with the baggy pants and pink sweatshirt? That's Toni Carter. We're going to invite her up for coffee." She strode out the door and down the hall. Lainie hurried to keep up.

Outside, Kelley walked casually over to the party of four, stopping in front of Carter. "Hi there. I'm Kelley Vickers. You're Toni Carter, are you not?"

The woman, who initially looked like she was going to walk around, stopped in her tracks. She stared daggers but remained silent.

Kelley smiled. "Oh come now. No need to be shy. I can see that you're interested in Paul Stafford's case." She gestured toward the woman's sign. "Why don't you come upstairs, and we can talk about it?"

Carter looked at the other three women, who had stepped back and stood watching the scene unfold. Her gaze jerked back to Kelley. "Why would I do that?"

Kelley shook her head, chuckled, and eased a little closer. "Just a friendly chat. We have coffee and tea." She paused momentarily. "I mean, a nice private conversation up there would likely be preferable to a less pleasant alternative, don't you think?"

The confrontational look on the woman's face began to morph into some combination of terror and rage. "What are you talking about?"

Kelley shrugged. "Simple choice. You can come upstairs and chat privately over a cup of coffee or we can have this discussion in front of a jury."

Toni Carter seemed to melt with fear.

Shaking her head, Lainie stared at Kelley. *Christ, this woman's good.*

Once upstairs in the conference room, Kelley stood by the door. "I'm going to grab a cup of coffee. Lainie? Black?"

Lainie nodded, not at all sure what was going on.

"Miz Carter? Coffee? Tea? We have bottled water if you'd prefer." She arched her eyebrows and waited.

Toni Carter shook her head and sat down, her look migrating toward the notebook computer on the table.

"Well, then, I'll be right back." With that she disappeared down the hall.

Lainie sat with the woman in uncomfortable silence. She wished she'd gotten Kelley to explain what the hell was going on. After what seemed like an interminable time, the attorney returned to the room, two cups of steaming coffee in her hands. Setting one in front of Lainie, who had taken a seat at the side of the table, she took the other cup down to her position at the end. Carter sat directly across from Lainie, twisting her head to look at Kelley.

"Sorry for the delay. So, I'm hoping that you can help me clear something up. I know that neither of us wants to get into any kind of protracted relationship. So, here it is. I have this recording that we got off Paul Stafford's message machine. Have a listen."

> *Paul Stafford. You will die for your sins and burn in hell for eternity. May the Lord have mercy on your soul.*

Kelley pressed a key on the computer after the message had played. "Now I think we'd both agree that the voice sounds an awful lot like you. If need be, we can go through a bunch of legal hoops to verify it but, hey, we're among friends here." She smiled as she gazed at the woman.

Toni Carter's look had morphed again. Gone was any sign of rage. In its place was fear tinged ever so slightly by confusion. She initially held silent. Lainie watched the woman's eyes as they flicked back and forth between Kelley and the computer. No doubt she was trying to compose an answer that would admit nothing but make this all go away. "What do you want?"

Lainie stifled a laugh before it came out. She had expected the woman to put up more of a fight.

Kelley folded her hands on the table, tilted her head slightly, and spoke. "Look, I don't want this to be any more complicated than it already is. Now, what I hear on that recording is a death threat—nasty stuff. But I understand that sometimes things are said in passion that perhaps we don't always mean. I'm sure that you probably don't really intend to kill him. So, I say, let's resolve this like reasonable adults. His phone number is private and unlisted. You tell me where you got it, and this unfortunate business between the two of us will just, poof, vanish into thin air." She held both hands up and gestured outward, as if releasing a pressure.

Carter stared.

"I can see that you're uncertain, and I understand. Tell you what, why don't you go home and think about it. Give me a call back with the information before three this afternoon." She handed the woman a business card. "If you can't bring yourself to do this, then I'm afraid we'll have to pursue some other options, one of which might be to interview your husband at his workplace. I think he's employed by the State Highways Division? But I'd hate to be playing this recording down there where everyone could hear. People always assume the worst and, heaven knows they talk." She smiled warmly at the woman.

Toni Carter stood and bolted out the door without a word. Kelley laughed. "Now that was fun."

Lainie saw the humor but contained the laugh. "How did you know the call came from her?"

Kelley arched her eyebrows. "Didn't you see her face? It told us everything. And, I might add, she didn't deny it."

"But before she came up, how did you know?"

She shrugged. "Lucky guess." The look on her face signaled that this particular line of discussion was over.

"Kelley, you know you can't follow through on your threat. I'm not sure that any court would actually consider that a real death threat." Lainie felt herself trying to find a solid spot to stand in this ever-expanding swamp.

She grinned. "We won't have to follow through. She'll cave. Bet you dinner."

Lainie looked at her, eyes wide. "And what if she doesn't? What if she just freezes and does nothing?"

"Then we go to plan B."

"And what is plan B?"

Kelley tilted her head back and grinned. "Oh, it's a good one. Her husband has a girlfriend. He'll be more than happy to help us."

Chapter 45

Lainie and Kelley sat in silence for a few minutes. Lainie teased at the conflict she felt over what had just happened. On one hand, she was delighted to see Toni Carter panicked and confused. But her concern about the information that Kelley had used, and more importantly, how she'd gotten it, worried her. She stood and walked over to the window, looking down on a protest party that had shrunk to three women.

"Kelley, I'm not going to ask how you got that information, but I suspect that it wasn't legal." She turned, leaned back on the windowsill, and waited for a response.

Kelley shrugged but remained silent.

After a moment, Lainie prodded her. "Well?"

"Well what? You said you weren't going to ask. And if I recall, you didn't pose a question." Kelley's face had become serious as she seemed to stare past Lainie out the window.

"I know you're into getting things done. And I do recall that you've got a mischievous streak. But Kelley, this is breaking the law. You know what can happen."

Kelley peered directly into Lainie's eyes. "When Paul gets here, take a good look at him. You think the police are playing by the rules? How do you think Paul's name got released before any formal announcement was made? Who was that *anonymous source*? And that self-righteous *thing* that was just up here, you think she's playing by the rules? Yes, I can follow the law and watch that man ground into hamburger by this massive, uncaring, and completely utilitarian machine. Or, I can go out on a limb and fight for him. Keep in mind, no one else is."

The last line cut deeply. Lainie closed her eyes, wanting desperately to hurl back a retort that would answer the challenge. Nothing came. She shook her head and looked away.

At that moment, the door opened. With Andi holding his arm, Paul limped over to a chair and sat. He had a walking cast on and no crutches. His face retained evidence of the beating. The bruises had faded to a lighter shade of blue with a tinge of yellow. His vacant eyes had sunk back into his head. His gaunt body seemed on the verge of collapse with each step. He stared down as he walked. After he sat, he kept his eyes down.

Andi had an anguished look on her face that Lainie had not yet seen. Her clenched jaw accentuated her thin face. Her eyes red and swollen.

Kelley nodded toward her. "Would you ask Elliott to join us?"

The research assistant left the room without comment. Silence took over.

Lainie wanted to say something to Paul. She wanted to talk to him, to apologize. But not in front of others. It felt private. For his part, he appeared to not even notice her, or anyone else.

Andi and Elliott returned and took their seats. Kelley cleared her throat and began. "Thanks everyone. Today's Friday. We have just over three weeks until trial. I spoke with the ADA this morning. She said she'd try to have the discovery materials to us sometime next week. If she puts us off, I could ask for a continuance. Depending on what the

statements look like, I might end up asking for one anyway."
She paused allowing the quiet to once again descend.

After a moment, she took a breath and switched direction.
"Paul, I have a few questions for you. First, have you ever
had contact with Robert Tell? He's that minister that rants
and raves all the time."

Paul kept his focus on the tabletop and shook his head but
remained silent.

"Okay. Your personal information, phone number,
address, like that. Have you given that out to anyone?"

He looked up at her for the first time. "Uh. Yeah. That's
on file with the school." The words came out without
expression. The tone mirrored the empty look in his eyes.

"Is it policy for the school to give out that information?"

He shook his head.

Kelley turned to the group. "I hope to hear something
back this afternoon, but I'm guessing that the callers who left
messages on your home machine got your information from
someone at the school. And that was very likely the same
person who released your identity to the press that first day."
She tapped a pen on her pad. "It doesn't really affect the case
but later, after we get an acquittal, this will help Paul in his
negotiations with the school district. For now, everything
hinges on those statements. We can't interview the students.
Their parents have refused. I think we've learned about all
we can learn without talking to them or at least talking to
other kids. Any ideas?"

Lainie watched and waited while nothing emerged from
the others. "One thing, maybe. What if I do some digging on
this guy Tell? If there's nothing else going on, it can't hurt
to at least have the information." She girded herself for a

rebuke from the boss, who had already made it clear that she didn't want to pad the bill.

Kelley tilted her head back and closed her eyes for a moment. She nodded. "Okay." She opened her eyes and stared at Lainie. "Dig up what you can. If you need Elliott or Andi, give them a call. Can you work on it tonight?"

Lainie's heart jumped. "Yes. Absolutely. I'll get on it right away."

"Okay then. Let's call it for today and plan on touching base tomorrow morning. I know tomorrow is Saturday and we won't keep you long. But I want everything that we've got fully organized by Monday. I'm going to press the ADA for those statements again early in the week and I want to make sure our ducks are in a row." She stood and gathered up her phone and writing material. "Andi, could you give Paul a ride home?"

Andi nodded and helped Paul out of his seat.

Lainie panicked. She wanted to talk to him today. She needed to make things right. "Paul, can I talk to you for a minute?"

He seemed not to have heard her. He turned and went out the door, Andi holding on to his right arm.

Lainie stood and started for the door when she felt the hand on her arm. She turned to see Kelley staring at her.

"Let him go."

She started to object but the look in her friend's eyes told her this was not a request. Kelley said, "He's not here today. Nothing you can say will reach him."

Chapter 46

Lainie threw herself into the research. One particular thing that seemed to stick in her mind was that Tell didn't seem to exist before fifteen years ago in Missouri. He seemed to come out of nowhere to be a high-profile reformer in the Evangelical community. *Reformer? What does that mean?*

She navigated to the article again. Scouring every word, there was no mention of him being a minister or pastor. She saw words like *advocate* and *activist*. But nothing about leadership positions. He surfaced again in Idaho with his own unaffiliated church.

She wondered why he left the mainstream Evangelical community. She went back through the Missouri article that referred to him as a *reformer*. In re-reading, she got the distinct sense that the term was self-applied. Quotes all came from him. Nothing from church leadership. And his main focus was youth.

She looked closer at the fuzzy photograph, an artifact of a time when hard copies were scanned with low resolution devices. There was no mistaking the face or the demeanor—passionate, arrogant, and confrontational. A curiosity in the image struck her. Several of the teenage girls were gazing at him rather than the camera, a look of adulation on their faces.

Despite the fact that they gave Lainie the creeps, nothing connected him to the case other than his apparent support for the three girls and his activism.

She knew they weren't asking the right questions. It occurred to her that this was just a recycled thought. But she had no idea what else to look for.

What was it they hoped to find in the girls' statements? She hadn't even thought about it. They'd been waiting for the package, complaining all the while. And yet there had been no discussion at all about what they might glean.

Lainie's initial reaction was that they wouldn't know until they saw the statements. But, no. There had to be something else. She felt as though it was right there—she could almost reach out and grab a tendril.

Mildred weighed in. *Step back a minute. Is he innocent or guilty?*

Lainie started to sweep the comment from her mind. And then it hit her. Yes, that was *the question*. Was he innocent?

The inner voice pushed harder. *Is he?*

"Yes!" The dam broke. She felt short of breath. Her chest pounded. The one question they'd refused to entertain held the key to understanding the case. If he was innocent, completely innocent, then the three statements wouldn't just have inconsistencies. They would be total fabrications. That was it. The entire thing was a lie.

She studied the old photo of Tell, still unable to connect all the dots back to him.

***

Lainie rose early the next morning, well before the sun. She gathered the printed materials and began to make a set of organized notes. The overall landscape seemed clear but the details down in the weeds still seemed fuzzy and disconnected. Why would the girls lie? What was Tell's connection and why now?

Kelley had already made coffee when she arrived. Elliott meandered in about five minutes after Lainie, looking like he'd just rolled out of bed. He grabbed a cup of coffee and plopped down in a chair. "Andi went to pick up Paul. She should be here in a few."

The statement struck Lainie as odd. If he just rolled out of bed, how would he know that Andi was on her way to pick up Paul. She shrugged and started placing copies of her documents on the table. As she composed the stacks of paper, she remembered the encounter with the protestor from the day before. "You hear back from Toni Carter yesterday?"

Kelley beamed. "Just like clockwork. Seems there's a Judith Danvers at the high school that had made it her business to disseminate information about Paul. Not only is that the source of the phone calls, but we can likely tie the vandalism on his house back to that as well."

Just as Lainie finished putting copies out, Andi arrived, alone.

Kelley looked up as the young woman came in. "Paul?"

Andi shuffled over to her chair and sat. "He didn't want to come. Said to go ahead without him."

Kelley looked at her with an arched eyebrow. Andi gazed at her for a second and then slowly shook her head. No other words passed between the two.

Lainie felt a pang of disappointment. With her revelations of the previous evening, she was certain that Paul would be encouraged. She was hoping to see a light in his eyes when he realized that they did believe him, or at least she did.

Kelley interrupted the thought pattern. "Okay, Lainie, you're up. Enlighten us."

Lainie sat straight in her chair and closed her eyes for a moment. Suddenly this seemed harder than she'd expected. Taking a deep breath, she opened her eyes to face the three. "Let's take a step backward. All along the three of you have been focused on poking holes in the case leading to either the charges being dropped or an acquittal in court. As Kelley said, our job hasn't been to prove his innocence but to make it hard for the prosecutors to prove his guilt." She paused, reluctant to utter the next words. "As for me, I started out assuming he was guilty. Grudgingly, I came around to your position." She nodded toward Kelley. "I limited my view to working the case."

She gazed down at the tabletop as she gathered her next collage of thoughts. Looking up, she stared into Kelley's eyes. "Paul's innocent." She waited for the onslaught of objection. Nothing came. Elliott doodled while Andi took notes. Kelley looked at her with head tilted and her mouth drawn into a tight, neutral line. Her eyes seemed to invite more explanation without actually asking for it.

The collective reaction confounded her for a moment. She recovered and plowed back into the issue. "Paul asked a crucial question the very first day we met. He wanted to know why the girls would lie. We chose not to consider that issue. We've been sitting here waiting on statements and not really knowing what we're expecting to find. The key to this entire case is going to be motivation. The statements may fill in some gaps or give us something to nibble on, but we need to look at them not as having flaws or inconsistencies but as being complete fabrications." She knew she hadn't given a compelling defense of her ideas.

Kelley shrugged. "But what if he really is guilty?"

Lainie shot back. "He isn't."

"Okay, if that's the case, let's talk about this motivation. Why?"

She took a deep breath and prepared for the leap. "Based on everything I've heard, I'm inclined to believe it has nothing to do with Paul. I think he's simply a convenient target of opportunity. The reason must have something to do with one or more of the girls, independent of him. This could be nothing more than an elaborate smokescreen."

To Lainie's surprise, Kelley arched her eyebrows and nodded. "Very possible. And if the statements are fabricated, Andi will spot it. That could be one reason why the ADA is delaying. She could be hoping that Paul will take the deal and she won't have to put what little she has out there."

Lainie bristled. "But shouldn't she be questioning his guilt rather than just looking to hide behind a deal?"

Kelley smirked. "Eve's not a bad sort. But she's got a huge workload and she gets her feed from the detectives. Steadman, in particular, has already convicted Paul in her mind. I'm betting that Lasorda has never given the guilt or innocence question a moment's thought." She paused and narrowed her eyes. "And, frankly, going to her right now with what you've got won't accomplish anything. You're going to need more than your gut if you're going to change her mindset. Anyway, enough of the speculation, fill us in on your research."

Lainie laid it all out for them, using her notes to keep her on track. The three listened without comment. Kelley sat with her hands folded and her gaze locked on Lainie as the other two fidgeted with pens and paper. As Lainie finished, she tossed an additional point. "One thing that struck me, and it may mean nothing. I couldn't find anything at all about this guy before the Missouri article. It's like he didn't exist."

Without looking up from his drawing, Elliott fired an interesting volley. "Maybe he didn't."

Lainie expected Kelley to comment in exasperation. Instead, the lead attorney narrowed her eyes, nodding slowly. "That would make sense. Yeah. Maybe he changed his name before that. Those kinds of records are mostly local and probably not available online. But there is one possible way. If he changed his name in Missouri, he would have been forced to provide a copy of the documentation to DMV to get his driver's license. Be tough to track that down." She glanced at Elliott with a single cocked eyebrow.

He glanced at her for a moment, then shrugged and went back to his doodling.

For the first time since she'd started working with this group, Lainie felt she knew exactly what had just occurred. The young hacker had just been given an assignment.

Her mind drifted back to Paul. "Do you want me to check on Paul this afternoon?"

Kelley stared at her for a moment and then shook her head. "No. He apparently wanted to be left alone today." She left it at that.

Lainie left with an uneasy sense that there was some undercurrent of communication or feeling to which she was not privy. Something had changed, and she remained in the dark about it.

Chapter 47

Lainie tried to abide by Kelley's admonition to leave Paul in peace. And she succeeded for about three hours. Late that afternoon, though, she picked up her phone intending to check to see if he needed anything like dinner or…. No answer on his landline. Then she remembered that Kelley had instructed him to unplug it because of the harassing calls. She tried his cell phone. Her call went to voice mail after four rings. "Hi Paul. It's Lainie. I was just checking to see if you needed anything. Give me a call if you do. Bye."

He probably saw my caller ID. She shuddered as she recalled her interactions with him since the story had broken in the media. The best that could be said on any day was that she ignored him. At worst, she all but agreed with the accusations to his face. "No wonder he won't take my calls."

If Mildred had other ideas, she kept them to herself.

***

After a night of tossing, flipping the pillow, and exploring every possible catastrophic possibility, Lainie could stand no more idle waiting. She punched a number into her cellphone.

"Hello."

She recognized the voice. "Good morning, Yolanda. This is Lainie. Is Kelley about?"

A laugh filtered out of the handset. "Ha. Come on, Lainie, you know better. She doesn't greet the world until after ten on Sundays."

Lainie sighed. "Yeah, I know. Was just hoping."

"Hang on. I'll roust her. It'll do her good."

After a moment of silence, she heard a faint voice in the background. "Hey, wake up. It's Lainie. She says it's important."

Next came a voice that sounded as tired as Lainie felt. "This had better be good."

"Kelley, I need to talk to you."

"Okay, so talk."

"No, I mean in person."

"Ugh. What's this about?"

"I can be there in fifteen minutes."

"This had better be good."

***

The condo never failed to impress Lainie. With Kelley a successful defense attorney and Yolanda the owner of an architectural and engineering firm, the place could have easily landed a spot in *Architectural Digest*. The solid oak furniture rested on plush ivory carpet. The walls sported complementary colors that Lainie would not have expected to work together—lavender and sage green. The artwork consisted of what she knew were original watercolors, mostly intimate landscapes and nature scenes.

Kelley greeted her wearing a robe and holding a cup of coffee. She looked as if she'd made a passing effort at running a brush through her blonde hair. She shook her head as she invited Lainie in. "I have coffee if you want some." She added a chuckle. "This had better be good." The smile on her face signaled that her initial irritation upon waking had subsided.

"Coffee would be great, thanks. The place is beautiful." Lainie walked over to a particular piece of art that she'd often admired—a small piece depicting a forest clearing with a downed tree and some ferns growing up around. "I just love this piece."

Kelley spoke over her shoulder as she walked toward the kitchen. "Yeah, yeah. You can dispense with the décor critique. What's up?" The words were gruff but the tone was amicable.

Lainie waited until Kelley returned with a steaming cup of coffee. "Thanks." She took the cup and sat in one of the wingback chairs. "I'm worried about Paul."

"I got that yesterday."

"I tried to call him last night. I wanted to see if he needed anything, you know, dinner or something." She added that last part in an attempt to fend off what she felt was likely to be a rebuke for ignoring the direction to leave him alone.

"And he didn't answer, huh?" She sipped on her coffee and turned toward the window.

"Yeah. Nothing."

Kelley gazed at her for a moment before responding. "It's hard, something like this. Some guys just don't make it."

Lainie set her cup on a coaster on the small table beside her. "Kelley, that's the second time you've said that. What do you mean?" She knew it wasn't like her friend to make meaningless, off-the-cuff statements, especially in response to a concern.

Kelley stood, walked over to the window, cup in hand, and stared out into the Sunday morning spring rain. The living room fell quiet. Lainie could hear the muffled sounds of Yolanda moving around in the back room. A clock on the mantle ticked as the pendulum swung back and forth as its face displayed the time—10:15.

"I get a lot of guys to defend. Truth is, most did what they were accused of. I give them the best defense I can; and they're entitled to that. People get upset at the notion of the guilty being acquitted. But if that happens, they should blame the police and the ADA for not doing their jobs. The guys, they handle it okay mostly. For a lot of them, it's just a game. They're out to beat the system so they can go out and do it again." She turned to face Lainie.

"Every once in a while, I get a guy who truly is innocent. This whole thing hits them pretty hard. Some of them make it. They harden up and fight back. We win some and we lose some. About three years ago I got this guy, a really gentle soul. They had him on child molestation, pre-teen nieces. He took it hard, really hard. Everyone turned against him, family, friends, work, everything. The system pounded him relentlessly. I did the best I could. He ended up killing himself just before the trial. Later we found out he was innocent. The girls had made up the story to get even with him. Some kind of grudge about him not letting them play with his iPad or some such crap. Some guys just can't make it to the other side."

Lainie sat, stunned. "You think Paul may be suicidal?"

Kelley shrugged but otherwise didn't respond to the questions. Instead, she continued with the rest of the story. "Steadman was the lead detective. When the truth broke, she just shrugged like it was no big deal. And then on to the next case."

"Why did you leave Paul alone? Why did you tell me not to bother him? Are you crazy?" Panic set in.

Kelley's response was not what Lainie expected. "Some guys, they just can't do it. I mean, even if we get him off, his life will never be the same. The system doesn't find him *innocent*. The best that happens in these cases is that the prosecution either drops the charges because they don't have enough evidence, or he's acquitted because the prosecution doesn't prove guilt beyond a reasonable doubt. Either way, he will always and forever be the man who was accused of sexual misconduct. Some people might believe his innocence, but most will just see him as one more pervert who got a free pass. Some people are not willing to live like that and it's their choice. I'm not going to get on my sanctimonious horse and tell him that he needs to toughen up and enjoy life. If he wants to end it, that's his right."

Lainie lashed out. "Well I don't have to sit back and let it happen."

Kelley smiled but a sadness filtered through. "He's not some lost puppy that you can rescue and take home. Even if you get him through today, there's tomorrow and the day after. Did you see his eyes the other day, Friday? They were empty. There's nothing left. It's not for you or me to decide whether his life is worth living. That's a decision only he can make. You can call and try to talk to him but please let him have dignity. God knows this has taken everything else he had."

Chapter 48

For all of the discussion, it finally came down to Lainie and Kelley each repeating things they'd already said. A very frustrated Lainie left just after one in the afternoon. She would do something, even if her friend wouldn't.

She tried to call him from the car—no answer. Between traffic and road repairs, she finally pulled into her own driveway at two. She didn't bother to put the car in the garage since she'd be going out later.

Once inside, she checked for messages—nothing. She considered calling 911. But she wasn't sure there was even an emergency. Maybe he was just sleeping. And the police would be the last people he wanted to see. Did it really matter what he wanted? After all, this was about saving his life. Was there anything left to save?

Mildred responded. *What do you think?* Not terribly helpful.

"He won't even take my calls. Why would he let me in the house?" Lainie could see herself outside banging on his door, all the neighbors watching.

And the alternative? Sitting back here and hoping for the best?

She grabbed her keys and purse on the way out the door.

As she drove, Lainie prepared to face Paul. She rehearsed what she wanted to say but kept stumbling over how to get him to listen to her or even let her in. When she turned the corner onto his street, she watched in horror as she approached the house. The realization of his new life slammed her. She was not prepared for what she saw.

The house, which had been a picture of tranquility when she'd been there before, had been transformed. Large splashes of red paint assaulted the exterior. Spray-painted messages underscored what the vandals intended.

Rapist!

Child Molester!

Burn in Hell!

Shattered windows gave evidence of rocks or other projectiles thrown in hatred. His car, which sat exactly where it had been when she'd brought him home that day, reflected the same sentiments. Gouges ran the entire length on both sides. All of the windows were broken. The same messages decorated the vehicle just in case people couldn't see the ones on the house. Trash and refuse littered the yard. The grass had turned green but had not yet started to gain any height. Otherwise, this could have easily been taken for an abandoned structure.

Tears formed in Lainie's eyes from sorrow or rage or a combination of the two. She parked her car behind his, turned off the ignition, and sat stunned for a few seconds. The light drizzle and low overcast made the three o'clock hour seem later. The house sat dark and still. She closed her eyes and shuddered, thinking about the possibility of what awaited her inside.

Taking a deep breath, she bolted from the car to the front porch. She rang the bell. "Paul." She called loudly, but not quite a shout. "Paul!" This time a shout. She pounded the door with the ball of her fist. "Paul, please, let me in."

Silence. No movement. No light. Nothing but the incessant rain. She glanced around at the neighboring houses. Lights shone from windows, but she saw no sign that anyone was the least bit concerned about this man.

She remembered the key—under the mat. Surely, he would have moved it. She stepped back and lifted the square of fabric that looked like a sturdy version of indoor/outdoor carpet. There it was.

She inserted the key and opened the door to a dark and deserted living room. Glass and rocks covered the floor. Some of the stones had paper wrapped around them, greetings of hatred, no doubt. Others sat bare, having served their purpose.

"Paul." She spoke in a normal tone. No answer. Silence. No movement. "Paul." Louder. She glided down the hallway, bursting through the first door on the left—a spare bedroom turned storage room. She considered the next door on the left and the bathroom at the end of the hall, but quickly decided that he was not likely in either place. The single door on the right—master bedroom—her instincts told her that she would find him there. She swung the door open. Nothing. On the far side of the bedroom sat the entrance to the master bath. No sound. She closed her eyes and prayed to whatever god or gods might be listening. "Please! No."

She shot across the bedroom and through the threshold to the sink and toilet area. Nothing at the sink. With trepidation, she opened the door into the bath and found him.

Chapter 49

Lainie stared in shock at the sight before her. Light streaming through the bathroom window illuminated the solitary figure. A shadow of a man wearing a green and blue plaid robe over a pair of what looked like yellow fleece pajamas sat huddled in the bathtub devoid of water. He faced the faucet with his knees pulled up against his chest and his forehead resting on his knees. His disheveled brown hair had apparently not seen a brush or comb in several days. She could see his upper body expand and contract as he breathed. His right hand, barely visible, held a box cutter.

She felt as though she had the breath knocked out of her. The air in the small room seemed to disappear. She eased toward him.

An inner voice stopped her—Mildred. *Wait. Lainie, listen. The words you say next will matter. We can do this.*

She closed her eyes, took one more step, and went down onto her knees, less than a foot from the side of the tub. She put her hand on his shoulder, which felt bony and frail. "Paul. It's me, Lainie." She gently applied pressure.

Paul kept his head down. "You shouldn't be here. You need to leave." The voice came out dry and empty.

She fought back tears. "Paul, if I live to be a hundred, a thousand, I could never make up for the way I've treated you. You have no reason to believe me or have any faith in me. But I'm begging you, please, listen to what I have to say now. Please."

He raised and turned his head, fixing a pair of haunted, sunken eyes on hers. "Lainie, I can't do it anymore. I need this to end." He dropped his head back onto his knees. He flexed his right hand, holding tight to the box cutter.

She held her ground, hand on his shoulder. "I believe in you, Paul. Not just believing you're innocent. I know that for a fact. But I believe in *you*. I believe in your life. Please, we can do this together."

He looked up again. The empty eyes now carried a suggestion of pain, sorrow, desperation. "I'm lost. I feel broken. I want this all to be over. Please leave. I need to be alone for this. Just go." His eyes began to fill with tears.

Yes, Lainie. You're doing it.

Lainie once again entreated the gods to keep her from saying the wrong thing. "I know, Paul, I know. And I know that just winning the case isn't going to fix everything. I know that life ahead is frightening. I can see that the road will not be an easy one. I promise you, Paul, I will walk it with you." She swiped away the tear rolling down her own cheek.

He sat for a moment, perfectly still except for his steady breathing. Then she felt a slight heave and the sound of soft sobbing.

She moved her hand to his head and gently stroked his hair. His sobs grew more pronounced. His right hand looked like it loosened ever so slightly. She reached over with her other hand and touched it. "Paul, can I have that? Please." She made no attempt to take the cutter from him.

Those few seconds the two remained in that position seemed like hours to Lainie. And then it happened. He dropped the cutter and held her hand.

***

She guided him by the elbow. "Don't worry about the place right now, Paul. Let's just get you a few clothes and get out of here, okay?"

He walked as if in a trance, easily guided by the pressure she exerted on his arm. For lack of anything better, she grabbed a pillow case from the bed. She picked up a pair of jeans and a shirt from the floor and stuffed them in. Opening the top drawer of the dresser, she pulled out a handful of underwear. The next drawer down held socks, several pairs went in.

Mildred prodded her on. *You need to hurry.*

She slid into the closet and jerked a couple of long sleeve cotton shirts off hangers and stuffed them in the pillowcase. That would have to do. She had toothpaste, soap, and the like at home. "Okay, Paul, let's go."

***

"It's not much for appearance right now. I've been using it as a storage room." Lainie and Paul stood in the threshold of her spare bedroom. She'd changed the linens at the end of the past summer. No one had used them since…. Not exactly fresh, but serviceable. "We can work on getting these boxes moved out tomorrow."

In the low light of gathering dusk, the room brought back unwanted memories. It was to have been a little girl's room. They were going to paint the walls peach—pink seemed too much. The few pieces of baby furniture they'd purchased had long since been removed. But the pain remained.

For the first time since *those days*, the room had a real purpose. Perhaps it could be a part of saving a life.

She showed him to the guest bathroom, pointing out the closet with the towels and the drawers with the toiletries. He followed her although she had no idea whether he actually understood anything she was saying. He had said nothing since he left the bathtub at his house. He stood in his robe and fleece pajamas staring blankly at the tub in her spare bathroom.

Lainie took him by the hand and led him back into his new bedroom. Moving him over to the bed, she sat with him, hand-in-hand. "Paul, there's a lot I need to tell you. So many things I need to say. But for tonight, I'm going to trust that you know I'm here with you and I hope that's enough. Tomorrow we start fighting back, both of us, along with the others. We're going to take back your life. I promise you."

Mildred whispered, *You did good, Lainie. You did good.*

Chapter 50

After showering and donning a set of clean clothes, well, relatively clean, Paul looked renewed, except for his face. Lainie looked into a pair of eyes that alternately seemed lost, empty, and hurting. He had not spoken much, answering only with monosyllabic words, head shakes, and nods.

"I'm going to put some dinner together. You okay with turkey vegetable soup?" She thought about something more substantial but, from the looks of things and what she'd heard from the others, he probably hadn't eaten in days.

He looked at her blankly, his mouth opened slightly. His head looked like it was wobbling. He said nothing.

She forced a smile and nodded. "Then soup it is." He sat on the sofa in the living room while she went into the kitchen and diced up a leftover turkey breast from earlier in the week. Tossing that in a pot of boiling water, she chopped onions, celery, and carrots. She added a can of chicken stock and some brown rice.

With dinner on to cook, she returned to the living room, followed by the aroma of the soup. "It'll be about forty-five minutes." Plopping down in the overstuffed chair facing the couch, she reached over to a small table and switched on a lamp. The room brightened.

He tilted his head, his eyes appearing to search hers. When he spoke, his voice came out low and unsteady. "Why am I here?"

Lainie leaned forward, hands folded in her lap. "With the stuff going on at your place, I thought this would be safer."

He looked around the room, hands clasped between his knees. "Why didn't you take me to the hospital or to jail?"

Although she didn't know why, the question hurt her. She had never considered anything other than her home. "Would you have rather gone to one of those places?"

"Would be less trouble."

She forced a smile, feeling a wave of sadness wash over her. "Paul, I wanted you here. That's all. I hope you don't mind."

He nodded and continued looking around the room. He seemed like a kid thrown into a new, strange environment and trying to understand.

Lainie stood and walked into the kitchen, returning with her landline handset. "I need to call Kelley."

He jerked his head and stared at her, fear in his eyes.

"It's okay. I just need to let her know you're here so that she doesn't send Andi over after you." She punched in the number and waited.

Kelley picked up on the third ring. "Hey. Everything okay?" Her caller ID apparently worked well.

She smiled at Paul as she spoke. "Yeah. Just wanted to let you know that Paul's here with me if you need to get in touch with him. We on for tomorrow morning?"

"You found that lost dog, did you?"

Paul watched her, his eyes narrowed as he listened.

"Yeah. All fine. We're about to sit down to dinner. What time in the morning?"

"Let's get a jump on it. How about nine? I'll turn the heat up on Lasorda first thing."

"See you then."

After she disconnected, Lainie placed the handset on the table.

"Why didn't you tell her?" He looked sincere.

"This is your life, Paul. If you want her to know, you can tell her. But as far as I'm concerned, this is between you and me." Looking at Paul, she realized there was so much she wanted to tell him. Mostly she wanted him to know how much she regretted how she'd been. The look on his face, though, told her that he was in no shape for such a conversation. He'd said only a few words the entire afternoon. And after they'd passed that bathroom crisis, he had remained dry-eyed, almost as if in a trance. But there was no hiding his pain.

Dinner was a subdued affair. He sipped some broth and drank some water but left most of the meat, vegetables, and rice in the bowl. His hand shook when he lifted the spoon to his mouth. Otherwise, his coordination seemed okay.

Lainie set down her spoon. "Paul, when was the last time you slept?"

He tilted his head. His gaze wandered as if he were trying to decrypt a garbled message and then returned to her, his eyes signaling confusion.

"I'm guessing it's been a few days."

He didn't answer.

She stood. "Tell you what. I have some Ibuprofen with Benadryl. That will help you get to sleep. I think you need some serious rest."

About an hour after taking a couple of the pills, his eyelids starting drooping. Lainie took him by the hand. "Come on. Let's get you to bed. Tomorrow morning will come early." She smiled.

214

He stood and allowed himself to be guided, as if a child, back to the spare bedroom.

"I'm just in the other room. Let me know if you need anything." She left him taking off his shoes and shut the door behind her.

After cleaning up and getting her things ready for the next morning, she started for her bedroom but noticed the light shining through from beneath his door. She opened it quietly to find him sound asleep in the bed. He'd apparently chosen to ignore the light. She gazed at him for a moment. In that instant, she felt overwhelmed by the desire to slide into bed next to him and hold him—to keep him safe until morning.

She backed out of the room, turning off the light and closing the door. As she moved into her own bedroom, she considered the queen bed that had once slept two but now served only her. Although she hadn't seen it coming, the bitterness she'd endured at the betrayal all those years ago had faded. She had a feeling that it had something to do with the man in the other room.

Chapter 51

Paul cleaned up nicely, although the look on his face remained a combination of flat and pained. He said little but complied with Lainie's instructions. "We need to leave in about five minutes." They had work traffic to contend with. Fortunately, Kelley had private parking, so they wouldn't have to hunt for a space. Still, they would be pushing it to get there by nine.

His walking cast had come off, much earlier than it should have. She wasn't sure how that had happened—probably somewhere between the jail, the hospital, and his time alone at home. The crutches had also vanished. He walked with a decided limp and leaned on anything available. But he never complained.

The others were gathered around the table by the time Lainie and Paul arrived. Paul poured himself into his chair across from the Andi and Elliott, nodding to them. Lainie occupied the seat next to him.

Kelley began the discussion. "First order of business—the discovery package. I just called Lasorda—tomorrow mid-morning at the earliest. Maybe as late as Wednesday. I warned her about a continuation. Honestly, I think she's playing for time, hoping Paul will cave on the deal. I believe she's nervous about the statements."

Lainie leaned back, tapping her fingers nervously on the arm of the chair. "Is it possible she knows something about them and she's trying to keep it from us? Could the delay be designed to make sure we don't have time to go through it?"

"Not her style, although it's possible. If she knows for sure that there's something wrong, she'll shine a light on it.

She knows it's better to sort it out rather than having it blow up in her face in the courtroom. Most likely she just sees things that make her nervous, like too much detail or very precise time estimates, things that would be easily challenged."

Her cellphone chimed just as she finished speaking. She glanced at the caller ID and shook her head. "This is Kelley Vickers."

Rolling her eyes, she gestured with her hand urging the caller to get on with it. "Well, yes, Detective Steadman, that is rather worrisome. And I do realize that he's not home. We decided, for his own safety, to house him someplace else." She leaned back in the chair, staring at the ceiling as she listened.

"Of course we will, Detective. I'm in the middle of a meeting right now but as soon as I'm done, I'll grab lunch, go pick him up, and we'll head down there. I'm thinking, maybe two-thirty, three. Will that work?" She looked as though she was trying to stifle a laugh.

"I hope you'll understand, Detective Steadman, and you know I hold you in the highest regard, but there's no way on this God-damned earth I'm going to tell you where he is. Now if you have an arrest warrant or any other kind of official document, I'm ready to jump and fetch. But absent that, you can just wait on us there."

Lainie cringed. Her friend seemed to have a passion for baiting Steadman.

"Well yes, certainly, and fuck you too. We'll see you at three." She disconnected. "Bitch."

Andi and Elliott watched, eyes wide, without speaking. This was the first time that Lainie had seen them react this way. She shook her head. "What was that all about?"

Kelley shrugged. "It seems the Smallwoods got some nasty harassment calls last evening. Person would call, breathe heavy, and then hang-up. At one point, a man spoke. He said something about the bitch deserving to die. I think that referred to the daughter. The police want to talk to Paul about it."

Paul's eyes narrowed. It was the first reaction Lainie had seen out of him—a good thing. She watched him shake his head.

Lainie jumped in. "That's bullshit. Paul was with me yesterday afternoon and evening. I know for a fact it wasn't him. Also, they can check his cell phone. In fact, they should be able to order up the records from the phone company and find out exactly who it was." This seemed like a problem they didn't need to even worry about.

Kelley laughed. "Ah yes, but now we're one step ahead of them. We know something they don't. So, while the good detective is bumbling about trying to pin this on Paul, we're going to find some more answers." She nodded in Elliott's direction. "To you, my good sir."

Elliott responded with his usual nonchalant shrug and went about his doodling.

Lainie leaned forward and pulled her chair up to the table. With her forearms flat on the top, she peered at Kelley. "I have an idea. Would you have any objection if I spoke directly with ADA Lasorda?"

"What do you want to talk to her about?"

"You know, I'm just going to lay a little groundwork. Once we get rolling, we're going to be throwing a lot of stuff at her. It could work to her advantage to let her know it's coming."

Kelley pushed her chair back from the table and stood. "I'm not sure *why* we would want to help her and, I have no idea what you're talking about but knock yourself out." She went to the door and turned to the group. "Let's hit it."

Andi and Elliott left the room together. Kelley was about to leave when Lainie offered a comment. "Those two. They are really good. You need to hang on to those guys."

Kelley shrugged. "Yeah, they're pretty good. They need to work on their poker faces, though."

"What do you mean?"

She laughed. "What, you haven't noticed?"

The question baffled Lainie. "Noticed what?"

"They're sleeping together."

Lainie stared for a moment. "Those two? Andi is sleeping with Elliott?"

"And what's so strange about that?"

Lainie shook her head as she walked over to the window and looked out. "Uh, I don't know. It's just that she's, you know...."

"Drop dead beautiful and he's kind of a gawky nerd? Or that she's six years older than him?"

"Yes. I mean, they seem an unlikely pair, I guess."

Kelley's mischievous smile warmed. "Maybe. But Elliott is crazy smart, he worships the ground she walks on, and he's loyal to a fault. He would do anything for her. Maybe she could have herself some buff stud, but she's brighter than that. She knows that these young, carefree years give way to a more settled existence. Elliott's in this for the long haul and I think that's what she's looking for. Oh, and don't tell them I know." She smiled at Paul and Lainie.

Chapter 52

Lainie drove Paul to his house to pick up some more clothing and a few toiletry items that she didn't have laying around her place. As the turned the corner on the approach, she girded herself for the visual onslaught. More than anything, though, she dreaded Paul seeing it. Recalling his state of mind the afternoon before as he sat huddled in the bathtub, she wanted to keep as much of that pain as possible at bay.

In the early afternoon light, even with the light drizzle, the paint splashes, broken windows, and slurs assaulted her. She could only imagine what it did to him. But his demeanor remained flat, as if he looked past it all.

She threw the transmission into park and turned off the ignition. "Let's get in and out. We'll swing by home and grab something to eat before we head downtown." She opened the door before he could respond.

They moved from the car to the front porch and into the house with hardly a pause. Lainie had kept the key from beneath the mat in her purse so she had no need to delay. Once inside, he pulled some slacks and shirts from hangers and folded them neatly on the bed. He got several pairs of jeans from a drawer and added them to the mix. From inside the closet, he pulled out a small, wheeled suitcase and packed his things.

He turned to her and nodded without speaking. His eyes, though, seemed to have more life than the previous day. He moved with a quicker pace, seemingly with purpose.

"Okay, let's be gone."

After a late lunch—leftover soup and a half peanut butter and jelly sandwich— Paul took the suitcase into the back room. He returned about ten minutes later wearing a pair of gray wool slacks and a navy cotton shirt. He had also changed from his sneakers into a pair of black leather shoes, not quite *dressy* but more formal than running shoes. He looked like a different person, almost normal.

They strode into the squad room at the Bellevue Police Department Sex Crimes Division at two-forty-five to find Kelley already there. Detective Steadman jerked her gaze to Paul as she remained standing beside the table. Detective Tom Burke looked up from his seated position and nodded, a neutral expression on his face. Steadman, by contrast, stared daggers and reached around to her back, presumably for handcuffs.

"Paul Stafford, you are—"

Kelley interrupted her. "Detective Steadman, perhaps before you start throwing the cuffs on him you might want to acquire some information from him. You know, that process we call... let's see, what was that word?" Her eyes widened and her smile broadened. "Oh yes, *Investigation.* That's it."

Lainie cringed. She shared some of Kelley's dislike for the woman but taunting and insulting her seemed too much. She spoke up. "Paul's ready to answer any questions you have, Detective." She tried to put a diplomatic spin on it.

Steadman narrowed her eyes, studying first Paul and then Lainie. She nodded and gestured toward a couple of empty chairs.

As Lainie and Paul sat, the detective pulled a pad and pen over in front of her. "Mister Stafford, where were you at about six o'clock last evening?" She held the pen in her hand and stared at him.

Paul looked over at Kelley, apparently remembering the instructions she'd given him. She nodded and then he responded, "I was at Miz Simpson's home with her."

"What time did you get there and when did you leave?"

He turned his head and looked toward the window, nodding slightly as if trying to recollect an elusive fact. "Uh, I think I got there about four, maybe. I stayed all night." The statement, although true, struck Lainie as sounding different than it was.

Steadman started. She stared at Paul and then at Lainie. She hadn't missed the connotation either.

Lainie jumped in. "I have a spare room, Detective. After his injuries, you know, down at *your* lock-up, we didn't want him to be alone." The sarcastic barb just made its own way out.

"Have you, at any time over the past week, made any phone calls to the Smallwood home?"

He gazed at her, curiosity in his eyes. "No."

"Did you make any calls to their home where you hung up when they answered?"

Kelley intervened. "He just answered that question. He said he didn't make any calls."

Steadman shot a retort back laced with venom. "I was asking for clarification. Now unless *Mister Stafford* has something to hide, I'd appreciate if he just answers the question."

Paul didn't wait for the okay. "No. I did not."

As the detective opened her mouth to continue, Kelley's cellphone chimed. She looked at the screen. "Excuse me, I need to take this." Rather than stepping out of the room, though, she connected while she continued to sit. "Kelley Vickers." She nodded. "Yes." The corners of her mouth turned up but did not evolve into a full smile. "That *is* interesting, yes. Thank you." She disconnected.

Steadman sat still watching her as if expecting to be let in on the subject of the call.

Kelley set the phone on the table. "Another case. Sorry. You were about to say?"

But Lainie knew better. If that had been about another case, she'd have left the room. That was Elliott. He found something.

Detective Steadman turned to Paul. "Mister Stafford, may I see your phone?"

Paul reached into his trouser pocket and retrieved his smart phone, setting it on the table halfway between him and Steadman. She picked it up and hit the power button. After a second, she handed it back to him. "Could you unlock it please." Her tone signaled that it was taking every bit of willpower she had to remain civil.

He put his thumb on the button for a second and then handed the phone back to her. She swiped and pressed the screen a few times before looking up at him. "Do I have your permission to have our IT guys take a look at this?"

Paul shrugged even as Kelley weighed in. "Detective, as entertaining as this is, it's painful to see you waste your time. He was with a member of my staff the entire evening and I think Miz Simpson can guarantee that he didn't call anyone. Besides, if you really want to solve this mystery, a court order to get their phone records should tell you what you need to know."

Steadman stared with what appeared to be pure, unbridled hatred at Kelley before turning back to Paul. "Do you have any other cellphones?"

"No."

The anguish on the detective's face intensified. Her mouth drew into a tight line and her eyes narrowed as she glared across the table.

Burke, Detective Steadman's partner, had remained silent and near motionless the entire time. If Lainie hadn't known better, she would have sworn that he was bored. A part of her suspected that he knew there was nothing to this line of questioning. She shifted to look at the confrontation between Kelley and Steadman. The detective did little to hide her contempt while Kelley put on a pleasant, nonchalant smile.

After a brief moment, Kelley stood. "Good then. If there's nothing else, we'll be going."

Looking at Steadman, Lainie was certain that it took every ounce of willpower for the detective to keep her mouth shut. Fists balled on the table, the woman sat rigid, her eyes fixed on Paul.

Kelley herded the group out the door ahead of her, calling over her shoulder, "Later."

Chapter 53

Once outside the building, Lainie reached over and touched Kelley on the arm. "Was that Elliott?"

"Bingo. All of the calls came from a burner phone. Nothing earthshaking there. He found the real gem when he looked at all calls to and from that phone. Most of them were from burners. All except one—our friend, Toni Carter. The plot thickens." She laughed. "It's going to take the police another few days to get that and even then, it's doubtful they'll look close enough to see the connection. You have to wonder how these guys ever solve any cases."

Lainie quickened her pace to keep up with her friend as Paul lagged behind a little. "I'm going to run Paul over to my place. I'm meeting with Lasorda at six at Tiffany's. I figure this'll go a little easier over a glass of wine."

Kelley shook her head. "Don't bother. I've already tried that. She doesn't budge, even with a healthy dose of alcohol."

Lainie shrugged as she walked. "She doesn't need to. I have no intention of asking her for anything. But I was wondering, could you ask Andi to drop over to my place and hang out with Paul until I get home?"

"Sure."

After they parted ways with Kelley, Lainie and Paul climbed into her Camry and she navigated through early work hour traffic toward her house.

"You need somebody to babysit me?" Paul's question came out flat, with a touch of resignation.

She focused on the road ahead of her. "Babysit, no. But like I told you yesterday, Paul, I care about you. So, I do want someone with you. I want you to know in no uncertain terms that you are not alone."

He turned his head and stared out the passenger window.

***

Tiffany's catered to the young professional crowd. Attorneys, accountants, and all manner of business professionals gathered there at quitting time to swap war stories, make professional contacts, or try to enhance their love life. The latter rarely worked. Most of the frequenters were more interested in money and power than love.

Lainie had just grabbed a booth and removed her coat when ADA Lasorda strode through the door, looked around briefly, and then made her way over. "Good afternoon, Counselor." She carried her raincoat over her arm and slid straight onto the bench."

"Thanks for meeting with me." Lainie signaled with her hand and caught a waiter's eye.

"What can I get for you?" The young man dressed in black trousers and a white shirt with his name stenciled on the pocket smiled at them.

Lainie spoke first. "One ticket, please. And I'd like a red wine." She turned her head toward Lasorda. "Eve?"

"The same." She nodded toward Lainie. As the waiter walked away, she continued. "I'm surprised that Kelley sent her assistant. I figured she'd do this herself."

Lainie started to respond but saw the waiter on his way back with two glasses of wine. She decided to wait. Instead of speaking, she nodded toward the young man.

"Here you are. Two red wines. Anything else I can get you?" He retreated after both of them shook their heads in unison.

Lainie took a sip and set her glass aside. "I'm not here on her behalf. This is personal."

Lasorda chuckled. "I'm sorry, Miz Simpson, I don't do personal. I assumed this is about the Stafford case. We're talking about a felony and we're doing it by the numbers."

Lainie nodded. "Yes, well, I don't really need anything from you. I'm not looking to cut a deal or ask you to do me any favors." She paused and gazed at the ADA for a moment.

"I don't come from a criminal law background. Mostly corporate, some civil litigation. So, you've probably noticed that I'm out of my depth. But I'm going to do something that attorneys I've known would never do. I'm going to lay my cards on the table for you with nothing expected in return, at least for now."

The ADA chuckled. "And to what do I owe this privilege?"

Rather than answer, Lainie reached into her purse and retrieved hard copies of the photos she'd taken at Paul's house. She laid them on the table, spreading them so that each was clearly visible. "This is Paul Stafford's house. I took them earlier today."

Lasorda glanced at them and shrugged. "He should call the police. On the other hand, this kind of thing can happen when you go around sexually assaulting teenage girls. Besides that, why show me? These have nothing to do with the case."

Lainie nodded. "I'm going to tell you some things. And before I do, I just want you to fully understand how

228

completely this man's life has been destroyed." She paused and took a deep breath. "Paul Stafford is innocent. And when I say *innocent*, I'm not using it in the context of you not being able to prove his guilt. I'm saying he did not do what they said he did."

The ADA took a sip of wine. "And you came to this gem of truth how?"

"I'm not here to offer proof. I'm not really even here to discuss the legal aspects of the case. I'm here because Kelley said you were competent, tough, ethical, and fair. And that's a compliment coming from her. I am just asking that you listen to what I have to say. It won't take any longer than it takes for you to finish that wine. After that, you can get up and leave."

Lasorda shrugged and picked up her glass again.

"You're stalling on the discovery package. Now I figure that you're too ethical to knowingly hide something. But you're also smart and strategic. I'm going to go out on a limb and say that there's something about those statements that bothers you. And they're really all you have. You figure if you delay long enough, it will put us in a crunch, and we'll overlook the problems. Delay too long and you risk a continuation, which also might work for you. Give you a chance to try and plug those holes."

The DA had lost the arrogant, bored look. She sat gazing at Lainie, her eyes betraying interest.

"Like I said, I'm not here to convince you. We will bring you evidence once we get the discovery package from you. But you can ask yourself, if he didn't do this, which I know is a very big 'if' for you, then the question that follows would be 'why?' Why would these girls make up a story like this if it wasn't true? That is the question."

Lasorda stared at her for a moment and then narrowed her eyes. "So what? All you're doing is laying the groundwork for an alternate set of facts. Nothing you say is compelling and I have statements from the girls. You have nothing to support your assertions." But the look on her face was anything but dismissive.

"Yes, I know. And without the statements, I am hobbled. The answers are likely not in them, but I believe they'll point me to where I can find what I need."

The ADA finished off the rest of her wine but continued to sit. "And why are you telling me this? Why not just wait until you have what you need and then give it to me?"

Lainie gazed at her for a moment and nodded. "Because when I do bring it to you, I am going to want a favor. If the evidence convinces you of his innocence, not just a lack of enough evidence to convict, but something that truly shows him to be the victim of a cruel injustice, then I would like for you to join me in publicly declaring his innocence. The system has stolen his life. It would seem a small step toward helping him get it back."

Lasorda gathered her coat and purse. "As you said, counselor, that is a big *if.*" She paused and looked at Lainie for a moment. "Come on. Follow me back to my office and I'll get you the package."

Chapter 54

Lainie walked through the door from her garage into the living room and caught the muted sounds of Andi and Paul talking in the living room. "I'm home." Hanging up her coat, she announced, "I come bearing treasure." She sauntered into the living room holding a manila envelope at about face level. "The discovery package."

Andi bolted from her seat. "What all's there?"

Lainie opened the envelope and pulled out the contents. "Just as we thought. The three statements." She waved copies of handwritten documents in front of her. "And some background stuff, all of which I think we have."

Paul sat transfixed at the sheets of paper. His eyes betrayed confusion and fear. After all, those three statements had ruined his life and, at the same time, held the key to his future.

"I haven't read them closely. Just picked them up a while ago from the ADA." Lainie tossed the envelope that contained several other sheets of paper on the dining room table.

Andi leafed through them quickly and then went back and started to read the first one.

"I'm going to give Kelley a call and see if she wants to do anything tonight." Neither Paul nor Andi responded. Lainie pulled out her cellphone and dialed.

"Hey. Anything worthwhile happen?"

Lainie smiled. "Got the discovery package. Andi's here looking at the statements right now. You want to get together tonight or wait until tomorrow?"

A brief silence ensued. "Let's do it tonight. That way we won't have to waste time tomorrow coming up to speed. Meet us down at the office as soon as you can."

Lainie disconnected and put the phone back into her purse. "Kelley wants to get started." She glanced at Andi. "I guess we need to take two cars. I assume you'll go home from there."

The research analyst nodded, grabbed her coat and purse on the way to the front door. "Yup. Paul, you can ride with me if you want."

Lainie winced.

Mildred offered her nickel's worth. *Is that jealousy we feel?*

Shut up. She collected her coat, purse, and keys, along with the package on the way to the garage.

***

Lainie stopped by the copier in Kelley's office and made photocopies of the statements for everyone. She walked into the conference room, lit by overhead fluorescent lighting, to find the others sitting expectantly. "Here you go." She gave everyone a copy of each statement.

Everyone around the table except Paul started reading. He sat and stared down at the paper shaking his head. In front of him, finally, were the words of three students that had brought him down.

Kelley pulled them all out of their concentration. "Okay, guys, let's get this over with." She turned to Lainie. "By the way, how did you manage to get these?"

Lainie shrugged. "It's like you said, she's tough and smart but she's not unethical. She knows something's wrong with these. I just told her that Paul was innocent and that we were going to prove it. And, voila, she gave them to me."

"You get a chance to look at them yet?"

Lainie nodded. "I gave one of them a cursory look in her office. I browsed another on the way to my car. Kind of tough by streetlight. I think that one was the Bufford statement. Writing skills aren't that great. She struggles with sentence structure and spelling. Except that in some places, it sounds very, I don't know, maybe polished? Anyway, that's about it."

Kelley turned to one of her assistants. "Okay, Andi. Do your magic. Can you have something for me by tomorrow afternoon?"

"Sure. I can have it tomorrow morning." Enthusiasm laced the young woman's words.

Kelley furrowed her brow. "Uh, no. I don't want you pulling an all-nighter. I may need you tomorrow. I suspect that things are going to speed up from here. Our goal is to nail this before it gets too far. Lainie, any thoughts?"

Lainie tapped her pen on her pad as she rattled through the explanation. "Yes. I still believe the key to this entire thing is the question Paul asked in the beginning—why? Thinking it through, these are three high school students and they've accused the high school principal. Logically that means that the motivation lies somewhere in the school. Since the students aren't connected other than through this case, I suggest that we pick one of them and drill down. The most likely choice is Caryn Smallwood. She claims to have had sex with him. The other two say he tried to coerce them, but they didn't go through with it."

Kelley considered the plan. "Other than the students, we've already covered the staff and faculty. What's left at school?"

Lainie thought about it for a moment. Her gaze floated from Kelley's face to the tabletop to Paul's face. "Teachers. Yes, I know we've spoken to them, but I think there's more there. When we interviewed them before, I don't think we'd really considered the possibility that the kids were straight-out lying. I think a more direct, forceful approach could produce some new information."

Kelley pursed her lips and exhaled. "Okay, Lainie. Do it. Andi, you have your assignment. Any questions?"

Andi shook her head as she gathered up the sheets.

Kelley looked around the room one more time. "Okay, folks, let's hit it." She stood and headed for the door, speaking over her shoulder. "Elliott, let's you and I have a talk."

Chapter 55

Lainie left the meeting energized. She had things to do, things that could make a difference. *Tomorrow morning* had a nice ring to it. As she drove, Paul sat beside her in the passenger seat looking out his side window. His demeanor as the group had girded for the coming fight seemed to improve. His eyes had tracked the speakers. She watched him nod a couple of times, thinking how it had only been a couple of days since....

She wanted to talk to him but, other than words of encouragement, she wasn't sure where to go with it. She had promised him they would talk more about what had happened between them earlier. More specifically, why she had treated him as if he was a combination of disease and criminal. Initially, her reluctance to have the discussion stemmed from his situation. But now she was afraid of what she would discover about herself.

Mildred offered her own observations. *Sooner or later you'll have to deal with it.*

Sometimes the little twit had a penchant for the obvious. The snarky remark didn't warrant a response. She turned the wiper switch from intermittent to continuous slow if for no other reason than to vary the sound.

"What made you change your mind about me?" Paul spoke without turning his gaze from the window.

Lainie glanced briefly at him and then returned her attention to the road. "It's complicated. But maybe that's not the right question. Maybe what's important is why I acted the way I did to begin with?"

"I just assumed it was because you thought I was all of the things they said." His words came out matter-of-factly, as if talking about some absent third-party.

She focused on the road as she tried to think of the right answer to that. Did she really think he was like that or did she just want to keep him at bay and that was a good excuse? "That's not a good assumption. But it is complicated. Maybe we can have a better discussion about this when I'm not driving on a dark rain-soaked road. But I'll tell you this and you can take it for what it's worth. My attitude toward you, both before and after the allegations, had more to do with me than with you. I've got problems that started long before I met you. It just seems that maybe you were meant to help me come to grips with them." In that instant she wondered where that particular notion came from.

Mildred responded to the question. *Probably from me.*

"Paul, I won't try to justify it. And explaining it so that it makes sense is not something I'm ready to attempt here and now. But I promise you this. I do believe in you. What I told you the other night at your place—I meant every word of that. I hope that one day you can find it in your heart to forgive me. For now, though, maybe the best we can manage is that you trust me to help you through this." She attempted to swallow the lump in her throat.

She sensed more than saw him turn and face her. She glanced over to see a look of curiosity. His head tilted slightly, eyes intense. Whatever coursed through his mind, though, did not make it through his lips. After a moment, he turned back toward the window.

Lainie smiled at him and offered, "Hey, I have an idea. I don't think either of us wants to cook tonight. Why don't we stop and get sandwiches and salads, along with dessert? We can call it a working dinner. I'm really anxious to delve into these statements."

He turned her way and studied her for a moment. "Sounds good."

Chapter 56

L ainie caught up with Clifford Taylor, the math teacher, in the teacher's lounge just after ten the next day. "Good morning. I'm Lainie Simpson. I'm with the team defending Principal Stafford. I wonder if I might have a few words with you." She looked around the deserted space—it would do if they could finish before anyone else wandered in.

He looked to be in his mid-fifties, his head bald on top with a band of brown and gray on the sides. He wore dark gray wool slacks, a light blue long sleeve shirt, and a wool maroon pullover V-necked vest. He looked up and considered her through narrowed eyes. "I've already spoken with your associate. I told her everything I know about the matter."

She smiled and sat across the small table from him. "Yes, I know. We're still gathering information and we just have a few more questions for you."

His face turned hard. "I told you I've said everything I intend to. I don't know anything about the case. Now, if you'll excuse me." He stood.

Lainie remained seated and eased the smile a bit without banishing it completely. "Mister Taylor, I have just a few questions. I'd prefer to get the answers here and now in a casual and relaxed setting. If not, though, there are other ways. Your choice."

The math teacher's face turned crimson. She could see him clenching his jaw. "You know, of course, that I can't discuss her academic performance without her parents' permission."

"Mister Taylor, surely you know by now that I have a court order for her school records. I have it right here in my briefcase if you'd like to refer to it. You can also call your office if you prefer. They can confirm that."

"Just ask your questions and be done with it."

The smile returned. "Thank you. And I promise, this won't take but a few minutes. What can you tell me about Caryn Smallwood?"

The words came out dripping with disdain. "Like I already told your associate," he paused as if to let the sarcasm sink in, "Caryn is an A student. I've never had any problems with her. And I don't know anything else about her."

Lainie nodded as she made notes. "So, you'd say she was a good student?"

"That's what I said. She's an A student." He folded his arms on his chest.

She sensed him dodging the question. "An A student is the same as a good student, and vice versa?"

His eyes narrowed and his facial features relaxed. "Not always the same, but, you know…." His words trailed off.

But she didn't know. "Tell me about her homework. Does she turn it in regularly and is it well done?" It was the first thing that came to mind.

"Yes." Emphatic. The red hue on his face deepened. "She always has her homework done without fail and it's flawless." He punctuated the words by stabbing his index finger onto the tabletop.

A vague amorphous tendril beckoned her toward something. But what? "And when you call on her in class, like to answer one of the homework problems, how is she at that?"

His color had returned to normal. His hands now sat folded on the table in front of him. "She doesn't like speaking in class. She prefers to give her explanations by writing problems and solutions on the board."

There it was. She could almost taste it. "So, if I'm understanding correctly, you would call on her for a homework problem and she'd go to the board and copy the solution from her paper. That was her explanation, right?"

"Yeah. That's about it."

Lainie scribbled notes quickly, anxious to get on to the next question. "What about tests?"

Taylor walked over and retrieved a notebook computer from the counter. He powered it up without speaking. After punching some keys, waiting, punching a few more, he used the trackpad to scroll. "So far this semester, we've had eight exams. She scored above ninety-five on seven of the eight." He opened his mouth then furrowed his brow, shook his head, and closed his mouth without speaking.

"What about the eighth test? What did she score on that?"

"Seventy."

Lainie stopped writing and looked up at him. "Anything special about that particular test?"

He punched a couple of keys and scrolled some more, staring at the screen. "No, nothing special. Quadratic equations—standard material for high school algebra." He seemed to be focused on something he hadn't noticed before.

An idea flashed into her mind. "For these exams, do you monitor them yourself?"

He spoke with his eyes glued to the screen, alternately pressing keys and scrolling. "No. Not usually. I have a teacher's aide that does that. I try to use that time for other things like preparing lesson plans, scoring homework, and the like." He turned his attention to Lainie. "But, you know, as I recall on that exam, I did monitor it. I remember my aide was out sick that day." He began to slowly shake his head.

The picture began to take shape. "Tell me about her, the aide."

"She's not bad. Punctual. Gets on well with the students. Follows instructions. You know, nothing special but it's really helpful having her around. Why do you ask?"

Lainie smiled at him. "No particular reason. I'm just gathering as much information as I can." She stood. "You know, I think that's pretty much it. I really appreciate your help." She handed him one of the business cards she'd had made up just for this case. "And if you think of anything else, please give me a call."

As she strode out of the room, Lainie could mentally see the entire picture of the case changing. Next came the English teacher.

Chapter 57

Lainie finished up with Taylor just before eleven. Rather than trying to corner Rosalee Chambers, the English Teacher, over the lunch hour, she decided to grab something to eat at the deli. Paul had remained at her house alone all morning. He seemed fine when she left but a kernel of worry huddled up in a corner of her mind. Taking lunch back would serve two purposes—something decent for both of them to eat and to ease her mind.

She left her car parked in the driveway and entered through the front door. A wave of complex aromas hit her when she opened the door. She detected curry, she knew that one. But there were others, subtler. From the threshold, she could see Paul in the kitchen stirring something in her large skillet with a wooden spoon. Dressed in jeans and a steel blue sweatshirt, he looked the picture of casual.

"Hey, I brought us some lunch. God, what is that wonderful smell? She strode through the dining room to stand beside him as he stirred.

"Just doing some curry. You had most of the spices. Hope you don't mind." He continued to look down at the pan of bubbling, thick liquid. "Thought maybe curried lentils over brown rice. I notice you have some red lentils in the pantry."

She smiled. Whatever else came of lunch, he certainly seemed to be in a better frame of mind. "I got some minestrone and a Greek salad at the deli. You hungry?" She walked over and set the two bags on the kitchen table.

He turned to face her, his head tilted—the look she'd come to associate with questioning or confusion. "I guess so." He turned his head and stared out the window for a moment.

Standing there, she could see the toll this had all taken on him. His body, trim when she'd met him, had turned gaunt. His clothes barely hung on his frame. He looked as if the slightest breeze would blow him over. Lainie reminded herself that, in the past week, she hadn't seen him eat much more than a bit of broth until the previous night when he ate half his sandwich and salad. Later he ate his entire piece of apple pie. Some expression had returned to his eyes, but they still remained set deep into his face. She fought off the urge to hug him, to hold him and tell him everything would be okay.

She turned and took a couple of bowls and salad plates from the shelf. "What do you want to drink?" Turning to the silverware drawer, she pulled out two soup spoons and salad forks.

He shrugged and furrowed his brow, as if trying to comprehend the question.

Lainie decided not to push. "Water okay?" She took two glasses from the cabinet and filled them from the dispenser in the fridge.

He remained quiet as he eased over to the table and sat.

She thought it odd that he could process the thoughts and information necessary to search through her ingredients and find what he needed for curry but struggled with a choice of drinks. A key difference struck her. Preparing the curry had developed from an internal motivation. He'd thought it through himself with no prodding. The question of drinks came from outside. So, he seemed to do okay with internal thought processes. Connecting with the outside seemed to come harder.

Lainie dished up the soup and salad, placing his in front of him and then getting hers. "There you go. The soup may be getting a little cool. Long drive from the deli."

He sat and stared at the dishes in front of him like he wasn't sure what to do with them.

She paused, her soup spoon in hand. "I hope this is okay. I mean, I guess I just assumed you'd like the soup and salad."

"Yes. But why are you doing this?"

Lainie shifted back in her chair with a start. "Well, I thought that you might be hungry and want to eat lunch."

He shook his head. "No. I mean, all of this." He gestured around the room. His eyes shimmered with moisture as he stared at her.

Lainie put her spoon down and folded her hands in front of her. "Paul, I'm just trying to help you."

"I know that. But you're my attorney, like you said." He gestured around the room again. "This is not attorney stuff. I don't understand."

Tears flooded into her eyes. She'd hoped that they had moved past that—apparently not. "I know. And as much as I might have wanted it to be true, I was never just your attorney." She started to tell him again that it was complicated and that she would one day share everything with him. But Lainie knew it would be a fruitless effort.

She could feel his stare. When she looked up again, the tears in his eyes had overflowed. He nodded and ate a spoonful of soup.

Chapter 58

Lunch with Paul had proved to be yet another gut-wrenching affair for Lainie. As she drove back to the school for her afternoon interview with the English teacher, she wondered if there would ever come a time when she and Paul could have a regular conversation without it ending in tears for at least one of them.

She pulled into the school parking lot just after one-thirty. Rosalee Chambers would be in class for another fifteen minutes. Since no meeting had been arranged, she planned to intercept the woman as she left the classroom. One of several small meeting rooms in the library seemed the best place to steer her for a private conversation.

Lainie stood by the door, checking e-mail on her phone, then for text and voice messages, and, as a last resort to stave off boredom, looking at her weather app. The weather guys predicted rain over the next several days. It figured—Seattle in the spring.

The bell rang and, within seconds, the door swung open and the horde of students flooded through the threshold bound for whatever awaited them next. After the last straggler, Lainie edged through the entrance. "Miz Chambers?"

The trim, mid-to-late twenty-something woman turned, eyebrows arched. "Yes?" She reached down and picked up her book and notepad.

Lainie strode forward and extended a hand. "I'm Lainie Simpson. I'm an attorney working on the Paul Stafford defense. Could I get a few minutes of your time?"

The teacher's face darkened, her mouth drawing into a tight line. "I've already spoken to the police and to one of your associates." She moved quickly through the door without a handshake, making her way down the hall.

Lainie hurried to catch up to her. "Yes. I know. We're getting ready for trial and we had just a few more questions, some things we were hoping you could clear up for us."

Chambers kept her pace, speaking over her shoulder as students whizzed by on both sides. "I've told you everything I know."

Lainie touched her arm and the woman whirled around to face her, eyes shooting daggers. "What part of *NO* don't you understand?"

Okay, let's bring out the guns. Lainie nodded her head over to the side of the hallway. Standing there face-to-face with the hostile teacher, she spoke slowly in a soft tone. "Miz Chambers, I assure you that'd I rather finish all this up in a private setting. But unless I get some answers from you now, I can promise you that I'll call you to the stand during the trial and pry the information from you in front of a jury, if that's what you prefer. Personally, I think it would be in everyone's best interest if we sort this out here and now." She forced herself into a neutral, non-aggressive but firm stance. She held the woman's gaze. "Why don't we find a room in the library? We can clear up the last few details. Then you and I will be done." She offered a very slight smile.

Settled into a small meeting room in the library, Lainie pulled out her notes and a copy of the statement Chambers had provided the police. "I understand that you're the one that initially brought this all to light. Could you go over how this information came to you?"

Chambers exhaled and rolled her eyes, the exasperation evident. "Like I told them, Caryn Smallwood came and talked to me about it. After that, I did exactly what our policy requires. I notified Principal Stafford's direct superior, which is the Superintendent." She clenched her jaw and folded her arms on her chest.

Lainie nodded and smiled as she made notes. "Good, thank you. It says here," she gestured toward a photocopy of Ms. Chambers' statement, "that this was on, let's see, oh yes, Monday, March thirteenth. What time of day?"

The teacher shifted her posture so that she was leaning back, keeping the same confrontational look. "It was just about eight-thirty. I remember because it was after homeroom and right before first period."

"And where did this occur?"

"I was alone in the faculty lounge. She came and knocked on the door. Told me she needed to talk to me." The woman apparently made no effort to hide her enmity.

Lainie furrowed her brow and looked up from her notetaking. "Any idea why she would come to you with this story, you know, as opposed to going to the school counselor?"

Chambers tilted her head slightly upward as if looking down her nose at her inquisitor. "I'd like to think that I have an excellent rapport with my students, that they feel comfortable coming to me with problems."

Lainie smiled. "That's excellent. I know how important it is that students have someone in whom they trust. Would you say that your relationship with her was exceptional in this way? I mean, she confided in you regularly?"

Chambers' gaze drifted toward the window. Her posture relaxed as she dropped her arms to her side. "I don't know that I'd go that far. There's never been anything this serious, so we've obviously never had this kind of conversation before. I'm just glad she trusted me enough this time."

"That's remarkable. I see from the records that she's in your English class. What time does that class meet?"

"I have her in third period, right before lunch."

Lainie tightened the rope. "Any idea why she would approach you first thing in the morning in the teacher's lounge rather than waiting, say, until right before or after your class?"

"No idea."

Something's missing here. "You seem to be very attuned to your students. Did you notice anything about her earlier, say, the previous week, that might have signaled any kind of problem?"

A darkness flashed over the woman. *That's it.*

Chambers recovered, cleared her throat, and turned her attention down and to the left, where some chalk dust had fallen. "Not that I recall."

"So, there was nothing at all that you can think of that might have been troubling her?"

The hostility returned. Chambers leaned back again, the arms back on her chest. "That's what I just said."

Lainie smiled inside. "And so, if I'm understanding this right, you have this girl who's doing okay, no problems. You see her every day. Everything seems right with her. Then, bam, Monday morning she's telling you that the principal has been forcing her to have sex and now she's so distraught that she seeks you out first thing in the morning."

Panic—the look that shot across the woman's face. "I just did what I was supposed to do. I listened to her and I reported it. That's all."

That's it. Time's up. "Miz Chambers, let's be honest here. Something's missing. You're holding information back."

The teacher's eyes widened and she squirmed in her chair. "I've told you everything I know. Now, if you'll excuse me…"

Lainie intervened in the escape attempt. "No, you haven't. There's something else there that you're not telling me. You may not even think it's important. But there's a man's life at stake here. It's not for you or me to decide what information is relevant. Your responsibility here is to tell the whole truth, all of it. It's up to the judge and jury to sort that out." She leaned forward toward the woman who sat across the table.

Chambers grew increasingly agitated. She unfolded her arms and rubbed her hands together on the tabletop. She shifted her gaze rapidly around the room. When she spoke, she started with the predictable self-defense. "I haven't lied about anything. Everything I told them was the truth. I just want to do what's right for the students. She shouldn't have to go through this."

Lainie nodded. "I know." She left it there.

The teacher nodded and looked down at the tabletop. "There was one thing. It's not really connected to this at all. But, you know, Caryn is an A student. She's probably going to attend one of the Ivy League schools next year. Her life shouldn't be destroyed this way."

Lainie let the silence work for her.

"She's always done stellar work in my class." Chambers paused and narrowed her eyes. "But this spring, she had a problem. I assigned a semester research project in British Literature that counts for thirty percent of their grade. Her paper was good, really good. Actually, it was too good. I remembered a similar one from a few years back, looking at the effect of beliefs and values in fourteenth-century England on Chaucer's *Canterbury Tales*. I remember it because it's such an unusual but rich topic. When I checked, her paper was nearly identical to an earlier one. She'd changed some of it, but the main points and citations were all the same." She shook her head as she stared down at the tabletop.

"When I confronted her about it, she didn't offer any explanation or excuse. She just bolted from the classroom. That was on the Friday before she told me her story. When she came to me that next Monday morning, she was in tears. She said that she'd cheated because of the stress she was under. She apologized and told me the entire story about the principal."

And there it was. "And so, she's going to fail for the semester? That means she won't graduate and will have to go to summer school. Maybe not get into that Ivy League school?"

Chambers shook her head. "I felt it best, under the circumstances, not to add to her burden. I told her that I'd omit that assignment. I will allow her to take a special comprehensive exam at the end of the year and use that in place of the research paper." The teacher looked up at Lainie, her eyes filled with questions and doubt. "You don't think…?"

Chapter 59

Lainie looked up at the gray, dismal sky outside East Rainier High School and smiled as she waited for Kelley to answer the phone.

Her associate dispensed with the small talk "Hey, what you got?"

"Jackpot!" Lainie almost shouted the word.

A laugh. "You don't know the half of it, girl."

She felt her eyes widen with wonder. "What?"

"We have a meeting with the ADA tomorrow morning at ten. Let's meet at my place, eight-thirty, and we can all swap war stories."

Lainie navigated to her house with a sense that things were falling into place. Despite the optimism, a worry tugged at the back of her mind. Something was still missing. The pieces made sense when looked at alone but not when you put them all together.

***

She didn't know when she'd had a more delicious meal. The curried lentils were seasoned to perfection. The brown rice was cooked to just the right consistency. The side salad was unique to say the least. Paul had tossed together some field greens that she'd had down in the crisper. Sliced purple onion, cashews, and carrot slivers nestled in the mix. Fresh sliced strawberries garnished the top. He had not dressed it but rather put a container of balsamic vinaigrette along with some lemon wedges on the table.

"Where did you get the strawberries?" She knew there were none lurking in the refrigerator.

He shrugged and narrowed his eyes as if concentrating. "I walked down to the store."

The nearest supermarket was a half-mile away. "Really? You just walked down there?"

He shot her a questioning look. "Yeah. I couldn't find any here." A simple answer.

Lainie opted for the lemon and some fresh ground pepper on her salad. She watched Paul nibble at his supper, hesitating frequently as though trying to figure something out. The lump in her throat refused to leave. He spent all this time cooking and even walked to the store for a garnish on the salad. And here he was eating very little.

She thought to ask him about it but, in the end, decided to let it go. After all, a more important subject filled her mind. "Paul, I need to tell you, we discovered the 'why' in all this today." She poured out the details of her conversation with Chambers.

He watched her without speaking, occasionally shaking his head. When she finished, he put down his fork and looked up at her. "I don't understand. Why say all of that just because of a paper? And why me?"

The last question was the one that tormented Lainie, mainly because she knew the answer and it devastated her. "As for the overall why, I don't know. People do crazy things when they think they're in trouble. As to the question of 'why you?' I can only surmise that you were just a convenient target. There doesn't seem to be any rhyme or reason other than accusing you would draw attention away from her."

He shook his head again, this time more rapidly. "I don't understand."

Before Lainie could continue the conversation, her ringtone sounded. She checked the caller ID before connecting. "Good evening, Reverend Polasky."

***

The minister, glancing up from her desk, motioned Lainie toward the chair sitting off to the side. "Thank you for coming down here. I hate to intrude on your evening."

Lainie wondered in passing why the minister had called in the evening if she hated intruding. After all, this conversation could have taken place during the workday. Instead, she nodded. "Not a problem." She opened the voice recorder app on her phone. "Do you mind if I record this conversation?"

"I'd prefer that you not. What I'm going to tell you is mostly just my opinion. Frankly, I'm worried that if it gets out that I spoke with you about this issue, it could have some unpleasant, if unintended side-effects. In fact, that's why I waited until after hours, when no one else is around. I'd really like it if we could just talk privately."

"We can do that." Lainie powered down the phone and set it on table beside the chair. "So, what's on your mind?"

"It's about Robert Tell."

Lainie started to say that she suspected as much but decided against commenting at all.

After a moment, Polasky began, soft and slow at first, as she appeared to pick her words carefully. "As you may have figured out, I have trouble considering Tell a minister. If anything, he might be considered more of an advocate for youth. He's come up with some structured outreach and programs for kids, mostly teens, and puts constant pressure on city and state government to fund them."

This was not news to Lainie. She'd seen the near constant stream of news stories. Before Paul's case, Tell's rants focused mainly on trying to secure grants for his programs. He railed on and on about the policies that prevented public funding of religious programs.

The minister continued, "He's really popular with young people. There are some adults, mostly women, that associate with his ministry as well, but it's really for the kids." She sat, wringing her hands in her lap. "Our church has had its share of youth that stopped attending, only to engage with Tell and his programs." She locked gazes with Lainie, worry in her eyes. "I have to say that I've prayed long and hard about this. I don't want this to be just sour grapes. But it's hard watching kids that I care about, that I've known for years, leave our church for him."

"What do you mean, 'leave the church for him'? You mean for his programs and activities?"

"Yes and no. I guess what I mean, what I fear, is that he is personally attracting the youth—not with his programs."

The words didn't surprise Lainie, but they did give her a bit of queasiness. A dark sense of foreboding eased its way into her consciousness. "You think that his relationship with these teens is more personal than spiritual?"

"I don't know what I think. But that is something that has crossed my mind and it frightens me."

Lainie started to mentally move the pieces of the puzzle around. A fuzzy mental picture began to emerge. "What makes you suspect this?"

"When he first came to town and began to recruit kids, I did some research. I found what you probably found as well—his history and reports of financial problems in Idaho. I called a friend of mine who serves a church in Coeur d'Alene. He told me that it was common knowledge that Tell had been having affairs with married women in his church. It blew up right about the same time he closed his doors—a couple of divorces and threats of violence. He disappeared and folks over there were left to pick up the pieces."

That sounded right in character with what Lainie thought of the guy. But still…. "Even if that was true, why the interest in young girls? If married women are his thing, why not just stick to what he's good at?" She winced at the thought of him being good in that way.

"There's more. My friend said that there were some rumors—nothing ever proven, no charges filed—that he'd also had inappropriate contact with some of the teenage girls. I researched as much as I could and found nothing. I even called the police in Coeur d'Alene but they didn't have anything on him."

"Maybe there was nothing to it." But her instincts told her differently. Everything about the guy—his apparent ease around kids and the way the girls looked at him—screamed confirmation of Janet Polasky's fears.

"Maybe. I don't know. Like I said, it's just a fear and I'd hate to unjustly accuse him of something like that."

Lainie weighed her options. Thus far, they'd only discussed Tell in the most general of terms. Nothing said so far had any direct connection to the case. "Reverend Polasky, I'm going to ask you something. If you can't answer it, I understand. But if you can, it could help salvage the life of an innocent man. Do you, by chance, know any of these girls—Caryn Smallwood, Marianne Thompson, or Deborah Bufford?"

The minister stared at Lainie, uncertainty in her eyes. "Let me say first that I can't discuss anything I've learned through conversations with congregation members. I guess as an attorney, you would understand that."

"Yes."

"I know Marianne Thompson. Her family attends our church."

And there it was. "But Marianne is connected to Tell's organization."

Polasky didn't answer.

But even this didn't really tell Lainie anything useful. She already knew that Marianne was associated with Tell—had been for nearly eight months. The only thing she'd really learned is that there had been rumors. "Do you have any reason to believe that her connection to Tell's church has anything to do with the case of Paul Stafford, the high school principal accused of inappropriate contact with the students?"

"No, not really. It just all seems too coincidental to me— Tell's background and his almost zealot-like advocacy in this particular case. For a guy who's been accused of sexual misconduct, at least in the court of public opinion, it just seems odd that he would take such an intense interest in a case that is already being handled by the authorities. It's almost like he's trying to fan the flames of a fire that already exists."

But how would Tell having sex with these kids connect to allegations against the principal? "Do you have any knowledge of Mister Stafford's case? I mean, did Marianne or her parents discuss it with you?"

"No, nothing at all. But even if they had told me things, I couldn't tell you."

"Anything else, then?"

"I would appreciate it if you could keep this conversation private. I don't think there is any factual information I've given you that you didn't already have. Everything else was just suspicion or rumor."

Lainie considered the request. It was true—the only new piece the minister had given her was conjecture and fear. "Yes, I will keep this confidential." The minute she'd said that, she wondered if she was truly willing to keep this from her team and from Paul.

Chapter 60

The group blew through the meeting in just under an hour. Lainie poured out her story to a collective look of lights popping on. She could see her three associates beginning to connect the dots. But if she thought she'd scored big, she felt one-upped when Andi plowed through her analysis of the three statements. Lainie listened and followed along on the marked-up documents the research assistant had provided.

When Andi finished, Lainie scratched the hair at her temple as she shook her head. "Still too many blanks in the narrative. We have the why on Caryn Smallwood, but not the other two? What's the thread that holds all this together?"

Kelley shrugged. "Dunno. And I suspect that we won't until we pull back some layers." She stood and gathered her documents. "You and I will start that process shortly." She nodded at Lainie. Turning to Andi and Elliott, she added, "You two stay available. Things are going to start happening fast now." She crammed everything in her briefcase and turned toward the door before stopping.

Kelley faced Paul and spoke gently to him. "We're going to do this, Paul. We know you're innocent and by the time we're done, the entire town will know as well. I promise you this."

He nodded at her, his eyes becoming moist.

Lainie watched the exchange with mixed feelings. She felt exhilarated that Kelley had joined the battle for his life. Her few words had clearly touched Paul but evoked a tinge of jealousy in Lainie.

Kelley resumed her bolt for the door. "Okay folks, let's hit it."

***

They met at the office of the District Attorney. The well-appointed conference room stood in stark contrast to the dark, depressing police station. Legal texts filled bookcases dominating an entire wall. The oval, cherry wood table served as the hub for ten padded swivel chairs whose blue and gray tweed fabric complemented the plush morning glory blue carpet. Photographs of the President of the United States, Washington Governor, and the current District Attorney adorned the walls. Lainie and Kelley entered to find ADA Lasorda and the two detectives already seated.

Lainie slid into a seat directly across from Burke and Steadman. Lasorda sat across from her at an angle. Kelley set her briefcase on the table and grabbed the seat next to Lainie, directly across from Lasorda. The scene struck Lainie like something out of a sports contest—the two opposing teams facing off.

Something seemed amiss. Kelley had become increasingly distracted after the pre-meeting they'd had in her office. Usually when she anticipated interaction with Steadman, she came in burning for a fight. Lainie observed that her friend and associate seemed more resigned, almost reluctant despite the ammunition in their arsenal. At one point, she nudged Kelley. Arching her eyebrows, she attempted to discern without speaking what was going on. A shake of the head was the response.

Lasorda took a quick glance at the team on her side of the table and then nodded to Kelley. "Okay counselors. You wanted to interview Detectives Steadman and Burke. Everyone's here. You're on."

Kelley closed her eyes for an instant before re-opening them and taking a deep breath. "Thank you." She nodded to the detectives. "And thanks for coming. I appreciate it." The tone was the sincerest that Lainie had ever heard her use when speaking to Steadman.

The detective narrowed her eyes. Her face exuded suspicion. She nodded and said nothing. Burke looked on, expressionless.

"Detective Steadman, could you tell me what, if any, assistance you gave the three students in developing their statements?" Kelley's words came out slow and calm.

The female detective reacted as if acid had been thrown at her. She jerked backward, her face transformed into a visual snarl. "What the hell kind of question is that?" She spit the venom-coated words across the table.

Kelley shook her head and let the silence settle in.

Steadman stared daggers as Kelley waited. "What are you implying?"

"I'm not implying anything. I simply asked a question." She tapped lightly on the stack of papers with her pen.

The detective looked over at her partner, who shrugged at her. Turning to Kelley, she hurled a response. "None. Nothing."

Silence, waiting.

Steadman's tone became more explanatory and less vile as she spoke. "The girls prepared their written statements at home. They came in and we interviewed them, going over the documents. We didn't make any changes at all."

Kelley nodded. "Is it customary practice to allow witnesses to write their statements at home and then bring them in to you?"

"No, not usually. The girls... and their parents requested that they be allowed to do it in the privacy of their home. There's nothing that prohibits it." Steadman's words came out sounding defensive.

"Okay. Thank you." Kelley seemed to glide past the subject as though it were of no concern whatsoever.

The female detective's demeanor had morphed from anger and hatred to one of curiosity. The thin tight line that had defined her mouth relaxed. Her eyes narrowed a bit. Her hands sat folded on the table in front of her. She nodded but said nothing.

"I understand that you took an initial report and did an interview before they wrote their statements. What instructions did you give them about the statements?" Kelley looked up from her notetaking.

Steadman took a deep breath and appeared ready to answer when Burke jumped in. "I can speak to that. I was there when she gave the instructions. Same ones we give to every witness. As much detail as possible. Be honest. If you don't know or can't remember, say so. Don't guess or speculate. Pretty much it."

The female detective nodded and then looked down at the table.

Kelley made some notes on her pad and then looked up, smiling. "Thanks." She shifted her gaze over to Lasorda and then back to the detectives. "Those are the only questions I had for you. You can go or, if you'd like, you're welcome to stay for our discussion with the ADA."

Burke and Steadman looked at each other, both appearing somewhat confused. Burke responded. "Uh, we'd like to stay, if you don't mind."

Kelley smiled. "Certainly." She flipped through the documents in front of her and pulled out a set of papers clipped together. "Please bear with me. I'm going to be giving you some copies of documents and you'll see multiple copies of each with different kinds of notes. I ask you to trust me that there's a point to all of this."

She handed each of them a document with three pages. "This is a photocopy of the handwritten statement of Caryn Smallwood. I'm giving you this so that you can verify what I'm working from. Can you tell me if this is a true copy of her statement?"

The three individuals across the table flipped through the three pages, moving their lips without sound. After a moment, Lasorda responded. "Looks like it, as far as I can tell." She offered a look that combined curiosity and confusion.

Kelley smiled. "Thanks. Hopefully you'll soon see why that's important." She handed each of them a second document with a couple of pages. "This is a text version of the statement. We simply transcribed it so that it would be easier to work with. We even left the misspellings in place." She chuckled. "If you could, please verify that this reflects the handwritten copy."

Steadman exhaled deeply. "Could we get on with this?"

"Of course. Sorry. I just don't want there to be any confusion about what we're working with." She organized another set of documents in front of her but held them there. "You can set those aside for now."

She passed out the new set. "This is the same document but you'll see that the front page has some words highlighted—'he fondled my breasts.' Down about halfway."

Lasorda's face betrayed no emotion at all. Burke narrowed his eyes as he appeared to read the document more completely. Steadman shot back. "So what?"

Kelley paused for a moment. "Doesn't that seem more like an adult term? I mean, I wouldn't necessarily expect a high school student to toss that one out there."

Steadman shoved the paper across the table toward Kelley. "Her words, not mine. They seem pretty clear to me. Not a lot of ambiguity. As for being adult terms, who knows, maybe she's got a good vocabulary. She's an A student, after all."

Kelley arched her eyebrows and shrugged. "Maybe. And you can see, if you turn the page, she used it a couple more times—same phrase. If those are her words, she certainly seems to like them."

Lasorda stepped in. "What are you getting at, counselor? I agree with Detective Steadman. It may seem a curious choice of words but it's not impossible. In fact, given the caliber of her schoolwork, I'd say it's not even improbable."

"True, true." Kelley gazed across the table, a hint of a smile finding its way onto her lips.

Lainie could see that her associate was ready to deliver one of the bombs. Curiously, though, Kelley didn't seem to convey the glee that she normally did when delivering such a blow.

More copies slid across the table. "These are the text versions of the other two girls' statements. Notice the yellow highlighting on both pages. Same term, same context. 'He wanted to fondle my breasts.' 'He tried to fondle my breasts'."

Lasorda stared at the new documents. Her eyes seemed to signal that she saw what Kelley had expected her to see. An air of resignation emanated from the ADA.

By contrast, Steadman's face darkened. Her eyes intensely scanning all three documents. Burke shook his head, almost imperceptibly.

Kelley let it sink in for a moment. "I call that a real curiosity." She grimaced as she slid more documents across the table. "If you'd look at these. They are also copies of the statements. You'll see four different color highlights on each. The colors are coded to specific phrases, each of which sounds more like an adult than a teenager. *Coerced me into having sex. Made suggestive remarks.*" She stopped with those. "Notice that those highlighted words are not only very adult, they are common across all three statements." She fell silent.

Everyone on the other side of the table remained silent. Lasorda stared at the three documents with the same look of recognition that she'd displayed earlier except that a hint of relief was included. Burke continued to shake his head. Steadman stared, her face continuing to darken, her eyes seemingly desperate to not see what she was seeing.

When Kelley spoke, it came out not a victorious gloat but rather as a reluctant call to consensus. "If you could, detectives, how would you characterize what you see here?"

Steadman closed her eyes as if she could shut out the truth. Burke glanced up. "Off hand, I'd say that the girls got help in writing their statements."

"And would that help most likely be from another student?" Kelley drilled down. Lainie knew that her friend was making sure they were all on the same page.

Burke shook his head. "No. An adult."

Kelley gazed at him for a moment. "In the interest of efficiency, I'm going to tell you what I think. Yes, an adult for sure but not one of the parents." She paused. "And it was not one of you." She paused.

Steadman opened her eyes and looked at Kelley, for the first time with anything other than hatred. She nodded.

"I have my own ideas about who it was but, since I have no real evidence, let's leave it for now. And I think it's fair to say that, although it does cast some doubt on the stories, it doesn't prove Paul Stafford's innocence. And that's my goal." Kelley gestured to Lainie.

"Miz Simpson has some additional information that might help. Lainie, you're on."

Lainie walked the group through the new information from Rosalee Chambers. She watched as their collective faces fell even further. As she concluded, she admitted the holes she saw. "So, this tells us the 'why' for Caryn Smallwood, I have to admit that I don't have a clue about the other two kids. And frankly, I don't think we'll ever know unless they tell us."

Lasorda shook her head. "Their parents have already said no. I guess we could bring them in and have the police interview them again." Her voice oozed resignation.

Steadman and Burke both continued to stare at the copies of the statements in front of them without speaking.

Lainie waded back in. "I don't think that's a good idea." She closed her eyes and prayed for the wisdom to do this right. "Look, I have to tell you, I think there's more here than we see. And I'm going out on a limb, but I'm willing to bet that the other two girls are also victims of this hoax. Interrogating them doesn't seem right to me." She paused as she watched the reaction on the other side of the table.

Lasorda furrowed her brow in what looked like curiosity. Burke shrugged but said nothing. Steadman seemed confused. She shook her head as if trying to shake water from her ears so she could hear better.

Lainie continued, "I think the best hope of getting at the truth while not destroying these girls would be to talk to one set of parents. I suggest Marianne Thompson's mother and father. She's the unlikeliest girl in the world to be a part of something like this. And if you look at the video recording of her interview with her parents there, they are engaged but seem reasonable."

Lasorda nodded. "I'll call and set it up."

Chapter 61

As the meeting broke up, Lasorda strode from the room as though on a mission. Burke and Steadman gathered their materials and spoke quietly to one another. Lainie watched as Kelley put her things together and kept an eye on the detectives at the same time. So far, everything had gone according to script. But what seemed to be unfolding was unfamiliar territory. Lainie put her copies into her briefcase and eased over toward the window to watch.

The two detectives started for the door. Kelley intercepted them. "Detective Steadman, could Lainie and I have a word in private with you?"

Burke narrowed his eyes and stared. Steadman looked over at Lainie and then to Kelley. "What's this about?"

Kelley shook her head. "Just another couple of questions, nothing major. And we didn't want to hold up the entire group." She looked over at Burke.

"I'll wait for you out front." He exited without waiting for a response.

Steadman leaned back against the table and faced Kelley. "So?"

"How well do you know Robert Tell?"

The color drained from the detective's face. She stared at Kelley for a long moment before offering a half-hearted rebuke. "That's none of your business."

Kelley nodded and lowered her gaze. She gestured to one chair and sat in the one next to it. "Look, Laura, let's clear the air here. We don't like each other. You don't like what I do, and I don't like the way you do what you do." She paused as she watched the other.

Steadman narrowed her eyes and shrugged.

Lainie now saw it. Only it looked far bigger and more menacing than she'd imagined.

Kelley continued, "This is that rare once-in-a-lifetime instance where our goals are aligned. We both want what's best for those three girls and we both want to see a perp taken off the streets. I'm asking you this here because I think that this is something we can do privately. No need to make a public issue of it."

Kelley's pronouncement stunned Lainie. As the hazy veil in this chain of events cleared, she could now see exactly where this was going.

Steadman nodded and lowered her gaze. "It's personal."

To Lainie's complete surprise, Kelley simply let it go. "Okay. Good." She looked down at her tablet for a moment before continuing. "I think it's probably a good assumption that you've never discussed this case with him." The words came out as a statement of fact. Kelley's face reinforced that. It wasn't even a question.

The detective nodded. "I would never discuss a case with anyone." An overly broad statement, to be sure, but Lainie got the gist. Apparently so did Kelley.

"I know that. Tell me, though, have you ever had discussions with him about the division's work in general. You know, things you look for, how to spot abused or exploited kids, that kind of thing?"

Steadman looked up, recognition in her eyes indicated that a light had popped on. "Yes. In fact, that's how I met him. He called our office and requested training on the subject of sexual predation. Because he works with kids, he wanted to know more about how to spot troubled children, signs of abuse or exploitation." Her eyes went wide and she drew back. "You don't think he…?" She didn't finish the question.

Kelley sighed. "Honestly detective, I don't think anything. The way I see it right now, Paul Stafford is guilty of nothing more than being in the wrong spot. It's easy to see why Caryn made up the story. But for the life of me, I can't figure out the other two. And more important, if you didn't help them with their statements, their parents didn't help them, and other students are out of the question, then who did? And why?"

Steadman stared. She looked like a woman who'd just been handed the worst news possible.

Kelley watched her for a moment. "I'm going to ask you for a favor, despite our differences. Please don't tell him we had this conversation. We need to gather facts and it may take a few days. No point in creating havoc"

Lainie knew this meant that Kelley didn't want the man warned. He'd already disappeared a few times and re-invented himself once.

Chapter 62

Lainie met Andi, Elliott, and Paul at Common Grounds. They had each polished off a couple of coffees and were debating lunch. "Hey guys." Lainie draped her coat on the back of a chair and pulled up to the small table.

"Sup." Elliott nodded, his signature understated greeting.

Paul gazed at her as if he wasn't sure how to greet her. Lainie smiled at him.

Andi turned her gaze from the menu, printed on a giant chalkboard in the front of the shop, to greet her. "Hi. How did it go?"

"About what we expected. Kelley went back to the office to catch up on some things. We can continue this conversation back at the office." Lainie turned her gaze to the large chalkboard. "We going to eat lunch here?'

Elliott offered one of his rare comments. "Paul said the Crusty Loaf is better. They have decent sandwiches as well as soups and salads. It's only a few blocks over."

Lainie shrugged. "Either way is fine with me." She remembered that she'd shared lunch with Paul at the Crusty Loaf. But that had been before.

"What's going to happen to the girls?" Paul's question came out of the blue and was not anything they'd spoken of.

As much as Lainie wanted to answer his question, she felt the pressure of being in a public place. "Why don't we talk about this later, back at my house."

His nod and furrowed brow told Lainie that he was worried about it, although he said nothing more. She wanted to explain about the different things that the ADA might take into account and the range of possible penalties but, knowing nothing about Juvenile Justice, she decided to let it go. She turned her attention back to lunch. "I say let's do the Crusty Loaf."

After lunch, Elliott and Andi headed to the office. Lainie and Paul started for home. He was his usual quiet self, seemingly focused on the scenery along the side streets as she navigated the suburbs. She wanted to talk to him about things. The case had changed today. The possibility of him being convicted had all but disappeared. The likelihood of exonerating him completely was a toss-up, but certainly not out of the question.

As of the time they left the meeting that morning, the trial was still on the calendar. She had no doubt that, between Kelley and Lasorda, it would not happen. The part that worried her was whether the ADA would drop the charges and smooth things over, which was her worst fear.

Luck was with her. She had no sooner pulled into the garage than her cell phone chimed. She retrieved it from her purse and checked the caller ID. "Hey, Kelley. Any news?"

"Yes. They left it on the calendar." She paused. "Look, I'll make this brief. You need to know and probably explain this to Paul as well. Eve's going to be under a lot of pressure to do something here. Children's advocates are going to be screaming for the trial, thinking Paul's guilty. Her boss is going to want this put to bed. The police are in a tough spot here. These kids are juveniles and we all suspect something else is behind this. But unless you and Lasorda can pry something out of the parents, we may have to cut our losses and take the dismissal. Sorry."

Lainie struggled to pull the meaning from the string of sentences. "Are you saying that she might end up taking this to trial?" After the morning meeting, she hadn't even considered that.

"No. Not a chance. She knows her case won't hold up. If she puts those kids on the stand, she could end up with an ethics violation trying to elicit testimony that she knows to be false. Also, like I said, she's a decent sort. She doesn't want to see them raked over the coals. Oh, by the way, she has an appointment to meet with the Thompsons tomorrow afternoon, two-thirty, at their house. But fair warning, they don't know you're going to be with her. Expect a hostile reception." Kelley laughed.

Lainie sighed. "Okay. I assume we'll meet up at her office around two. I'll connect with you in the morning."

***

They had a quiet dinner—leftover minestrone and a small salad. Paul opted for the soup, of which he ate maybe three or four bites.

Lainie put her spoon down and gazed across the table at him. "I'd have thought that you'd be happy. You're pretty much off the hook here. The case against you is non-existent and, depending on what Marianne's parents say tomorrow, you could be completely exonerated by the end of the week."

He peered into his soup bowl, spoon stalled just above the surface of the liquid. He furrowed his brow and shook his head. "I know they were wrong, but it shouldn't ruin their lives."

She couldn't believe what she'd heard. "Paul, I appreciate that you're not vindictive, but these girls didn't give a second thought to ruining your life."

He shrugged. "I'm an adult. I'm supposed to know how the world works. Stuff like this happens and I should have been able to handle it. I crumbled and that's my fault. But they don't deserve it. They're just kids."

Lainie thought about his words. They were kids but, then again, anything that happened to them would be through the kids' system anyway. "I'm sure that whatever trouble they're in won't be anything like what you've been through. Their cases will be handled through the juvenile justice system."

He set the spoon down beside the bowl and looked up at her. "What are you going to say to her parents?"

This was indeed the question. What do you say to parents when their model child does something completely out of character that nearly ruins a man's life, including a near suicide attempt? "I don't know yet. I guess I'll tell them what I know, which is only part of the story. I hope that they'll be willing to talk to Marianne and find out the answers to all the questions we have. I mean, I don't want to see her interrogated by the police any more than you or her parents do. But if they won't help, then I don't see any other choice. The ADA is not likely to just dismiss the charges and then let it all slide. People are going to want an explanation."

He nodded and stared down at his soup bowl, which was still more than three quarters full. "Okay."

As she watched him, a disturbing thought entered her mind. What if during his beating in jail he'd suffered brain damage. His near suicide attempt had been after that. And since then, he appeared to have trouble processing information. He seemed to struggle to understand what people told him. He spoke little. A lump formed in her throat.

She could feel her heart aching for him. He had tried to get her to date him. His infectious smile and disarming way of bumbling along had almost endeared him to her.

And then came this case. She'd turned on him. All he seemed to want was for her to believe him. He'd almost begged. But Lainie Simpson would not be made a fool of again. She would not be left with a handful of spaghetti, watching her life walk out the door. She would never again have to apologize to herself for being gullible.

And this was the result—a gentle, kind, and broken man sitting in front of her, struggling to come back from the brink. She paused on the cusp of telling him all of it. Lainie wanted him to understand why she'd been that way. Surely, he'd understand.

Then she realized that she didn't fully understand.

Chapter 63

Lainie met Eve Lasorda at the District Attorney's office just before two the next afternoon. They decided to ride out to the Thompson's together. She noticed that the ADA seemed more reserved, a distracted look on her face, worry in her eyes.

"I appreciate your doing this for us. This will mean a lot to Paul."

Lasorda nodded. "Yeah, well, this seems like the best idea all around. I have to say that this is one of the squirreliest cases I've ever dealt with. I get the Smallwood girl, you know, the distraction. But the other two—makes no sense. And on one hand, I don't have any real desire to put them under intense interrogation. But if we can't make this work for us today, I'm not seeing any other options."

Lainie nodded as she looked out the passenger side window of the ADA's deep blue series 5 BMW. After a brief pause, she glanced around at Lasorda. "Paul's worried about what's going to happen to the kids."

The ADA shrugged as she drove. "Go figure. They screw his life up to the point where he can probably never make it completely right, and he's worried about them. Takes all kinds, I guess."

"He just wasn't prepared for something like this. I mean, I watched the man crumble right in front of my eyes." She shook her head, tears starting to form.

"You know, people never think about what this kind of thing does to an innocent man. Everybody assumes that once someone is accused and charged, they're automatically guilty. I tell you, I live in fear of putting the wrong man away. I'm just glad the governor put a moratorium on capital punishment in Washington. I can't imagine what it would be like to send an innocent man to his death."

Lainie reflected on the fact that this could have happened to Paul—an innocent man's life was nearly ruined, almost ended. She shook it off as they rounded a corner in an upscale suburban neighborhood.

"Just up here, if I remember. I came out here initially to meet with the parents when this thing first fired up." Eve craned her neck looking at houses on the right-hand side of the street. "Ah, there it is, two one three."

She parked in the driveway but left her harness buckled. "Okay. Like Kelley told you, they don't know you're coming. I told them *we* needed to talk to them. Didn't say who *we* were. So, expect some pushback. I'll try to run interference to get us in. After that, you're up. Make it good." She released the harness, opened the door, and slid out.

Lainie reached down at her feet and retrieved her heavy briefcase, which carried the documents, some photographs, and a notebook computer. "Show time."

The Thompsons were apparently ready for them. The door opened within a couple of seconds of Lasorda ringing the bell. The two attorneys stood facing a man and a woman, both with somber, troubled looks on their faces. "Please, come in."

Eve stepped in first. Once Lainie entered and the door shut behind them, the ADA spoke. "Thanks for meeting with us, Mister and Missus Thompson. This is Lainie Simpson. She's an attorney representing Paul Stafford." The tone of her introduction suggested embarrassment and apology.

A change swept over Mr. Thompson like someone had tossed icy water over his head. The somber, pained look turned to rage. His facial muscles twitched as he clenched his jaw. His eyes initially widened and then narrowed abruptly. His breathing came in deep breaths as he glared at Lasorda. "We told you. They cannot talk to our daughter."

Lainie noticed that Ms. Thompson had a much different look on her face. She glanced at Lainie, closing her eyes and then bowing her head as if in resignation.

Lainie stepped forward as Lasorda nodded in her direction. "Actually, we're not here to speak with Marianne. We're here to talk to you." She held her briefcase handle with both hands, to avoid the awkwardness of the absence of handshakes.

He glared at her. "You've got some nerve, showing your face here after what that man did." His arms hung at his sides with fists clenched.

Lainie lowered her gaze and nodded. "I understand how you feel. And I'll try to make this as quick as I can, I promise."

"We have nothing to say to you." He used the pronoun *we* although his wife's demeanor suggested the two were not of a single mind.

Lainie nodded. "I know. And I don't have any questions for you. I've come to tell you some things. I asked Assistant District Attorney Lasorda to accompany me for two reasons. First, I want to be clear with everyone that I'm not trying to sneak around and conduct business in the shadows. Everything I'm saying and doing I want to be out in the open. Second, everything I'm about to share with you, I've already told her. If you doubt my word, you have only to ask her."

An uncomfortable silence descended and cloaked the group for a moment. Ms. Thompson broke the impasse. "We can sit at the dining room table." She paused and shook her head. "Better than standing around, I guess."

Lainie positioned herself across the table from Mr. Thompson, who sat next to his wife. Eve parked on the far end of the table. "Before I start in with the things I want to talk about, I want to show you some photographs." She took out the same photos she'd shared with Lasorda a few days before. She turned them so that they were right side up to him and gently slid them across the table. "There are pictures I took last week of Paul Stafford's home."

Mister Thompson glanced down and then glared at her. "We had nothing to do with that." He sat with his arms folded on his chest. "But I can't say that it upsets me very much."

"Understandable." Lainie nodded. "Probably also worth saying that his life is being destroyed pretty much like his home is."

"Maybe he should have thought about that before he...." His words trailed off into silence.

Lainie took a deep breath and bit her tongue. "Yes, well, I'll put these aside for now and get to what I wanted to talk about." She reached into her briefcase, which was situated on the floor beside her chair, and pulled out three sheets of paper that were stapled together. Handing a copy to each of the parents, she spoke softly. "This is a photocopy of your daughter's statement to the police." She caught his eye as he looked up from the paper. "Have you read this?"

He glanced down at it and then immediately up. "I looked at it, yeah."

Lainie considered him for a moment and then glanced at his wife. "Yes, you looked at it. From the look on your wife's face, I'd say she read it word-for-word, probably a couple of times."

Ms. Thompson did not take her eyes off the paper in front of her. Her eyes appeared to be filling with tears.

"And I'm going to take a guess here, but I'd be willing to bet that your wife knows what I'm about to tell you. I suspect she's known it all along." Lainie pressed gently.

Ms. Thompson continued to stare down, shaking her head as though willing away the entire mess.

"Mister Thompson, that statement is a fabrication. There may be an element or two of fact buried in there somewhere, but anything relating to Paul Stafford is simply not true."

Thompson's face went beet red. He pounded a fist on the table, his jaw clenched even tighter. "My daughter is not a liar."

Lainie shook her head. "No. She's not. And that's why I'm here." She shifted in her seat and placed her hands flat on the tabletop in front of her. "I'm a defense attorney. If all I wanted was to see Paul Stafford acquitted or the charges dropped, I wouldn't be here. I'd be out celebrating with my client. All three of the statements are fabrications. I can sit here and walk you through the proof if you like, but I think Missus Thompson already knows. Some of this may be your daughter's words but the key parts, the accusations, are not. We've gone over all of this with the police and the ADA. If you doubt my word, ask Miz Lasorda."

He jerked his head toward Eve, who lowered her head and nodded.

When he turned back to Lainie, some confusion had found its way onto the mask of rage.

Before he could respond, Lainie continued. "I'd like you to see something." She reached down and retrieved the notebook computer. Opening it, she depressed the power button, waking it up from sleep mode. The media app was up, and a video queued. She moved the device to the center of the table, offset by a couple of feet so both the Thompsons and she could see it. Eve, sitting at the far end of the table, had the best view.

Before depressing the play button, she explained, "This is not anything you haven't seen. It's your daughter's interview with the police and the two of you were there. I'll be starting and stopping it from time to time with some explanation. What you're going to see first is a confident, smiling, sincere-looking young woman. Watch the way that she makes eye contact and describes things." Lainie pressed the play button.

Mr. Thompson watched, a pained look on his face as though he were re-living a nightmare. His wife looked up at the video from time to time but appeared to focus all of her attention on the paper in front of her. The young girl on the screen glided through her statement with apparent ease. Then Lainie stopped the show.

"What you're going to see next is where she begins to talk about an interaction with Principal Stafford. Watch the change in her demeanor, her speech, and her interaction with the police." She pressed the play button again.

A change swept over the girl in the movie. She began to stutter and pause. She lowered her head and wouldn't look at Laura Steadman, who was conducting the interview. The detective prompted her a couple of times with questions like, "And then what happened?" and "What did he do then?" Marianne continued to stumble, shaking her head almost imperceptibly. Finally, she managed to get a couple of sentences strung together but stopped abruptly in mid-sentence.

After a couple of attempts to prompt her again, the detective filled in the rest of the sentence for her, in the form of a question. "And you said here in your statement that he told you he wanted to fondle your breasts. Is that correct?"

The young girl looked as if she was trying to disappear. Her shoulders and arms pulled in to her side. She rigidly stared down. The nod was barely visible. Lainie hit the pause button again.

"You see the difference? When she discussed being at school, hanging out in the lunchroom, and talking to her friends, she seemed relaxed, sincere, and almost conversational with the detective. The minute she hit the point where she supposedly interacted with the principal, she changed like day into night."

Mr. Thompson shook his head. "That means nothing. She was just embarrassed by what that man put her through. That's why she acted that way." He glared, although a sliver of doubt appeared to hover in his eyes.

Lainie studied him for a moment without speaking and then hit the play button again. The young girl returned to her calm, pleasant conversation with the detective. The scene repeated itself several times, always in the same sequence. When the video ended, she said, "Mister Thompson, you had it right the first time. Your daughter is not a liar. She did fine right up until the point where the story turns to Paul Stafford and then she clams up. I think you know as well as I do, she struggled with something that she knew in her heart was not true."

She closed the notebook and put it in her briefcase. "Your daughter is without a doubt becoming a fine young woman. She's respected by teachers and students alike. She's an exemplary student with a wonderful life unfolding in front of her. And to be honest, I have no idea why she did this. As I said, we know the statements are not true. We know something about how all of this started. But how your daughter came to be involved, I don't have a clue."

The couple across the table sat, he with a stunned look on his face, she with tears dripping on the pages in front of her.

Lainie pushed just a bit harder. "But here's the problem. Making a false statement to a police officer is a misdemeanor crime. As the photos earlier showed, Paul Stafford's home and his life have been all but wrecked. And as I said earlier, we have enough here to get the charges tossed. But all of us, you, me, and Paul Stafford, we all want the truth. And I can promise you, no one wants to see your daughter hurt."

She paused and gazed to the end of the table, catching Eve's eye. "I can't speak for the District Attorney's office or the police. But I am pretty confident that if your daughter can talk to them and help straighten this out, the legal consequences would be far lighter, especially since she's still a juvenile. I'm pretty sure that Miz Lasorda is not going to take this to trial, but if she did, Marianne would be called to testify. If she lied under oath, that would be perjury, a felony, much more serious."

Lainie let the words and the reality settle for a moment. "I won't take any more of your time tonight." She wanted to offer them something—comfort, encouragement, anything—but she could see that they had stopped listening, descending into their own personal hell, perhaps.

Chapter 64

Lainie dragged herself into the house just after five-thirty that afternoon. The session with the Thompsons had left her physically and emotionally exhausted. The aroma, a combination of ginger and garlic, hit her full on as she walked through the door between the garage and kitchen. "Something smells delicious."

Paul stood at the stove, a wooden spoon in his hand, stirring a mixture in her large skillet. The floral apron over his jeans and tee shirt seemed a bit comical. He twisted his head to look at her. "Nothing special. Just some chicken stir fry."

Lainie arched her brow. "Hmmm. Didn't know I had any of that stuff here." She nodded toward the pan.

He returned his gaze to his creation. "I walked down the store and picked up some things."

A fleeting thought crossed her mind. This seemed a lot like having live-in help. He seemed to be keeping the place straight and had dinner ready for her in the evening. She almost popped off a humorous comment about it but thought better of it.

Staring down at the concoction, Paul changed the subject. "How did your meeting with Marianne's parents go?" The question came out soft, with a hint of pain.

Lainie played it down. "About what you'd expect. They didn't want to believe that their daughter would do something like that. Hit them pretty hard. Hopefully, they'll talk to her and get her to come clean."

He continued to stir as he stared at the vegetables, his head nodding slowly as if trying to process the information.

She shed her raincoat and started for the closet. "I'm going to get changed. Be out in a few." As she made her way to the master bedroom, she heard her cellphone ring. She'd left it on the kitchen counter. After an abrupt about-face, she strode toward the sound. The caller ID read *Abramson, T.* A moment of doubt coursed through her mind until it clicked—Paul's ex-wife.

Lainie pressed the connect icon. "Hello." She strolled into the living room as she spoke, prepared to move down the hall if the conversation warranted it.

"Hi. This is Terri Abramson, you know, Paul Stafford's ex-wife. I'm sorry to bother you but I'm really worried about him. I don't have his phone number so I went over to his house and, God, the place is wrecked. And he wasn't there." The voice sounded frantic.

Lainie strode casually toward her bedroom. "Yes, I know. We have Paul put up here at my place until this is all over."

An awkward silence descended. When the woman spoke again, the tone had evolved into confusion. "Oh. I didn't know the two of you were—"

Lainie interrupted. "We're not. I have a spare bedroom at my place, and we couldn't leave him there. You saw his house. Once he is exonerated, he'll go back and get the place fixed up, I'm sure." She didn't have the slightest idea how that might happen, but it sounded good.

"Okay, good. I was wondering if I could come over and see him?"

"That's something you'd need to talk to him about. Hang on and I'll get him." Lainie ambled into the kitchen and handed the phone to Paul. "It's Terri." She left him alone and made her way back to the bedroom and changed into jeans and a sweatshirt.

Dinner turned out to be a subdued event. Paul seemed pre-occupied, moving his food around the plate rather than eating.

Between bites, Lainie, prodded him. "You're missing a great meal here. This is fantastic."

He glanced up at her and nodded. He spoke after a long moment of awkward silence. "Terri wanted to come over and see me. I told her where you live. I hope you don't mind." His eyes conveyed genuine concern, as if he was a kid expecting a scolding.

"Of course I don't mind." She paused as she searched his eyes for some hint of how he felt about it. "She seemed really worried. You don't talk to her much?"

He shrugged and went back to shifting the positions of the chicken and vegetables.

After dinner, the two of them did the dishes. Rather than stacking the dishwasher, Lainie washed them by hand. Paul took them from her, dried them, and put them away. Lainie thought it interesting that he knew where everything went. Just as they finished wiping down the counter and stove, the doorbell rang.

She opened it to find Terri Abramson. "Come in." She turned toward the hallway, which Paul had just transited on his way to his bedroom. "Paul, Terri's here."

He'd apparently heard the bell and shuffled into the living room, his socked feet dragging the carpet.

His ex-wife strode across the room and embraced him tightly. "Hey there. How you doing?"

Lainie felt a pang of jealousy. "I have a pot of fresh coffee and the hot water's on for tea if you'd like some."

Paul spoke up. "I'd like coffee, but I can get it." He turned to Terri. "Anything?"

"I've got some things to do back in my study. Give me a shout if you need anything."

The two nodded but said nothing as Lainie skulked back to her writing desk.

She emerged an hour and a half later to find Paul sitting on the couch with a cup of coffee, staring out the front window. "Oh, Terri leave already?"

He turned his head in her direction, as if surprised by the sound. "Yeah. She just stopped by to check on me."

Lainie eased over and sat down beside him. "It's like I told you, there are lots of people who care about you."

Paul furrowed his brow as if trying to decipher what she'd said. He shook his head as he spoke. "She feels sorry for me. Just pity."

She touched his shoulder. "Paul, there's a big difference between someone feeling bad about what's happened and pity. I don't know Terri very well, but off-hand, I'd say that she's not the type to dole out pity."

He looked down, his head nodding slowly.

His mannerisms, especially when responding to things said to him, worried her. "I need to ask you something, and please don't be offended. When you speak or do things, you seem to be fine. You make sense when you talk. You manage complex tasks like getting what you need to make really good meals. But when I or anyone else speaks to you, it's like you have trouble understanding. Are you okay?" The question sounded stupid, but she couldn't think of any other way to put it.

He gazed up at her for a moment. "Yes. I guess. I mean, I can think okay. And I seem to be able to say what I think. When other people say things, I understand the words. I just have to think about how they fit together and what the overall meaning is." He paused for a moment, studying her as if looking for understanding in her eyes. "But I notice that it's getting better."

"Paul, maybe you should see a doctor and have tests done. You could have some serious injuries that you don't know about." She almost said *from your episode at the jail*, but she thought better of it.

He shrugged. "Why? What good would that do?"

She smirked. "What good? I'll tell you what good. If you have brain damage from your injuries, then the state is liable."

He shook his head. "It's getting better. And I just want all this to be over, so I can go back to being a person again."

Chapter 65

By ten that evening, the day had taken its toll on Lainie. The interview with the Thompsons and then the visit by Paul's ex had left her with that feeling of trying to cram ten pounds of rock into a five-pound bag. She felt like her mind and her heart had maxed out. Her cellphone chimed and competed with the call of her bed. She glanced at the caller ID and frowned. *Why would she call at this hour of the night?*

"Hey Kelley, what's up?"

"You see the six o'clock news tonight?"

"Nope. Dinner and then had a visitor. Anything in particular?" She leaned on the kitchen counter and stared into the living room at Paul, sitting on the couch.

"I was going to call you earlier but it slipped my mind. Yeah, that guy Tell. Maybe just more of his blowhard bullshit, but you may want to catch a re-run at eleven."

Lainie glanced at the clock. "Okay. Will do. Anything on for tomorrow?"

Kelley's response followed a brief pause. "Maybe. I didn't get a chance to talk to Lasorda today after your meeting so I'm not really sure about her intentions. The trial's still on but I can't believe she'd let it go that far. Elliott did manage to uncover some interesting stuff."

The last statement piqued Lainie's interest. "What?"

"Eh, too complicated for the phone. Besides, he'd do a better job of explaining. Why don't we try to get together at nine?"

"You want Paul there?" Lainie suddenly found it odd that they had taken to deciding whether they want their client present during discussions.

"Yes. He needs to hear this."

After the phone call, Lainie parked in the overstuffed chair sitting across from the sofa. The information that Elliott had found something new had no effect on Paul. He nodded and shrugged. They chatted idly about everything and nothing until eleven. She felt a little uneasy about him sitting there watching whatever sewage spewed from Tell but couldn't think of a diplomatic way of getting him out of the room.

The local news had the story buried three deep. It came on just after the first commercial break. The perky blonde anchorwoman, organizing a small stack of papers introduced the video footage. "In the ongoing story of a sexual assault case involving East Rainier High School principal Paul Stafford, Pastor Robert Tell held yet another rally near City Hall today."

Her in-studio image cut only to be replaced by a video recording of the firebrand minister.

> *We learned today that there's been a delay in the trial. We should have expected this. The servants of Satan are marshalling their forces to attack these three young innocent girls who have done nothing but relate their nightmare. This is what happens when we entrust our most precious resource, our children, to Godless snakes of the night. Even now they are plotting to rip the young women*

*apart, to put every aspect of their lives under
a microscope. To blame them for the evil that
was visited upon them.*

He swept a shock of dark hair from his forehead, his brown eyes flashing. He held a book to his heart with his left hand while holding his right arm in the air, fist balled. "We will not stand idly by and allow this. We will take to the streets. We will march to the lair of these serpents. We will hold back no effort to protect our children."

The image cut back to the anchorwoman. "Pastor Tell did not offer any specifics about his plans. The District Attorney's office responded saying that the case was still under investigation and that there was no delay. They would not comment on any developments in the case citing their reluctance to try the case in the court of public opinion." And the station cut to commercial.

Paul watched the screen with little visible reaction. He tilted his head slightly and furrowed his brow as if trying to take it all in and make sense of it.

"I know that we asked you this before, Paul, but have you ever had any issues or contact with this guy?" Lainie couldn't figure out why he'd chosen to champion this particular case.

He gazed at her for a moment and then shrugged. "No. I mean, I've seen him speak on TV before, but I don't recall ever having met him."

Chapter 66

Lainie and Paul beat the rush and arrived in the conference room about ten minutes ahead of the scheduled meeting. They were early enough that the regular protest crowd outside the building hadn't shown up yet. Kelley had opened up and remained in her private office going over some papers. Andi and Elliott hadn't yet shown their faces.

Lainie set her briefcase down beside her chair. "You know, I think I'm going to run across the street and grab some coffee and stuff. What would you like?"

Paul shook his head, almost imperceptibly. "I'm okay. Thanks." The words came out soft and slow.

She stopped by Kelley's office and got her latte order before heading over to the small bistro. "What do the kids normally drink?"

Kelley chuckled. "Get 'em lattes. They'll like it or do without."

When Lainie returned, she brought lattes all around, even for Paul, along with a bag of black currant scones. By this time Andi and Elliott had taken their traditional seats, side-by-side. Their off-beat affection for one another had become a bit more obvious with time.

Kelley broke off a piece of scone and held it up in front of her face as she spoke. "You got no business parading these things in front of me. I have a hard enough time as it is." She added a chuckle. "Lainie, why don't you fill us in on the meeting yesterday before Elliott swamps us with technical jargon."

Lainie sucked some of the foam from the top of her latte before setting it aside. "Pretty much what we discussed ahead of time. I didn't go into a lot of detail."

Andi jumped in. "How'd they take it?"

"About how you'd expect parents to take that kind of thing. As for Mister Thompson, it was disbelief at first, then, well, I guess you'd say despondence." After a brief pause, she added, "I did get the impression that Miz Thompson already knew that something was wrong with the statement. Nothing I said seemed to surprise her.

Kelley studied her for a moment. "And?"

Lainie knew exactly what she was asking. "I gave them the pitch, you know, having her come in and clear things up. I guess we'll see soon enough."

Kelley scribbled some notes on her pad as she spoke. "I hope so. I mean, we can discredit the statements easily enough and we even have a motive of sorts. And that will be enough to get the case tossed. But it doesn't prove his innocence. Just because the statements are constructed doesn't mean they're false."

"But they are false." Paul's voice exuded desperation.

Kelley eyed him for a moment. "Yes. You know that and we know that. And I suspect even the prosecutor and police know that. But that doesn't mean that they've exonerated you. It just means that they won't convict you. In fact, if nothing else happens between now and Monday, I suspect that Lasorda will simply drop the charges for lack of evidence. After that, finding the truth is a more complicated problem."

Paul looked from one face to another around the room, a look of urgency in his eyes. He appeared on the cusp of throwing another argument out but instead shook his head and fell silent.

Kelley offered up a smile and moved on. "Okay, Elliott, you're up."

Lainie was caught off-guard by the young man's passion and focus. Up until this point, he hadn't even appeared to show much interest in the case.

He leaned forward, tapping his finger on the table to emphasize points. "I was able to get some video footage from the school. I used the dates of the supposed incidents as anchors and looked at both sides of them by five school days, just on the chance that the girls were off by a day or so. We got footage from the hall cameras, which show the entrance to the admin offices, where the principal hangs out. We also have footage showing both entrances to the lunchroom and inside the lunchroom."

He paused, narrowed his eyes and nodded, as if organizing facts before he spoke. "Nothing at all showing any of the girls going into the office any time either side of the dates. This is most important for Caryn Smallwood, who said the sex happened in the principal's office. She was nowhere near that office at any time during those days. The other girls said he hit on them in the lunchroom. Again, no sign of Paul in or around the lunchroom on any of those days." He fell silent and moved his gaze from one face to the other. No one had questions.

He leaned back and slouched into his usual "nearly asleep" position. "I also went back and looked at the lunchroom footage from last fall, when Paul did talk to Marianne. You know, the discussion he told us about." She turned his computer so that Kelley, sitting on the end, as well as Lainie and Paul sitting across the table, could see. He depressed a key and a video began to play. Although there was no audio, it wasn't hard for Lainie to interpret what was going on.

Paul stood with his back to the camera. Marianne faced him with several other girls around her. They stood about three feet apart. She could be seen speaking, smiling, and then laughing. He nodded and appeared to say something. After a few seconds, he turned away from her, waving in the process. He strode out of view of the camera.

Elliott hit another key and the video froze. "So, nothing there. Looks like it went down just like Paul said—a short, casual conversation. He didn't linger. She didn't appear intimidated or offended to me. Besides, she had other girls around her at the time and there was no reaction from any of them." He shrugged.

Kelley pulled her chair closer to the table and broke off another piece of scone. "Okay, again, this doesn't prove that there was no sex. It just means that the statements are wrong. And it brings us back to the same place we always end up. We need for one of the girls to come clean. That's the only way that I can see to prove him innocent. Otherwise, it ends up as a 'not enough evidence' case, which will leave Paul in that in-between land."

She glanced down at the papers in front of her and then continued slowly. "Here's the complicating factor. This Tell guy, he's paving the way to push back if the credibility of the girls is questioned. While I personally don't care about him, other than to think he's an asshole, this goes into the mix with all of his other crap. And it becomes political. As far as the case goes, it won't make any real difference. They can't convict Paul without evidence. But it can make his ongoing life miserable."

Paul hung his head and closed his eyes.

Chapter 67

The group finished up before eleven. Lainie wanted clarity on the plan, the contingencies—just in case. She knew, though, that everything hinged on Lasorda's decision. Kelley said that she'd contact the DA's office that afternoon.

The lead attorney shuffled her papers together and stood as the meeting broke up. "I'll call Lasorda this afternoon. If we don't get something by nine on Monday, I'll file a motion to dismiss. I suspect she won't oppose it." She smirked and shook her head. "And as far as we're concerned, the case would simply fade into oblivion. Not sure how hard she'd lean on the kids for the false statements. They might just shuffle it off on the juvies and call it a day. Anyway, why don't you two meet us here, say, eight-thirty?"

Lainie nodded. "Okay. But give me a call right away if anything breaks." She turned to Paul. "Let's swing by the Crusty Loaf and grab a sandwich."

He forced a smile and nodded.

***

Saturday morning dawned clear. Lainie rose just after six, an anxious feeling eating at her. *I need to get on those chapters. I promised Meg.* Over the last few days, she'd largely ignored her fictional dilemma. Her editor wanted a developing love interest by the end of the second novel. But Lainie hadn't a clue as to how that might happen.

She parked in the large, overstuffed chair with her cup of coffee and stared out the window waiting for inspiration.

"Good morning." The voice floating in from the hallway pulled her out of her reverie. Paul shuffled barefoot wearing a pair of jeans and a navy-blue tee shirt. This was the first time that she'd actually heard him greet her quite like that. Up until this point, he usually just nodded and avoided her gaze.

"Hey there. Coffee's still somewhat fresh." She nodded toward the kitchen.

He glided into the living room holding his cup with both hands. He eased down on the couch, placing his cup on a coaster sitting on the coffee table. As he sat there, he gazed down as he wrung his hands. "Lainie," he spoke without looking up. "I know I've been really weird. I could actually feel myself being that way but I couldn't seem to stop."

He paused and looked at her. "But I wanted to thank you. You know, for… I guess for everything. I couldn't have gone through this without your help."

To say that this caught her by surprise would be an understatement. She nodded and smiled, although it seemed to require more effort than she'd expected. "I wish we could have done more, I mean, to stop all of this madness before it really started. No one should have to experience what you've been through."

He chuckled, a rarity. "People go through worse." His face grew serious again. "I'm getting better. I can feel it. I just wanted you to know how grateful I am."

Out of the blue, a realization hit her. She'd forgotten to do the grocery shopping Friday afternoon. "Oh crap. It's Saturday and I didn't get to the store yesterday."

He shrugged. "I can walk down there if you like."

Lainie laughed. "I'm not thinking so. I need to buy groceries for the week. And Saturday doesn't work well for me."

He returned her laugh. "I remember."

She recalled the day that she'd backed into him, setting all of this in motion, quite by accident. Lainie shook her head. "Yeah, I guess you do. You got the short end of that straw."

Paul smiled softly. "Oh, not so much. If that hadn't happened, I wouldn't have had a good attorney. Maybe I'd be in prison already. Maybe I'd be...." His words trailed off as the smile faded.

An uncomfortable silence swooped in. Before she could attempt a resurrection of his good mood, her cell phone rang. Her screen showed the number as blocked. She glanced at the clock. "Who would be calling at eight on a Saturday morning." She connected. "Hello."

"Lainie, this is Eve Lasorda. Sorry to roust you on a Saturday. If you're willing, I need you in my office in half an hour. The Thompsons are bringing Marianne in to talk to us."

Chapter 68

Lainie cursed the Saturday afternoon leisure drivers as she navigated through work zones and backed up turn lanes on the way to the District Attorney's office. "Shit! Could you please get the lead out? For God's sake, just make the freaking turn."

She pulled into the parking lot some forty minutes later, shaking her head and muttering under her breath. She bolted from the car, briefcase in hand, headed for the large masonry and glass building. As she approached the door, the thought occurred to her that it was Saturday afternoon. Would the door even be open? As she drew closer, she saw Lasorda standing just inside. As Lainie strode up, the ADA opened the door enough to let her in and then allowed it to close and lock behind them.

Eve's words came out in a clipped, no-nonsense cadence. "Miz Thompson has Marianne in the second-floor conference room with Detective Steadman. Mister Thompson is in my office. I think you should hear what he has to say first." She strode toward the elevator.

Lainie wondered whether having Steadman there was a good idea, although she couldn't say why it bothered her. Something teased at the edge of her mind. She shook her head and shrugged.

Mr. Thompson presented a very different image from the angry, confrontational father she'd spoken to the previous Thursday. He wore a haggard look, a downcast face staring at the hands that he wrung in his lap. He remained seated, not reacting as Lainie and Eve entered.

"Good afternoon, Mister Thompson." Lainie started to say that it was good to see him again, but likely that wasn't what he needed to hear. "Thank you for bringing Marianne in." At least she hoped it would be something worth thanking him for.

He looked up at her, puffy bags beneath his red, bloodshot eyes. "We tried to talk to her, like you said." He shook his head, a look that combined confusion and fear in his eyes. "But then she started saying strange things, things that we didn't understand. It's like she's someone else. Please help us."

The words hit Lainie like a punch in the stomach. She had been anxious to interview the girl, but now…. She struggled to catch her breath and looked over at Lasorda, who likewise wore a troubled look. "Mister Thompson, I'm an attorney. And I represent the man she accused. I'm not sure that I'm really the right person to help."

He shook his head. "Marianne's a good girl. Something's just gone wrong. We can take her to a therapist or something, but the trial's coming up and I don't want her in trouble. We need to do something today." The words came out frantic, grasping.

She looked again at the ADA with an arched brow.

Eve provided a soft, reassuring response. "Lainie, I don't want that girl interrogated. And you asked to talk to her. This is your chance."

Lainie shook her head. "I don't know, Eve. This seems awfully risky, I mean to Marianne. It's one thing to interview a witness to get information. But if she's having… problems, maybe she needs someone who's trained in this kind of thing. I'm just a lawyer."

The ADA implored her, "I know. But could you at least give it a shot. We can shut it down if it looks like it's not going well."

Mister Thompson shifted his gaze back and forth between Lainie and Eve, but said nothing.

Lainie sighed. "Okay. Let's try. But, seriously, if things start to slip, I'm going to call a halt." She turned to Mister Thompson. "And you also need to be watching and shut it down if you have any concerns." She wondered in passing how much liability she would be assuming.

If her parents appeared to be nervous wrecks, Marianne Thompson seemed anything but. She sat, hands folded motionless on the table in front of her. A soft smile painted her face, her eyes bright and welcoming.

Detective Steadman sat in a chair against the wall, a dark, troubled look on her face. She nodded but didn't speak as Thompson, Lainie, and Eve entered the room.

Lainie took a quick look around at the players before taking a seat at the table directly across from the young woman. She set her briefcase on the floor at her feet and placed her hands on the table in an effort to anchor herself. The Thompsons sat on either side of their daughter while Lasorda parked at the head of the table.

"Hello, Marianne. May I call you Marianne?" Lainie smiled.

The question drew an even more welcoming smile. "Of course."

"I'm Lainie Simpson." She reached across, offering her hand, which the young girl shook. "When I spoke with your parents the other day, I tried to be really honest with them so I'm going to do the same with you. I want you to know that

I work for Principal Paul Stafford. I'm his attorney. And I'm representing his interests. I just want to make sure that you understand that."

Marianne nodded, the smile never leaving her face. Serenity—that was the look. Her dreamy hazel eyes framed by her mousy blonde hair locked on Lainie's. Her relatively tall stature—maybe five eight or five nine—accentuated her trim build. She tilted her head slightly, eyes wide, as she spoke. "Oh. How is Principal Stafford?"

The question stunned Lainie. How should he be after all that he'd been through? She looked over at Eve and then at Steadman but neither displayed any reaction. She shook her head. "Well, I guess I'd say he's had kind of a hard time with all of this." The question caught her off-guard.

But the young girl acted as though this was the most natural conversation imaginable. "I'm sorry to hear that. I hope he gets better." She paused and looked down for a moment. "Anyway, please tell him that I said hello."

Lainie's confusion and distress deepened. Could this be a conversation with a young girl that had accused a man of attempting to coerce sex from her?

Mildred, for once, appeared to be on her side. *Yes. Something's not right here.*

She ignored the voice and bought some time to organize her thoughts to this new reality by reaching down into her briefcase and retrieving a copy of Marianne's statement. She placed the copy on the table between them. "Marianne, I've been reading over the statement that you gave the police. I have to say, this is a well-done statement. It has a lot of details. Very thorough."

"Thank you." She nodded, the smiling look of peace on her face not changing.

Lainie glanced at the two parents, both of whom looked bewildered. Mr. Thompson gazed at his hands, resting on the tabletop and subtly shook his head. Ms. Thompson stared at some indefinite point in space midway between the surface of the table and Lainie's eyes.

"Could you tell me a little about how you organized it? I mean, it must have taken a lot of effort to remember it all and set everything in the right order." She tried to pick her words carefully. Nothing felt familiar or right.

The gentle smile evolved into a soft laugh. "It was hard." She paused and narrowed her eyes, allowing her gaze to drift downward slightly. "I mostly just prayed about it—a lot."

"When you say you prayed, do you mean, like up in your room? You'd pray and then do some writing and then maybe pray some more? Like that?" The introduction of religion put Lainie even further off balance.

Marianne looked up and to the right as she appeared to think. "Well, maybe some of it. But mostly we prayed down at the church." She finished with a definitive nod, the smile returning.

Lainie made a note on the pad in front of her—*We?* "Marianne, when you say 'we,' who are you talking about?"

"Oh, that was Debbie, Caryn, and me. And of course, Pastor Bob." Her hands remained folded, unmoving on the table in front of her.

The delivery unnerved Lainie. The girl seemed in a trance. "Help me understand here. When you, all of you, prayed down at the church, was it like a silent prayer where each of you prayed for yourself?" Now Lainie was definitely out of her element. This seemed more like spiritual counseling than lawyering.

The soft laugh returned. "Not really. I mean, yes, some of it. But Pastor Bob had to help us. We can all talk to God, but our souls are not ready to hear his voice. That's why Pastor Bob spoke for us and then helped us to understand God's word."

"God told you what to write?"

"Yes. But it was hard to understand. He first had to help us see that what we remembered wasn't right. You know, human memory is really flawed. So, the first thing is that he helped us to know what had really happened."

Lainie knew she needed to nail this part. "If I understand what you're saying, you all prayed and then Pastor Bob revealed to you what God had told him, you know, about what actually happened."

The smile broadened, and Marianne nodded firmly. "Exactly. Once we understood what had happened, then he helped us to write it all down."

Lainie looked over at Eve, whose face had darkened. The ADA nodded discretely.

"Marianne, can I ask you, when you spoke with Detective Steadman about your statement, is that why you hesitated at certain parts? You didn't really remember that well and you were relying on God for those details?"

The dreamy look returned. Marianne's gaze drifted slightly up and to the side, a faraway look in her eyes. "Yes. I mean, now that God told me those things, I know that they're true. I just don't really remember it that well."

And that was it—finished. That should have been enough for Lasorda. Lainie looked down at the ADA with arched eyebrows, hoping that Eve caught the question. Can we end this?

Lasorda gestured with a slight shake of her head. The message was clear—*Don't stop now.*

Lainie mentally organized the next set of questions. Raising her gaze to rest on Marianne's face, she continued, "Could you tell me how all of this started?" The question felt right.

Marianne shrugged. "Oh, yes. That's easy. Caryn got in trouble at school. I heard her talking to some friends about how the English teacher accused her of cheating and it was going to ruin her life. I'm not really good friends with her or anything, but I overheard it. So, I talked to her. I told her that God could help her out. She laughed at me, well, at first. But I told her that he helped all kinds of people. She just needed to give him a chance. So, she agreed to see Pastor Bob. And then he asked Debbie and me if we would be willing to help out, you know, to do God's work."

Something didn't fit. Why would he do this to get a cheater off the hook at school? As Lainie tried to assemble the puzzle pieces in her mind, a horrendous image flashed across her mind. She needed to end this.

Mildred disagreed. *You can't. You're in the middle of the swamp. You can't leave her here alone.*

Chapter 69

Middle of the swamp—that was an understatement. The worst part was that Lainie had no sense of where solid ground might be found. She decided to take a step back. "Marianne, how did you know that Pastor Bob would help Caryn? After all, she didn't know him and he didn't know her."

The young girl drew her mouth into a tight line and shook her head. The look seemed one of frustration at Lainie's apparent lack of understanding. "God doesn't work that way. He helps anyone who asks. Pastor Bob tells us that all the time. We need only turn to him and ask."

"Then Pastor Bob helps a lot of people with their problems?"

Her smile returned. "Yes. Well, I'm sure he would help anyone, but mostly us kids. He says that the people around us don't understand just how painful and serious our problems are. But God knows. He helps us to find the way."

Lainie cringed at what she wanted to ask next. "Marianne, has Pastor Bob ever helped you out with a problem."

A dark look swept across the girl's face. She lowered her gaze. "We're all sinners. The only path to redemption is through God."

But that wasn't an answer. And, on reflection, Lainie knew that the question was not relevant to her case. Still, she held her silence and waited.

Marianne glanced over at her mother and father, lowering her gaze after that. "I'm sorry, Mom, Dad. I made mistakes. I sinned." She looked up, plaintively at her mother. "I wanted to tell you but I couldn't." Tears formed in her eyes but she said nothing else for a few moments.

Lainie, meanwhile, couldn't help feeling that she'd wandered into something that no one here at the table was prepared for. She glanced over at Eve, whose eyes reflected the same sentiment. When she shifted her gaze to Steadman, a very different look awaited her. The darkness that had crossed the detective's face had evolved into a combination of rage and grief. Somehow, though, Lainie knew this was not meant for her or for Paul.

Then she remembered why she was reluctant about Steadman being there. She was Tell's lover.

Marianne's voice interrupted her wild careening thoughts. "I know, I should have told you. Last summer," the young girl lowered her gaze and wiped at her eyes with her hand. "I let a boy use my body. I sinned and God punished me." She sniffed and wiped again. "He put a curse on me."

Silence enveloped the room. Lainie desperately wanted to tell the girl to stop talking. The group didn't need to hear this. She didn't want to hear this.

But the confession continued. "I was just starting to go to Pastor Bob's youth meetings. So, I talked to him about it." She looked up and around the table, her eyes shining, the smile returning to her face. "And he told me about God's love. He said that God forgives all sins. That he could make me pure again." She closed her eyes as if reliving some wonderful moment.

"We prayed together at the church. He held my hand and we talked. He told me that God was ready to help me." She nodded, glancing at each of her parents.

Steadman looked on the verge of collapse. She seemed to be gasping for breath.

"And then he took me to this special place. It was kind of like a hospital only smaller. God was there with us. We talked some more. And I talked to other people. They held my hand and assured me that everything would be okay. And then they let me sleep. Pastor Bob said that when I awoke, I would be cleansed and pure again." The smile broadened, eyes bright and clear.

"And I was. I felt God's hand on my shoulder. I felt his love. Pastor Bob said that I might be sick for a couple of days. That was just God and Satan fighting but the devil had no chance. My faith was too strong, he said." She put a hand on her mother's shoulder. "I promised God that day that my body would never be used by anyone but him again."

Lainie's sense of fear strengthened, along with a growing sickness in her stomach—*but him*. This was the end for her. She looked at Eve with a resolute shake of her head. Lasorda nodded back and stepped in.

"Marianne, you remember me, right? I'm Eve Lasorda."

The young girl shifted her gaze to the ADA. "Of course. That's a wonderful name, Eve."

"Thank you for sharing this with us. Can you tell me, though, how do you give your body to God?" Eve seemed to struggle with the wording but the question was clear.

A broad smile broke out over Marianne's face. "It's wonderful. The most sacred and holy of rituals. But I can't talk about it outside the church. That would be blasphemy."

Chapter 70

Lainie left the District Attorney's office horrified and enraged. As she navigated through the Bellevue streets, intense sadness and despondency set in. By the time she pulled into her garage and made her way into the house, a pervasive emptiness had replaced everything. "I'm back." She called toward the living not knowing whether Paul was even there. It didn't really matter anyway.

Within seconds, he appeared at the threshold between the dining room and kitchen. His eyes asked the question she knew was on his mind. He stood watching as she dropped her keys in the hall basket and shed her raincoat.

"I'm going to put some water on for tea. Want some?" She avoided his gaze, focusing on the shiny stainless-steel kettle. She didn't really listen for his answer. Reaching for a decorative ceramic container, she pulled two tea bags out and placed them in cups. Lainie stared at the kettle, waiting for the familiar whistle. She felt Paul's gaze but couldn't bring herself to meet it. She had envisioned the scene where she could tell him that his life belonged to him again. The twist with Pastor Bob was never part of what she imagined. How could any joy or happiness emerge from this mess?

Her mind wandered to Detective Steadman. She hadn't struck up a friendship with the woman. She'd barely even spoken to her. And certainly, the detective was no friend of Paul's. But Lainie could find no joy or pleasure in this development. Given she had crumbled when her lout of a husband had dumped her, she could only imagine what Steadman was going through. The kettle whistled.

She handed Paul his cup and moved slowly and silently into the living room, then eased into the overstuffed chair. He set his tea cup on the coffee table and dropped onto the couch. She could see the persistent question on his face.

Lainie looked up and closed her eyes, taking a deep breath and not knowing how to even start this discussion. She briefly considered whether she could ethically share it with him.

Mildred offered her own assessment of the issue. *Screw the ethics.*

She opened her eyes and waded in. "Paul, what I'm going to tell you is for you alone. Let me say, before I start, that I hope I can finish without falling apart. What I learned today is beyond anything I could have imagined."

His eyes opened a little wider and he tilted his head. She could see a tentativeness, even fear. As she opened up and related the experience, the color drained from his face. His tea sat untouched. She could see him struggling for breath, shaking his head gradually as his eyes became red. Tears streamed down his cheek.

As she finished, he stood, wobbling as he centered his weight on his legs. Continuing to shake his head, he stumbled toward the back room, saying nothing. He went into his room, closing the door behind him.

Lainie watched him until he was no longer in view.

Mildred offered her assessment. *You did the best you could with it.*

She didn't know how to argue with her conscience on this one. He deserved to know why tragedy had been visited upon him. And yet the knowledge perhaps made things worse. "Maybe there was another way. Maybe he didn't need to know everything."

He's an adult. He will figure it out. Mildred was being uncharacteristically kind to her.

Lainie sipped her tea and stared out the window. Every few minutes, a feeling of grief would stick its nose in. She banished it. Then rage showed its face. She refused it a toehold on her emotions. Mostly, she felt helpless, overwhelmed by the future that this young girl faced. And her parents—what must they going through? Then she thought about Deborah Bufford, the young girl with the learning disability. Was it the same with her? Did she give her body to God too? She closed her eyes tightly, hoping to shut everything out, unsuccessfully.

After about an hour, Paul emerged, eyes red and swollen. He made his way down the hall on unsteady legs. He walked over and sat on the couch. He gazed down and shook his head. "Sorry." He stared at his hands, resting in his lap. "I couldn't help thinking about how I reacted to this. It was a rage, a hatred like I've never known. And then it hit me, that's how people thought about me." He raised his head to meet her eyes. "That's how you thought about me." Tears filled his eyes again.

Lainie could feel her heart breaking, not just for him but also for herself. His statement was so unfair, and yet it was true. She remembered that first night, how repulsed she was, how much she hated him. She tried to salvage something of the moment. "It's not the same thing, Paul."

He looked at her for a moment, making no effort to wipe the tears. "Yes. It's exactly the same thing. But the worst part is that I can see now why people hated me. They thought that

I was guilty of that thing, just like I think Tell is guilty. I don't know any more about him and what he actually did than what you knew about me that first night."

"No, Paul. You're wrong." Her voice came out firm, almost harsh. "There's a big difference." But she knew he was right. Lainie shook her head and lowered her gaze in defeat.

Her own tears began to gather as she searched for some way to make life right again. Paul saved her.

"Lainie, I'm sorry. I'm not going to get weird on you or anything. I guess I'm just maybe overreacting a little. I never expected this, ever."

She looked up to see him dabbing his eyes with a tissue. He picked up his cup of cold tea and took a sip, grimacing in the process. He exhaled and slouched down. "Will the girls get some help? I mean, rather than being punished or anything like that?" A hint of hope shone through in his gaze.

Lainie nodded. "Yeah. I'm sure of it." She started to add that it was likely to be a long road for them. But she left it at that. She glanced at the clock. Six o'clock already. "Hey, it's getting kind of late to be starting dinner. Why don't we go out and grab a bite?"

A faint, soft smile painted his face. He nodded. "Okay."

She was just about to get her jacket when the doorbell rang. She glanced out the side window to see a car with which she wasn't familiar. It looked like a Mercedes, although she couldn't see the identifying logo. The first thought that occurred to her was that it could be one of her old attorney friends. Except that she didn't have any old attorney buddies other than Kelley, who didn't drive a Mercedes.

She opened the door and her heart dropped.
"Hello Lainie. Long time."

Chapter 71

Lainie stared at the unwelcome face. "Yes. Seven years, three months, and a few days, give or take. What do you want, Jason?" She stood squarely in the doorway, preventing his entry. She could feel Paul behind her staring.

Her ex-husband had changed. The wavy dark hair had thinned and become streaked with gray. His full, muscular build had shifted its load slightly—less around the shoulders and more around the gut. Pouches of pasty skin surrounded his bloodshot eyes. He'd been drinking again.

He offered a version of what had once been a heart-stopping smile. "I just wanted to talk. Can I come in?" He was dressed in charcoal wool trousers. The buttons on his light blue shirt strained against his stomach and his midsection rolled over his belt.

She started to hurl an insult at him and tell him to get the hell off her porch.

Mildred intervened. *You're better than that.*

Lainie stepped aside and gestured him in with her head. Turning, she unenthusiastically made the introductions. "Jason, this is Paul Stafford. Paul, this is my ex-husband, Jason Simpson." With an open hand pointed toward the couch, she offered him a seat without speaking.

Paul looked first at her, then at him. "Uh, I'll be in the back room." His words came out shaky and uncertain. He turned and shuffled down the hall. She'd been meaning to tell him about her divorce, not that it was any of his business. Still a lot of how she'd acted stemmed from that. She just hadn't gotten around to it yet.

Jason peered at her, his eyes narrowed. "I'm sorry. I didn't realize you had a live-in boyfriend."

Lainie rolled her eyes. "That would be none of your business." She started to correct the misunderstanding but decided against it.

He looked down at the hands folded in his lap. "I made a mistake. Leaving you. I know that now."

She laughed in spite of her anger. "Mistake? No that wasn't a mistake. A mistake is when you put too much salt in the rice. Or when you add a column of numbers incorrectly or take a wrong turn. You knowingly destroyed our marriage. You knew exactly what you were doing."

He shook his head. "Yes, okay. I was wrong. I thought that maybe we could, I don't know, try to get to know each other again."

She sat, her hands resting on the arms of the overstuffed chair. "No thanks. I know you about as well as I want to."

He leaned forward, pleading in his voice. "Lainie, we had some wonderful years together. You can't just throw them away."

She shook her head and smirked. "First, I didn't throw them away. You did. Second, yes, there were some good years. And I'll carry the memories with me for as long as I live. But I don't want to relive them, and I don't want you in my new life."

He leaned back, glaring at her. His eyes exuded an icy hardness. A menacing tone entered his voice as he spoke. "And yet you'll take up with a rapist, a child molester."

Her rage almost boiled over but she held it in check. Taking a deep breath, she put on her sweetest, most insincere smile. "I see that you've slipped with age. Time was when you were pretty good about checking facts before you ran your mouth." She arched her eyebrows as she spoke.

"What the hell is that supposed to mean?"

Lainie shrugged. "Nothing. Nothing at all." She stood. "Now, if there's nothing more, I've enjoyed this little trip down memory lane, but I've got other things to do." Without waiting for a response, she strode over and opened the front door, standing aside gesturing him out.

"I can see that forgiveness is not one of your strong suits." He remained seated.

Her smile softened and her words came out genuine, which surprised her. "Whatever you might think, I have forgiven you. I don't hate you and I don't bear you any ill will. I have another life and you are not a part of it."

As Jason shuffled through the door and out to his car without looking back, Mildred commented. *Well done. I'm proud of you.*

Chapter 72

With Jason out the door, Lainie's first choice for dinner would have been The Salty Sockeye, the Gilman Village spot where she and Paul had eaten. But the late hour and weekend traffic discouraged her, and they settled for a local Red Robin.

With their orders for burger and salad up, they sipped on iced tea and tried to work around the silence that followed them into the restaurant. She'd felt the awkwardness when Jason had walked through the door. She didn't think Paul had overheard his denigrating remark about him. Still, the discomfort persisted.

"Look, I'm sorry about Jason. I haven't seen him in over seven years. Then, bam, out of the blue he shows up." She shook her head.

Paul shrugged. He looked like he wanted to ask a question but, instead, he picked up his glass and sipped.

"Our divorce wasn't as amicable as yours." She once again started to relate the details but found it easier to return his shrug.

He eased into a different subject. "What's next, I mean with my case?" He ran his index finger slowly around the rim of his glass as he stared at the iced tea.

Lainie cleared her throat and shifted gears back into her best legal voice. "We haven't discussed it but I'm pretty sure the first order of business on Monday will be for Lasorda to drop all charges. Either she or her boss will have to make a statement to the press. I've asked her to stress your innocence when she does. I'll check with her again on Monday."

He looked at her, a smile in his eyes. "Thank you." He turned his head and looked out the window. The clatter of plates and voices in the popular family eatery seemed to fade to a comfortable blanket of white noise. His voice came out soft and slow. "I know I told you once already, but I am truly grateful to you. I don't think I could have made it through without you."

***

Kelley called the group together for a meeting at nine on Monday morning. Although the trial was technically still on the calendar, she assured them that, by then, the charges would be dismissed. Andi and Elliott nodded in unison. Andi looked over and smiled at Paul, who looked exhausted.

Lainie still wondered how they might move Paul's innocence more into the public eye. "You mind if I call Lasorda? I want to try and push her a little on the statement they make to the press. After Saturday, I figure she owes me big time."

"Knock yourself out. If she makes the statement, probably not going to be an issue. Not sure how her boss would handle it if he decides to do it himself. All in all, though, I'd say your chances are good. If they just say they dropped the case because of evidence, it makes them and the police department look bad. If they can say that they identified the true villain, everyone comes out okay. Well, everyone except Tell. But even the case against him would be dicey, unless they can get those three girls on the same page. My guess is that there are some tough times ahead for them."

Paul spoke up, for the first time in several meetings. "I guess this means that all of this is coming to an end for me. I know that I gave you a retainer. How do we settle the rest of the bills and stuff?" He held a pen in his hand, apparently ready to write down any critical information.

Kelley grinned and arched her eyebrows. "I got a plan."

Lainie spoke up. "Before we close the books on this, I want to make sure that the DA's office follows through on that press conference exonerating Paul. I'll call Eve and see what she has planned."

Chapter 73

Lainie stood to the side and back, flanked on one side by the District Attorney and on the other by the Bellevue Chief of Police. A low, steady stream of murmuring floated up to the podium from the crowd of reporters gathered for the press conference.

The Assistant District Attorney visually checked with her boss, who nodded. She stepped to the microphone and began. "Good morning. I'm Assistant DA Eve Lasorda. I want to thank you all for coming. We have a brief announcement which will be followed by a Q and A session."

She took a deep breath and glanced back at Lainie. It had come down to this. They had the complete story. But there was no clean way to tell it without tipping their hand with regard to the ongoing case. The biggest problem for the DA and police, of course, was that Robert Tell, as far as they knew, was not aware of the latest developments. They did not want him getting wind of this before he could be apprehended.

Eve continued, "Over the weekend, we made substantial progress on the case involving the three young girls who reported sexual misconduct at East Rainier High School. Up until this point, Principal Paul Stafford had been the primary suspect. We now know for certain that he was not involved in any inappropriate behavior. The allegations against him were completely false. All charges have been dismissed. I speak for both the District Attorney and the Chief of Police," she glanced back at the DA and the Chief, before going on, "in conveying our deepest apologies to Mister Stafford for the pain he has endured."

Several hands went up in the audience, but Eve did not appear to notice them. She continued, "Based on our new information, we are close to making an arrest. I will have more information for you later in the week."

More hands went up, along with the shouted questions. Lasorda pointed to a young man near the front. "I'll take questions now starting with this gentleman."

"Mitch Connors from the *Seattle Post Intelligencer.* Who is the new suspect?"

"I'm not at liberty to provide that information at this time, since the individual is not in custody. I promise that we will publish it as soon as an arrest is made." She pointed to a middle-aged woman on the other side of the room. "Yes, with the navy blazer."

And so it went. Most questions were not answered as they probed too close to what no one wanted to say. Lainie thought that the authorities probably hoped everything would just go away—that the press and public would lose interest. But she doubted that would be the case. She'd seen what public opinion had done to Paul. It was relentless. Sooner or later, Lasorda and company would have to come clean.

But for that day, she had what she wanted. Paul was innocent and the world knew it.

Chapter 74

After exiting the elevator, Lainie and Paul made their way down the corridor in the Bellevue School District Building. She glanced at him as they walked. For this meeting, he wore a pair of medium gray wool dress slacks, a pale-yellow shirt, a blue and yellow striped tie, and a navy blazer. It was the first time she'd seen him in anything resembling dress attire. It all hung loose on his gaunt body. All things considered, though, he looked good.

Entering the second-floor conference room, they found Kelley already chatting with several men dressed in suits and ties. Glancing around, Lainie spotted Kelley's briefcase on the table and claimed the seat next to hers.

A lone woman sat in a chair at the far end of the table, reading through some notes. Paul had strolled over to her and she stood as he approached. After they exchanged words, the woman put her arms around his neck and hugged him. He returned the hug briefly before they parted, nodding and smiling.

"Who's that?" Lainie eyed the woman as Paul sat.

"Oh, that's Beth Tanis. She's the assistant principal." He brushed the non-existent wrinkles from his trousers as he spoke.

Lainie felt a pang of something not quite like jealousy but, maybe. The woman appeared closer to Paul's age and was beautiful. And apparently, she liked him. "Looks like she never stopped believing in you."

He shrugged and shifted his gaze over toward the woman, who had turned her attention to the papers in front of her. "I don't know. I mean, now that the story's more or less out, I guess it's easy to believe. Not sure what she felt a few weeks ago. I haven't spoken to her since I left."

The words cut Lainie for reasons she struggled to identify. Yes, it was easier to believe in someone once you had all the information. But when the case first hit her in the face, her reaction was to not believe in him. She wondered if she'd ever be able to forgive herself.

Mildred offered some insight. *Nothing you can do about the past. Let it go.*

And yet was she willing to let Jason's betrayal go? She knew that she had to. There is a difference between forgiving and not wanting to go through it again.

Kelley returned to her seat as the men situated themselves on the other side of the table. She turned and smiled to Lainie and, down past her to Paul. "Hey, I didn't notice you come in."

A stately late-fifty-something man on the other side of the table opened the discussion. "Let's get started." He paused, tapped his pen on his pad, and then continued cautiously. "I have to say that I'm curious, even a bit confused about the reason for this meeting. After all, Paul Stafford has been completely exonerated. We're anxious to have him return to his position." He offered what looked like a rehearsed smile. "With full back pay, of course."

Kelley nodded. "Yes, well, I'm afraid it's a bit more complicated than that. A lot has happened between the time you let him go and today." She reached inside her briefcase and retrieved the now well-used photographs of Paul's house. Laying them out on the table between her and the men, she leaned back. "These are pictures taken of Mister Stafford's house about a week ago."

The man glanced down at the horrific representations. "Yes. Very unfortunate. But I'm not sure that I see the connection to the school." He folded his hands on the table in front of him.

"Ordinarily, I might agree with that assessment. But here's where it gets interesting. In addition to the physical damage you see here, he received numerous vile, threatening phone calls. As a note of interest, we were able to track down the origins of those phone calls. Not surprisingly, there is a connection between the people who made them and the people who did this damage." She let that hang in the air for a moment.

Lainie winced internally. She hadn't heard that and tried not to let her confusion show through her veneer.

Before Kelley could continue, the man retorted. "Yes, well as interesting as that is, I'm still not connecting the dots."

"Okay, then, allow me to help. The phone calls came in to his landline. That line is not one that he uses. It's a holdover, if you will, from the good old days. The only reason he still has it is that it's bundled with his cable and internet access. He uses his cellphone for everything these days. The landline number itself is a private, unlisted number. The only place that it's recorded, other than the phone company, is at the school. He has, unfortunately, neglected to update his contact information in his personnel file."

"Proves nothing. He could have given that number to someone and not remembered. Maybe someone at the phone company gave it out. We don't release that kind of information."

Lainie could see a hint of doubt in the man's eyes, though. She pictured the wheels turning in his head, trying to navigate a way out of this.

Kelley sighed. "I figured you'd go there. I'll skip the suspenseful back and forth. We interviewed one of the callers. We have the name of the person at the school who gave out his phone number and address. And, if you're interested, I suspect that the anonymous leak of information to the media on that first day probably came from the same person."

He cleared his throat and nodded. "Since I've not seen any legal papers, I can only surmise that you don't have enough to file a suit against the school."

She laughed. "And you would be dead wrong. I figure that if we pushed ahead, we'd be looking at a mid-seven-figure payout." She shook her head. "But Paul, our client, didn't see it that way. He doesn't want your money, the foolish man." She grinned.

"Then what does he want?"

"I'll let him speak for himself." She leaned in and looked past Lainie at Paul. "You're up."

Paul gazed at the man for a moment and then down at the table again. "Three things. First, I'd like my attorney fees from the criminal case covered by the school district."

The man across the table shot back quickly. "This has nothing to do with your representation in the criminal case. They are two very different issues."

Paul shrugged. "Yeah, maybe. And I don't care. However we frame it or consider it, all I want is for these people to be paid." He gestured toward Kelley and Lainie. "You can either pay them directly or we can go the legal route. Then you can pay me and I'll pay them."

Kelley interjected, "And I can promise you that the amount will be considerably lower if you simply pay the bill directly."

The man stared across at Paul, a hint of anger in his eyes. "Okay, let's set that aside for a moment. I can't agree to anything like that here and now. We'll come back to that. What else?"

Paul leaned in, his forearms on the table. "The three girls." He shifted his gaze to Beth Tanis. "I understand that Caryn Smallwood had an academic problem. That should be handled in accordance with standard procedures. But as far as for the other two girls, I assume they are academically eligible for graduation. I don't want this case to interfere with that. They graduate on schedule."

The man glanced down at the assistant principal, who nodded subtly. "Okay."

Paul took a deep breath. "Finally, I want my contract terminated effective today."

The statement apparently caught the school district representative off-guard. "I don't understand. You've been cleared. We're looking forward to having you back."

Paul smirked. "Let's not be naïve here. I can't come back and work at the school and you know it. I can't walk down the hall and look teachers, advisors, and administrators in the eye. Parents are not going to want to work with me. You don't want me here any more than I want to be here."

A brief but uncomfortable silence fell over the room until the man responded. "Would you at least agree to serve out the year?"

"No. The budget for next year is done. Miz Tanis is more than capable of leading the school through the remainder of the session. In fact, I'll take it one step further, she should be your choice for the principal position. There is no finer administrator in the district." He glanced over at Tanis, who simply shook her head. Paul smiled at her.

The meeting adjourned with the school representatives promising to get back to Kelley on the legal fee issue. Paul and Lainie strode down the hall toward the elevator. "I think you caught 'em by surprise, Paul."

"I guess." He walked on without pausing.

Once inside the elevator, Lainie broke the silence. "So, what next?"

He stared at the elevator wall. "I should go home and get my house cleaned up."

Three hours later, Lainie pulled up into Paul's driveway. They sat for a moment looking at the wreck that was his home. "You need some help? I'd be glad to come over and lend a hand."

He gazed at the scene. "No, that's okay." He turned his body to face her and reached out, taking her hand. "Lainie, you've done enough for me already. It's time that I start doing for myself. I've got a long road ahead. I have to take that first step at some point. Might as well be now." He squeezed her hand and then opened the car door and got out.

Before she could react, he opened the back door, pulled out his luggage and backpack containing his clothing, and shut the door. Lainie started to get out of the car but he began walking toward the front door. He turned about halfway and waved, a soft smile on his face.

She felt, just for an instant, like she'd felt that night when Jason had left. Except, of course, Paul was not betraying her. He was simply going home.

But it still hurt.

Chapter 75

Lainie pulled out of the driveway as Paul unlocked his front door and entered without looking back. She tried to leave him behind as she navigated out of the neighborhood, back through city center, and into her own neighborhood. She focused on re-imagining her life. She hadn't lost Paul. She'd never had him. She hadn't even wanted him.

Now she had the entire weekend stretched out in front of her and no obligations, other than the novel. She'd implied to Meg that another few chapters would be heading her way shortly. The terms *few* and *shortly* were notably short on specificity. But Saturday and Sunday would be hers. She would answer to no one—get up when she chose; go to bed when she chose.

Mildred declined to comment.

And dinner—whatever she wanted. She didn't have to worry about what anyone else would like. She had her life back, such as it was.

***

Saturday and Sunday flew by. Lainie plowed through three chapters, barely taking time to eat. She gave a passing thought to going grocery shopping, something she'd neglected to do on Friday evening. Remembering the last time she did that on Saturday, she opted to wait until Monday morning.

The weekend behind her, Lainie got an early start, she finished shopping, and pulled into her garage before eleven.

As she walked into the kitchen through the door from her garage, she heard the ring from her cellphone, nestled in a pocket of her purse. Retrieving it, she glanced at the caller ID. She connected and put the phone to her ear. "Good morning, Eve."

"Hi Lainie. Was wondering if you were free this afternoon. I'll buy you a cup of coffee."

Lainie smiled. "A cup of coffee as in one that you pour from the pot at your office?" An inside joke from her old law firm.

"Naw. Let's keep it casual. How about we meet down at Common Grounds. Two o'clock work okay for you?"

***

Lainie draped her raincoat over the back of her chair as she sat down at the table. Eve had already downed half a cup. "Couldn't wait for a sunny day?"

Lasorda shrugged and smiled. "Around here, I'd be waiting until July."

"Let me grab a cup. Be right back." Lainie ignored the fact that Eve had offered to buy her a cup. Feeling extravagant, her cup of coffee became a cappuccino. After all she'd been through, she deserved a treat. And, given the agreement that Paul had wrangled out of the school board, she had been able to bill for her services without the guilt of him having to pay for it.

She returned to the table to find Eve having slipped into a more serious demeanor. "How's he doing?"

Lainie thought about it for a moment. "I don't know. I guess he's just starting to rebuild his life, whatever that entails." She shook her head to clear the thought.

Eve nodded and glanced over at the window. "They found Robert Tell." She shifted her gaze back to Lainie. "Bullet in the back of the head, about fifty miles north of here."

Ripples of nausea rolled through her stomach. The cappuccino no longer looked that good. "You're not thinking Paul…?"

The ADA smirked. "No. Not at all. Laura Steadman turned herself in this morning. Given everything that happened, I just thought you'd want to know."

The image of the detective's darkened face flashed through Lainie's mind. She recalled Steadman's demeanor as Marianne Thompson told her story. "What's going to happen to her?" After the way Steadman had treated Paul, it was hard to generate a lot of sympathy. On the other hand, she'd also been betrayed. It occurred to her that this entire case had been about betrayal. There were no winners.

Eve narrowed her eyes as she appeared to consider the question. "I don't know, honestly. I mean, it has all the trappings of first-degree murder. And I haven't spoken to or seen Steadman, but it doesn't make any sense to me. The only thing I can think is that she had some kind of psychotic break."

Lainie considered that, as far as she knew, Eve didn't know about the relationship between Steadman and Tell. She would know soon enough, though.

The ADA forced a smile. "Here's the really strange part. She asked Kelley Vickers to defend her. Do you believe that?"

"Really? She asked Kelley?" It sounded pretty far-fetched.

"Yup, and to make things even more weird, I think Kelley's actually going to do it." Eve shook her head and laughed. "There could be some conflict of interest stuff there, but if they sort that out, it ought to be one interesting case. Fortunately, it's not mine." The mirth faded as she continued, "But I also wanted to meet with you to thank you for what you did with Marianne Thompson. Her parents also asked me to thank you."

Lainie furrowed her brow. "For what? All I did was question her."

Eve chuckled, allowing the laugh to soften to a smile. "No. You treated her with dignity and respect. Most defense attorneys would have butchered her. I can't think of any case where I've seen such a display of humanity. Pretty humbling."

Lainie wasn't used to these kinds of compliments. "Thank you. Honestly, though, I think it's going to take a lot more than respectful words to heal her."

Chapter 76

June came and went with July bringing several weeks of uninterrupted sunshine. Lainie found herself out and about more often. It turned out that Thursday afternoon was the very best for grocery shopping, right around two. With most civilized people still at work, she had her pick of parking spots and plenty of room in the grocery aisles. By that time of day, the shelves were stocked, and harried shoppers hadn't had time to pick them over.

She'd tried to phone Paul a couple of times, but it always went straight to voice mail. She considered that he might have her blocked but dismissed the thought. He'd seemed genuine in his gratitude and he somehow didn't seem the type to intentionally ignore people. Still, he hadn't returned any of her calls. Then again, she'd been paid. He didn't owe her anything.

Mildred had a different view. *You're wrong, Lainie. He owes you his life. Others may have helped him or even believed in him. But you were there when he needed you most. He won't forget that.*

She listened to her conscience. There might be any number of different reasons for him not answering or calling back. He had a lot on his plate.

This patience finally gave way to a need to know. Early on a Thursday afternoon, nearly two months after the school meeting, she navigated across Bellevue and into his neighborhood. Pulling into his driveway, the condition of his house stunned her. The structure was completely refurbished. Windows had all been replaced. No graffiti remained. His car appeared newly painted. He had been busy.

Neither the ringing of the doorbell nor a solid knock on the door produced a response. She peered through a lacy curtained window into a dark house—no movement. But the view into the house extended through the kitchen and out a partially visible back window. Something or someone moved in the back yard.

Lainie made her way around the side, glad that he didn't have a fence. She emerged into an open space. Paul stood, his back to her, watering an L-shaped garden. He wore jeans and a faded rose-colored tee shirt. His body seemed to have regained some of its weight, but he was still thin. He remained stationary, almost immovable except for his right hand that directed the flow from the nozzle to the right and to the left.

"Hey stranger." She put on her best smile.

He turned, apparently surprised, and then his face brightened, or so it seemed to her. His hazel eyes lit up and the corners of his mouth turned upward softly. "Hi Lainie. How are you?"

She shrugged. "Ah, a master gardener now, I see."

He laughed. "Well, I'm unemployed. Figured I'd stretch the food budget." He gestured to the garden plot on his left. "Zucchini, tomatoes, romaine lettuce, and some radishes. Do people really eat radishes?" He scrunched his nose. He glanced at the section of the garden to his right. "And then I thought, maybe some color, something pretty—annuals. The pictures showed yellows, reds, oranges, blues, and a bunch of purples. Don't even know their names. Here's hoping."

Lainie nodded. "How've you been?"

"Okay, I guess." His face grew more serious. The smile disappeared. "Some days are better than others. But, all in all, getting better."

He released the nozzle and dropped the hose to the ground. Walking over to the back patio, he turned and faced her, squinting against the southwestern sun. "I got a call from the Thompsons. Marianne wanted to see me."

She arched her eyebrows and waited.

"She's over at Fair Oaks Center, you know." He looked down and shuffled his sneakered shoe across the concrete.

"And?"

He looked up. "And what?"

"Did you go? What did she want?" Lainie could see the pain filling his eyes.

He nodded. "Yeah. I went over. She just, you know, wanted to apologize. To ask my forgiveness." The volume of his voice trailed off.

When he didn't continue, she prodded. "And?"

He shook his head and turned to the side, looking over at the garden. "What do you say to something like that? What happened to me was bad, unfair for sure. But nothing compared to what happened to her. She was betrayed by someone she should have been able to trust. Kids shouldn't have to deal with that, ever."

He turned back toward her and forced a smile. "She's got a good family though. They're going to stand by her, and that's what she needs. And I also ran into this woman minister over there. I think her name was, let's see, something Polasky. I think she's planning to work with Marianne."

With the discussion paused, the sound of birds and insects created a pattern of comfortable white noise.

Mildred prodded her. *It's okay. Ask him.*

She took a deep breath and gazed at him. "Paul, I was hoping that you'd stay in touch, maybe call."

He turned toward her and studied her for a moment. "Why don't we go inside. I'll put the kettle on for tea."

Chapter 77

They entered the house through the back door into the kitchen. The place was immaculate. Lainie looked around in wonder. This guy definitely shattered the stereotype of the slovenly male.

Paul walked over and turned the knob on the range. A blue flame leapt to life on the back-right burner. He filled a copper kettle with water and set it on to heat. Opening the bottom drawer of a cabinet and pulled out two boxes. "Let's see, I have regular black tea and an herbal spiced peach."

Lainie initially thought the peach an odd choice for a single guy to have around. But, then again, he didn't seem to fit that stereotype either. "I think I'll try the peach, thanks."

With their cups of steaming, aromatic tea in hand, they migrated into the living room. She remembered the last time she'd been to his house and how it might have ended had she not gotten there soon enough. And the time before that, carrying the carrot cake in from the car because he was still on crutches. She'd seen the room in good times and bad.

"I see you've put a lot of work into the house. It looks fantastic." She took a sip of tea and then set it on a coaster. He sat on the sofa. She took a wing back chair facing him.

His face darkened. He seemed to struggle as he spoke. "Yeah. Well, I went out and started to work on it." He shook his head and he seemed to search for words. "Then my next-door neighbors came over and started to help me." His eyes wandered to the window. "And then they came from other houses. All to help me." He sniffed and wiped his eyes with a handkerchief. "I'm sorry. I have problems with emotions right now." He forced a smile. "But, it's getting better. Not as often. Not as bad. Anyway, a guy down the street owns a window company. They replaced all of them for free. Another family had my car fixed up." A tear trickled down his cheek. "I tried to tell them no but...." He wiped his face. "Sorry. It's really overwhelming."

Lainie smiled. She would have taken his hand or put her arm around him had he been sitting next to her. "I know. I'm sure it is."

Paul cleared his throat. "About calling you." He turned to look out the window. "When you came over here that day. When you, well, you know, pulled me out of the bathtub. Lainie, I had never imagined a place that dark. It was like I couldn't breathe. If I tried to move, vines and webs kept me. The more I struggled, the tighter they squeezed. I was ready to give up. Then I saw, no, I felt this light. It felt good, warm, right. When I tried to move toward it, everything loosened. I knew that was where I needed to go. It was like I wanted to laugh and shout. Everything was perfect. That place, it was the bathtub with the box cutter. I was so ready, Lainie."

He turned back towards her. "Then you were there. You said you believed in me. You said you cared. Your words, they were like this shimmering gold lifeline hanging right there in front of me. When I grabbed it, you pulled me out. You walked with me. The darkness got lighter and then there was color. You saved my life."

He stood and walked over to the window, parting the curtain and looking out into the late afternoon light. "I was so screwed up." He smirked. "I guess you knew that, though." He turned toward her. "I lost touch with reality. When you said those things, I guess I read too much into them. I heard what I wanted to hear. I built up this fantasy world around me. I'm sorry."

He paused and smiled, nodding his head. "But, you know, as I got better and re-asserted my grip on reality, things cleared up for me. I was able to make sense out of it all, at least to the extent that any sense can be made of it. Anyway, I just thought that trying to put everything back together in my head, inserting some time and distance between us would be a good thing. I didn't want to cause you any discomfort or embarrassment after everything you did for me."

Lainie struggled with this explanation. "I'm sorry, Paul, what is it that you read into my words? I'm not understanding."

He shrugged and looked away. "It's really nothing. I'm better now so it's not a big deal. It's just that when you said you cared about me, you know, I just read too much into it."

He seemed like a little kid caught with his hand in the cookie jar. She said, "So, if I understand, when I said I cared, you thought I meant that I was in love with you?"

He shook his head. "I wouldn't say that I thought it. Maybe I started to wish it." He smiled. "But, don't worry. When I began to come out of it, I was able to put it into perspective. So, it's not a problem." He rambled on.

"And so, you thought I loved you. But now you think I don't. And it's okay. Is that it?"

"No. I didn't say it's okay. I said that I understand and that I'm getting better. I can't just turn that stuff off like a switch."

She stood and walked over to him. "And how did you come to this conclusion that I don't love you?"

He laughed. "That was the easy part. Once my head started to clear, I remembered that you didn't even *like* me." He ambled back over to the couch.

The words cut her like a knife to the heart. Lainie closed her eyes to stave off the tears. "Paul, I guess it's time that I came clean with you." She stood and moved over to the front window where Paul had stood only seconds before, looking out into the early summer afternoon. "I wanted to talk to you about this so many times, but it never seemed right, with all that was going on."

She turned to face him, her hands clasped in front of her. "I think I told you once or twice before, the way I was had more to do with me than with you." Her smile felt sad. "Do you remember meeting my ex-husband?"

Paul nodded.

"We were married for about eight years. He's a doctor." She smirked. "The perfect setup, huh—a doctor and a lawyer? Anyway, after years of trying, I got pregnant. And for me, it seemed the most wonderful thing in the world. But something changed between Jason and me—a coolness, a distance that had not been there before. In my excitement over our baby, I ignored the signs. Then, let's see, when I was three months along, I miscarried. I started that day with cramps and spotting. It got worse. I called Jason, but he was out of his office. He didn't answer his cellphone, so I called a cab to take me to the hospital." A tear trickled down her cheek as the memories flooded back.

With her legs beginning to tremble, she eased into the overstuffed chair, wiping her face with a handkerchief. "So, I lay there in the hospital bed, alone, as the doctor delivered the news. I ended up calling Kelley, who dropped everything and came to the hospital. Jason showed up later with some excuse. Actually, I've forgotten exactly what it was. But at that point, I was glad to see him and wanted so much to believe everything would be okay."

"I'm sorry, Lainie." Paul opened his mouth as if to continue but shook his head and fell silent.

"Fast-forward two weeks. I had gone back to work, probably sooner than I should have. I came home one day, I think it was a Tuesday." Lainie wasn't sure about the day or even if it was important. "I heard him shuffling around in the bedroom. I called out to let him know I was home and then started throwing some dinner together—nothing special, spaghetti and a salad. I figured I'd change after I got things going. And just as I was about to drop the pasta into the boiling water—I'll never forget it—he strolls in tugging two pieces of rolling luggage behind him."

And suddenly she was back there, all those years ago. "He spoke as casually as if he were ordering a pizza. 'I'm leaving. I'm sorry, but I can't do this anymore.' I stood, spaghetti in hand, staring at him. It was like I couldn't understand what he was saying. He hung his head and continued, 'There's someone else. She makes me feel young again, in love. I'm sorry.'"

Back in the present, Lainie's tears flowed freely. "Without another word, he rolled his luggage out the front door and was gone."

Silence blanketed the space between them for a few minutes. Paul's gaze seemed searching, as though he himself was trying to understand.

She closed her eyes tightly and wiped her face again. Sitting up straighter and locking gazes with him, she continued, her voice stronger. "After that, I fell apart—quit my job and opened my own law firm so I wouldn't have to work with other people. But then there were the clients and I couldn't work with them either, so I holed up at home writing. As long as I was alone, I was able to hold it together, oddly enough... until I met you."

A quizzical look crossed his face. His head tilted slightly to the side and his brow arched.

"You made me care and I didn't want to. I fought it. I looked for every possible reason to not like you. But, against every instinct, I found myself drawn to you, all the while determined never to be hurt like that again. Then came the accusations. And, honestly, Paul, when I heard them, the only thing that went through my mind was that I had once again been betrayed. I never gave an instant's thought or consideration to the possibility that you could be innocent. Wallowing in my own self-pity, I did everything I could to hurt you. I am so ashamed to admit it, but it was as though this was my chance to punish Jason by taking it out on you." She paused and smirked. "Yeah, I know, stupid."

Lainie felt something she never thought she'd feel again—love. "And as much as you may think I helped you, Paul, you saved me. I never thought I would trust anyone again, but I trust you. There are no words to tell you how sorry I am that this has cost you so much. I wish with all of my heart that I could take it back and do it over again. But the best I can do is to share this with you and hope that you will find it in your heart to forgive me." A smile broke through.

"As for loving you, I think it's fair to say that your first impression was right. When I said I cared, it did mean that I loved you. And I knew it at the time. I just didn't know how to say it. Actually, I didn't even know how to feel it. Paul, it's going to take time for me to adjust. But I want, with all of my heart, to try." Aware that she had begun to ramble, Lainie fell silent and waited.

He repeated, "Lainie, I'm sorry. I never meant to cause you pain."

She sat dumbfounded—him causing her pain? She searched for the words she needed but before she could speak, he continued.

"But, if you're serious, then maybe we could start with lunch. I know this great place down in Gilman Village, in Issaquah. They do a really great grilled salmon salad. And they have good pasta, too."

In an instant, she moved from her chair to the couch to sit beside him. Taking his hand in hers, she gushed, "Pasta sounds good."

The End

Epilogue
18 Months Later

Lainie watched as the water in the pot came to a boil. She was adding salt when she heard the front door open. She called out, "Hi, Hon, I'm in here. Dinner will be ready soon." The stove clock told her the time—5:15 p.m.

From the living room, she heard what sounded like a cross between a grumble and a grunt, as the soft footfalls receded down the hallway toward the bedroom. A brief darkness crossed her mind. They had been married nearly one year. In fact, their first anniversary would be coming up next month—December.

It wasn't like Paul to come home morose. He was usually upbeat. He'd taken a position as the principal of an alternative high school. The job had, at least so far, been perfect for him. He worked with budgets and the school board, leaving the hands-on work with students to his vice principal.

She set the pasta down on the counter and turned toward the hallway, calling out, "You okay?"

After a moment of silence, he emerged from the bedroom with his jeans and sweatshirt on. "Yeah. I'm okay."

She met him halfway down the hall and kissed him. "You sure? You could have fooled me?"

"It's just Friday and I'm worn out." A smile washed over his face. "I've decided, though—I'm never letting Vicki go on leave again. Either that or they need to give me two vice-principals." And then it was as though the dam burst. "I spent the entire afternoon refereeing a pissing contest between a teacher and the parents of a brat. I could have sworn that I was the only adult in the room."

She laughed. It was so *Paul*. "That, my love, is why they pay you the big bucks."

"Well… they either need to make the bucks *bigger* or make sure that my vice principal is never gone again." He kissed her. "So, dinner? What can I do to help?" But then he stopped mid-step. "Oh, I forgot." He turned and slipped back into the bedroom, bringing out a paper bag.

"What, did you stop for some wine? A bold Merlot or something?"

He raised his index finger, waving it back and forth as a censure to her. "Tsk, tsk, now. You know you can't drink." He shrugged and grinned. "But I did stop and get a couple of cannoli." He held up the bag enticingly.

"Paul," she feigned exasperation, "I'm going to end up fatter than I already am." She patted the pronounced bump that was her stomach.

He laughed—a genuine laugh that made him so endearing. The laugh that came from his heart. "Come on, let's eat. We can tear into the Cannoli tonight while we watch a movie, what do you say?"

"Okay, okay. The bread's in the oven. I'm about to put the pasta on. You can throw together a salad, if you don't mind."

After they finished and as Paul was stacking the dishes, he turned to her, a serious look on his face. "Maybe we could talk about the room tonight. We can't wait until the last minute. We need to get it painted and we might even want to replace the carpet in there, depending on the colors. And then we still have to get it furnished."

A wave of anxiety rushed through her. She'd been through all this before and remembered all too well how it had turned out. "I don't know, Paul. We still have a few months."

"Yes, we have a few months. But we've also put this on the back burner for months already. It's like, whenever I bring it up, you clam up on me. If nothing else, at least talk to me about it. What is it about furnishing the room that bothers you?"

She took his hand and led him into the living room. They sat on the couch in silence together for a moment before she took a deep breath and poured it all out. She dumped the years of pain and humiliation onto his shoulders as he sat and listened, eyes moistening. "I'm afraid, Paul. I'm terrified of wanting this child so bad and then having it ripped from my life... of having you ripped from my life. I don't want us to ever change." Tears streamed down her cheeks.

He drew closer to her. "I know, Lainie. And I know, from experience, that there's nothing I can tell you right now that will make that fear go away. I can only say that you saved my life once. And in the process, you completely changed it for the better. Right now, you are my life. "He broke into a grin. "You and that sassy little girl in there." He gently touched her stomach.

"I understand that all of this makes you feel horribly vulnerable. I get that. But to be in love, to bring a child into the world... that is the essence of vulnerability. When something is as precious as what we have, then losing it would be devastating. I promise you, Lainie, I am here with you now. We are going to raise our daughter, you and I. And

I will do everything humanly possible to make our life the best. I love you."

She put her arms around his neck drawing him closer. His arms wrapped around her back. They held each other closer and tighter. She closed her eyes and savored the moment. And then she felt a kick in her stomach. She smiled.